The BABY TRAIL

THE
BABY TRAIL

A Novel

Sinead Moriarty

ATRIA BOOKS

New York   London   Toronto   Sydney

ATRIA BOOKS

1230 Avenue of the Americas
New York, NY 10020

ISBN: 0-7434-9676-0

First Atria Books hardcover edition March 2005

10 9 8 7 6 5 4 3 2 1

Designed by Dana Sloan

ATRIA BOOKS is a registered trademark of Simon & Schuster, Inc.

For information regarding special discounts for bulk purchases,
please contact Simon & Schuster Special Sales at 1-800-456-6798
or business@simonandschuster.com

Printed in the United States of America

For Troy

ACKNOWLEDGMENTS

Sincerest thanks to my U.S. agent Emma Parry, to my editor Greer Hendricks and all at Atria Books.

Warmest thanks to my editor Patricia Deevy, Michael McLouglin, Grainne Killeen and everyone at Penguin Ireland. Thanks must also go to Tom Weldon, James Kellow, Hazel Orme and all at Penguin UK, for their support and encouragement.

A big thank-you to my agent Gillon Aitken, Sally Riley, Lesley Shaw, Ayesha Karim and all at Gillon Aitken Associates.

Thanks to Lis Leigh and the Tuesday-night writing group in the City of Westminster College.

Thanks, Paul White, for your great advice.

Thank you, Mum and Dad, for always being there.

Thanks, Sue and Mike, for being my cheerleaders.

Thanks to my friends, for their enthusiasm.

Most of all, thanks to Troy, for absolutely everything.

The BABY TRAIL

*H*ello, I'm Emma. I used to be a normal, happy, level-headed person. I had a great husband, lovely friends, a job I enjoyed and a very lively social life—until I decided to have a baby and turned into Kathy Bates in Misery.

It all began so innocently. I had it all planned out: come off the pill in December, have sex, be pregnant by January, have the baby in September, get a personal trainer in for November and have my figure back and the baby into a nice routine by Christmas so I could sashay around the festive parties looking like Liz Hurley after her baby. Not that I am comparing myself for a minute to Liz—or Elle or Catherine Zeta Jones, for that matter.

In fact I've been told I'm the image of . . . Sonia (the little redhead who sang those annoying pop songs for Stock Aitken Waterman), Fergie (I starved myself for weeks after that) and Julianne Moore. My best friend Lucy told me I look like Julia Roberts in Pretty Woman, but that's what best friends do—lie to make you feel better.

Anyway, let's rewind to the beginning, when I was still relatively sane. . . .

ONE

*M*y New Year's resolution two years ago was to get pregnant. Top result, I thought, as the previous year I had given up drink forever after dislocating my shoulder in a dive bar on New Year's Eve—well, New Year's Day at 6:00 A.M., to be precise. I lasted a week. I thought that this resolution would be a lot more realistic and should be a piece of cake to achieve—off the pill, some sex and Bob's your uncle.

It was high time I had a baby. I was thirty-three and although I may have felt—and, truth be told, behaved—like I was twenty-five, it was time to knuckle down and get up the duff. I told James later that night when he came home from work. He seemed pleased—if a little surprised that I was feeling broody as I'd rough-handled his nephew over the Christmas holidays. I reminded him that little Thomas had turned the TV off at a key moment in *The Sound of Music*, the scene in the cemetery when the Nazis are chasing the von Trapps—I mean, come on, it's a life-or-death situation. And I had merely nudged him gently aside. It wasn't my fault that the child had no sense of balance, fell down and hit his head on the video recorder.

"That's not how Imogen saw it," said James.

"Well, Imogen is highly strung, uptight and neurotic," I said, smiling sweetly at James—who is very handsome, by the way.

When I first introduced him to my family I could see they were

3

surprised, shocked, even. Before James, I had gone for a guy I thought I could save—you know, the tortured artist, unshaven, grubby and dirt poor. But then I met James and he saved me—from myself, mostly.

He's tall, has chocolate-colored hair, lovely brown eyes and a killer smile. His nose is a bit big, but it looks good on a man. It did worry me, though: what if we had a daughter and she inherited it? Mind you, they can do wonders with surgery.

James's sister-in-law, Imogen, was a nightmare and had never liked me. She had wanted James to marry an English rose, some boring, horsey private-school chick just like her, who would sit around in twinsets and pearls talking about ponies, gymkhanas and "maaahvelous" recipes. She was horrified when James produced me—Irish, passionate about everything, opinionated and, worst of all, a redhead.

To be honest I don't think James's parents, Mr. and Mrs. Hamilton, were too thrilled with me either. They had hoped that James would only spend a year in Ireland, training the Leinster rugby squad, but instead he met me and decided to stay for good. However, after three years of me studiously scraping my hair back into velvet bows and donning "respectable clothes" when we went over to see them, they had come 'round. I also held my tongue—unusual for me—when Mr. Hamilton talked about ridding England of its immigrants. "Send the lot of them home and let us get on with it. Coming over here, sponging off our government, taking our jobs and then whingeing about it. Send them all back, I say. That'll stop the buggers."

I was going to point out that two of my uncles and my brother were immigrants and ask if he wanted me to bugger off right now or would it be all right if I finished my apple crumble? But then I looked at James, who was shaking his head and mouthing "no," so

I thought better of it. Besides, Daughter-in-Law of the Year, Imogen, had piped up, "I so agree, Jonathan, this country just isn't the same anymore."

James thought Imogen was "nice" and refused to criticize her out of loyalty to his brother, Henry. There were only the two of them in the family, so it was important that they got on. Henry had christened me Paddy (better than Spud, but still not terribly endearing) on our first meeting. Despite this little hiccup we got on quite well in an odd sort of way. He was obsessed with horse racing and seemed to think that because I was Irish I'd been born and reared in stables—a bit like Jesus, I suppose, if you think about it. He was always asking me what I thought about horses and jockeys I'd never heard of. I have an unfortunate habit of never admitting I know nothing about a topic. Ask me any question, no matter how obscure, and I'll have a shot at answering it. So Henry and I had long chats about horses, bloodlines, jockeys and trainers. We once had an hour-long conversation on what it was about Dawn Run that had captured the hearts of the racing public. Henry reckoned it was her refusal to give in.

"She was an extremely tough horse, all right," I said, nodding and praying he wouldn't ask me any direct questions about her career history.

"Wasn't she?" said Henry. "That win in the Gold Cup when she was headed between the last two fences and just managed to get her nose in front again on the run-in really summed up her desire to win."

"I'll never forget it," I lied.

"But what a tragic end to a glittering career."

What did he mean "tragic"? Hadn't he just said the stupid horse had won the race? "Oh, it was desperate," I said, shaking my head and sighing.

"So brave of her to try to repeat her earlier victory in the Grande Course de Haies at Auteuil. A broken neck. What a way to go! She was definitely one of the brightest lights to grace the National Hunt," said Henry, his eyes misting.

"So sad," I agreed, thinking, Come on, Henry, get a grip—it was a bloody horse, not a member of your family.

Anyway, back to Imogen: When I grumbled on about her being a witch, James jumped in to defend her: "She may be a little overprotective, but that's only to be expected in first-time mothers. I'm sure you'll be the same."

"James, I think it's fair to say that I'll never be anything like Imogen. I am not boring, uptight or neurotic."

"No, darling, you're spontaneous and just a little insane."

"Better mad than boring. I'll make a brilliant mother though, won't I?"

"Yes, darling, you will. Now, shouldn't we stop talking and get down to baby-making?"

"Absofuckinglutely!"

A week later I phoned home to tell my mother about our decision to have a baby.

"Hi, Dad, it's me."

"Oh, hi, how are you?"

"Grand, you?"

"Grand. How's himself?"

"Fine. Any news?"

"Not really. Well, your sister's in the doghouse. Some poor eejit turned up here on Friday night in a dinner suit with a big flower and a box of chocolates to take her to a ball, but she was off at some party in Cork. The poor fool was sitting here like a lemon while we tried to call her. In the end your mother felt so sorry for him she offered to go to the ball herself. That got rid of him, all right," said Dad, as we both giggled. "Oh, here's Barbara now. I'll let her fill you in."

"See you, Dad."

"Hello."

"Hi, Babs. What's going on?"

"You mean apart from our mother losing the plot completely and accusing me of ruining her life? God, I forgot about the poxy ball. What's the big deal? He's a total nerd anyway. I only said yes because he cornered me in the library and I couldn't think of a good excuse quickly enough."

"In the library? Were you lost?"

"You're hilarious. I was trying to find Jenny so I could cog her notes. Anyway, I went to Cork to a mad party and had a great time. I would have had a shite time at that crappy ball."

"So you didn't forget?"

"Well, okay, not really. But if you saw the state of him you'd understand."

"Bit mean, though."

"Yeah, I know, I know. I'll go and hunt him out in the library tomorrow and apologize."

"Careful! The library twice in one week? Bad for the image."

"I'll wear a wig. Oh Jesus, here's Mum. I'm off before she starts spraying me with holy water."

"Hi, Mum," I said, trying to stifle giggles.

"Funny, is it? Funny to bring disgrace on your family? Some poor young lad all dickied up with a beautiful corsage turns up at the door to take her to a ball and she's off gallivanting at some rave party in Cork. Well, the poor boy nearly died, as did we. We had to bring him in and feed him stiff drinks. He was as red as a beetroot.

I was mortified myself and, to make matters worse, it turns out he's Liam and Eileen McGarry's son."

At this point my mother paused for dramatic effect, but it was lost on me: I had no idea who these people were. "Who?"

"You know, Liam and Eileen McGarry from the golf club and isn't Liam the captain this year, so the whole place will be talking about what an ignorant so-and-so we've raised. I'd say that boy will never go outside his front door again. It's a dangerous age for boys, you know—the percentage of suicides among boys between the ages of eighteen and twenty-five is very high."

I decided to step in. "Mum, relax. I'm sure it'll be fine. She's going to apologize to him."

"Pffff. Anyway, enough about that young pup. How are you?"

"Great, thanks. Actually, I've decided to have a baby."

"What do you mean?"

"I mean, I've decided to have a baby. I'm going to get pregnant."

"Lord, Emma. I hope you haven't broadcast this around."

"What do you mean, broadcast?"

"Well, these things are best kept private. Why does everyone nowadays feel they have to tell the world their private business? I blame that Oprah Winefrid myself."

"It's Winfrey."

"What?"

"Her name is . . . oh, never mind. Just think, this time next year you'll be a granny."

"Could be."

"What?"

"It doesn't always happen overnight, you know, especially at your age. It's not always that straightforward, Emma."

"Well, thanks for all your support. Hopefully at the grand old age of thirty-three my ovaries haven't totally shriveled up."

"There's no need to be dramatic. Just keep your business private and get on with it."

"Fine, I will. I'd better go now and hop on James before my biological clock stops."

Your cycle is twenty-eight days, so you should ovulate (isn't that just the most cringe-making word? It sounds like something fish do) midway. On day fourteen, when James came home from work, I was waiting for him.

Instead of greeting him from my usual horizontal position on the couch, eating chocolate biscuits in my pajamas and Gap hoodie, I was waiting for him in the bedroom in my garter belt and stockings, which hadn't been trotted out since our honeymoon a year ago. I had lit scented candles and left only a small lamp on in the corner of the room. My thighs and stomach look a lot better by candlelight—believe me.

Stunned not to find me on the couch, James walked into the bedroom, sniffing the air suspiciously. When he saw me in my garter belt he began to look really worried. "Okay, what have you done? You crashed the car, didn't you?"

"No, I did not. I just thought this would be a nice surprise for you. Make a change."

James sat down on the bed and took my hand in his. "It's all right, darling. The most important thing is that you weren't injured. Just tell me how bad the damage is."

"James! I did not crash the car." I was getting frustrated now and the garter belt was digging into my waist. I had starved myself for weeks before the wedding and that was a lot of meals ago. "I wanted to surprise you and inject some fun into our midweek routine."

"Fine, but is there anything you want to tell me? I promise, no matter how bad it is, I won't get annoyed."

"James!"

"Aha, I know. Your parents have separated and your mother's moving in with us?"

"No, they have not. What do you mean, my parents have separated? Do you think they might? Why should they? They get on really well."

"Emma, I'm just trying to figure out what you've done."

"For goodness' sake, stop being so suspicious. I just felt like spicing things up a bit. And, besides, I'm ovulating." I had to admit it before he cast any more aspersions on my parents' marriage. I thought they seemed happy enough. Granted, they weren't Mr. and Mrs. Mike Brady, but they got on all right.

James looked a bit taken aback. "What?"

That's the problem with men who've been brought up in all-male households and go to single-sex boarding schools—they tend not to be very *au fait* with the inner workings of the female body. When we first moved in together James called from the supermarket one night to see what I wanted for dinner. I asked him for chicken tikka and a twelve-pack of Tampax Supers as I'd run out. He nearly passed out. He just wasn't that relaxed around feminine hygiene products. But, as my friend Jess said, it's all about training. I was working on him, slowly but surely.

"I'm ovulating—you know, popping eggs—so we need to go for it. It's day fourteen. Come on, let's get to it."

"Right, right, of course, yes. Do we have time for foreplay or should I just shoot from the hip, as it were?" said James, laughing, as he whipped off his tracksuit.

TWO

I met James three years ago in a pub—as you do. At the time I was coming to the end of a relationship with a total loser called Ronan who was a "freelance journalist" and "aspiring novelist." During the six months we were together, Ronan wrote one eight-hundred-word story for *In Dublin* magazine and one chapter of his novel. The magazine paid him sixty quid for the article, which was the only money he earned in our time together.

So for six months I supported Ronan—bought all his drinks, drugs (apparently they boosted his creativity), a new printer for his computer and even paid his rent. At first I thought he was wonderful because he was so different—poetic, lyrical, artistic—but as I got to know him better, I began to see him for what he really was: a lazy, scabby dreamer. Also his tendency to break into poetry—initially charming—got on my nerves. Besides, as I discovered, it was always the same quotes from the same six poems.

The first time she met Ronan my best mate Lucy thought he was a tosser, and told me straight out that I should ditch him. Although I knew she was right, I continued to see him in some lame hope that his genius would rub off on me. I also thought that by subsidizing him, I was helping him to focus all his energies on his novel—which I naïvely thought would be a literary masterpiece, and which, needless to say, he would dedicate to me for all my help and support during his early days.

However, when I got to read the long-awaited first chapter, two things became abundantly clear: Ronan did not have a talented bone in his body and the drugs he smoked had fried his brain. It was time to move on.

The night I met James was the one after I had read Ronan's drivel. The usual crew I met up with on a Saturday was out, and Ronan, as always, arrived with no money. Lack of funds, however, did not affect his thirst and I was up and down to the bar like a yo-yo, buying him pints with whiskey chasers, while Lucy rolled her eyes up to heaven and quizzed him on the theme of his novel.

"I don't understand how you think a book about a guy who speaks only in rhyming couplets could be commercial," she argued.

"But it's not supposed to be commercial. I would never sell my soul for financial gain. It's aimed at poetry lovers, particularly admirers of Patrick Kavanagh."

"Well, if you don't want to make any money out of it, how do you plan to support yourself?"

"A true artist never worries about where his next meal comes from. Besides, I have my freelance work to pay the bills," said the smug would-be author, as he threw back yet another pint he hadn't paid for.

I nearly choked on my own drink. In the last six months I had paid all his bills as well as his rent. He was really beginning to bug me. I'd have to get rid of him. Lucy was right. He was not boyfriend material.

When Ronan turned 'round to bore one of my more tolerant friends about his book, I moaned to Lucy about my job. It was simple: I hated what I did. I was a senior recruitment consultant in Parson, Mason and Jackson and, due to the Celtic Tiger, was earning good money—although the Ronan fund was putting a serious dent in my salary. The hefty commissions I was bringing in were the main reason I had stayed there so long. But I was bored senseless and really wanted to try something else—namely makeup.

I had always been obsessed with makeup—trying every new brand on the market as soon as it hit the shops—and I was fascinated by the way makeup artists transformed models for photo shoots. I had done various short makeup courses and often made up my friends if they were going to weddings or balls. I really believed I had a flair for it, but I was afraid of taking the first step. For the first few months I'd have to work free of charge to gain experience and the thought of not having any income terrified me. God forbid I'd turn into a sponger like Ronan!

Poor Lucy had been listening to me moan about my job for years. "Do you really want to leave?" she asked.

"Yes. I swear, Lucy, this time I really mean it."

"So you're not just saying it because you're going to be thirty in ten days' time?"

"Well, that does have something to do with it, but only because I can't bear the thought of being in this job at thirty, when I swore to myself that I'd be gone by twenty-eight."

"Okay. Well, then, if you really want out, you're going to have to stop spending money on losers like Ronan, and take the plunge. So what if you're broke for a while? At least you'll be happy. You've been giving out about your job for years, so you should do something about it."

"You're right. I *have* been moaning for years. You know what, Lucy? I'm going to do it this time, I really am. I'm going to hand in my notice."

I was feeling very brave, largely due to the four vodkas I'd just consumed, but also because, as Lucy had pointed out, my thirtieth birthday was looming and the thought of waking up on that day in the same job terrified me. Thirty was a milestone—a sign. It was time for me to change my life and stop drifting along. Ronan would have to go too: I no longer liked him, never mind fancied him, and he was too expensive. I'd tell him later and on Monday I'd resign. Hurrah, I was finally taking control.

I went to the bar to order a bottle of champagne to celebrate my new life. When I had fished my money out of my purse I looked up to see a tall, dark, handsome guy standing beside me ordering drinks. "What are you celebrating?" he asked, in a posh English accent—-smiling at me. He had a great smile.

Cute and English. I liked that, no baggage. Irish guys always had baggage—somehow you always knew someone who knew someone who had gone out with them, shagged them, snogged them or fancied them—and at some stage that baggage would inevitably turn up to haunt you. At least with an English guy all his exes would be tucked away in England—out of sight, out of mind.

"I'm celebrating my decision to get out of the rat race and follow my true desire to be a makeup artist." I beamed at him. "By the way, I'm Emma."

"Very pleased to meet you, Emma. I'm James. Good luck with your new career. I did the same thing two years ago and it was the best decision I ever made."

"Really? What did you do?"

James told me he used to work in corporate banking but found it deadly dull. What he wanted to do was be a top rugby trainer— well, he admitted that what he had really wanted to do was play rugby for England, but when that didn't work out he opted for the more realistic goal of being a rugby trainer. On his thirtieth birthday, he'd handed in his notice, sold his Porsche and his loft apartment overlooking the Thames and taken a job as assistant coach to the Titans. A year later when the Titans' captain, Donal Brady, decided he wanted to move back to Dublin and play for Leinster, he persuaded James to come with him. So now James was the assistant head coach of the Leinster team.

A kindred spirit! It must be fate. It had to be. How could I possibly have just bumped into this gorgeous guy at this turning point in my life if it wasn't meant to be? Just as I was imagining what our children would look like, Ronan staggered over. "I'm dying of thirst. What are you doing? Brewing the stuff?"

I glared at him. "I'll be there in a minute."

"Well, hurry up, you've been gone for ages and I want to get another few in before closing time," said Ronan, looking huffy.

A normal boyfriend would have been jealous because I had been talking to James—well, flirting outrageously would be closer to the truth—for ages. But not Ronan: all he wanted was his drink. If I had been having sex with James at the bar Ronan wouldn't have cared, as long as he had his pint.

"Fine. I'll bring them over," I said, through gritted teeth.

"Well, hurry up. Lucy's giving me the third degree about my book," he said, and then, spotting James's cigarettes on the bar, his eyes lit up. "Can I borrow one?" he asked.

"Are you planning on returning it?" said James.

"Ha-ha, I suppose not. Do you mind?" said Ronan, who was already pulling open the box.

"Help yourself," said James drily.

God, I wished he'd just piss off and disappear—Ronan, not James.

"Mind if I take two—one for the road?"

Christ, he had no shame. I was mortified.

"Take three," said James. "That way you won't have to come back."

The sarcasm went over Ronan's head as he pulled another cigarette from the pack. Turning to me as he left, he said, "At this rate you'd better get me two drinks. If you need a hand carrying them, give me a shout."

James looked at me, eyebrows raised. "Boyfriend?"

"Kind of," I mumbled.

"Interesting. What does he think of your new career move?"

"I haven't told him yet, because he's going to be one of the casualties of my planned maneuvers, along with the job I'm in now," I said, giving him my flirtiest smile. I know it was mean to denounce Ronan but, come on, the guy was a prat and James was gorgeous.

"I see. And when exactly are you planning on telling him?" he asked, grinning back.

"No time like the present," I said, looking over at him as he gulped half of Lucy's drink while she was talking to someone else.

"How do you think he'll take the news?"

"He'll miss the cash flow, but I don't think I'm 'deep' enough for him."

"What attracted you to him in the beginning?"

"He was the exact opposite to anyone else I had ever gone out with. I thought I'd give the sensitive, poetic type a chance for a change. It turns out the poetic types are broke, self-obsessed and really dull."

"How did you meet?"

"At a poetry reading," I said, beginning to laugh. "He gave a very dramatic reading of Patrick Kavanagh's 'Canal Bank Walk.'"

"Poetry reading?"

"I was trying to inject some culture into my life." I shrugged.

"Well, I'm not big on poetry, but if you fancy a drink some night . . ."

"Order me a white wine, I'll be back in a second," I said, throwing all the how-to-get-your-man—play hard to get, never show him you like him early on, make him wait, always say you need to check your diary, blah-blah-blah—advice out the window.

I charged over to Ronan, threw a pint and a whiskey chaser in front of him, told him I didn't think it was working out and that the two traits I deplored most in a man were scabbiness and laziness, both of which he had in abundance. I wished him well with his novel, sprinted back to James, knocking people and drinks aside in my eagerness . . . and we've been together ever since.

THREE

Couldn't believe it, I wasn't pregnant! I'd been sure my swollen stomach was a little baby growing inside me. Instead it was all those muffins I'd been eating. Very disappointing, as I now had the double whammy of not being pregnant with the guilt of having eaten the muffins in some self-indulgent fantasy that it was a craving. Damn, now I'd have to go to the gym to de-swell my non-pregnant stomach.

I decided it was time to take control and focus on being healthier to help my fertility along. Apparently there's a lot you can do to "aid the process," as I found out when I came across Winifred Conkling's *Getting Pregnant Naturally: Healthy Choices to Boost Your Chances of Conceiving Without Fertility Drugs* on the Internet.

Winifred says that diet is key, and suggests that men should avoid cottonseed oil and cycling, while both partners should enjoy good orgasms, biofeedback, meditation, visualization and massage, as well as quitting smoking and recreational drugs, and limiting computer use.

Right. Well, I had no idea what cottonseed oil was—it sounded like something they used to eat down in the Deep South in the days of slavery—but enjoying good orgasms sounded fine to me, and I'd get James to stop cycling and smoking.

I looked up biofeedback: ". . . using safe, battery-operated, electronic instruments, biofeedback techniques measure and feed back subtle changes in cortical brain waves (EEG), cortical blood flow (HEG), muscle tension (EMG) . . ." Bloody hell, it sounded like some form of torture. I wouldn't be having any of that. I'd be sticking to the massages, orgasms, healthy eating, gentle exercise and lots of green tea.

James came home later and I made dinner. He stared at the plate for a few seconds. "What do we have here, then, Emma?"

"Steamed vegetables and tofu."

"Tofu?"

"Yes, it's supposed to be really good for you and I was reading all about fertility today on the Internet. We need to change a few things."

"Oh really, like what?"

"Like our diet and our lifestyle. We have to give up caffeine, alcohol, fatty foods, processed meat and just stuff with additives in general."

"So what does that leave?"

"Well, vegetables and fruit, tofu and green tea. Oh, and you also need to stop smoking and cycling. It squishes your balls or something."

James winced. "And after we've finished this delicious feast, what's for pudding? Sheep's testicles?"

"No, smart-arse, sex and massages, actually. . . . Oh yeah, and good orgasms."

"I see. Well, that part sounds great, but I'm not sure if I'll have the energy for the sex and orgasms if all I'm eating is rabbit food," said James, waving a piece of broccoli in the air.

He had a point. While he rustled up an enormous plate of

pasta, which he chomped with glee, I pushed my dry, tasteless vegetables and even less appetizing tofu around my plate.

An hour later we were in bed. Well, James was in bed having his post-sex cigarette (he swore it would be the last one he smoked . . . ever) while I was attempting to do a handstand against the wall.

"What are you doing?"

"Handstand," I puffed.

"Any particular reason?"

"So the sperm can swim downstream more easily."

"You're joking?"

"Do I look like I'm joking?" I said. This gymnastics lark was tough going.

James began to laugh. He thought it was hilarious. I, on the other hand, was not having such a fun time as all the blood was rushing to my head and I was feeling dizzy. I was never the most agile and couldn't even do a decent forward roll in school, never mind a handstand. My arms were shaking and I collapsed in a heap on the floor, hitting my leg on the bed as I fell. James was doubled up on it, hooting.

"I don't know what you're laughing at. The sperm will be confused now. They won't know which way to swim. You should have held my legs up in the air. We need to take this seriously, James. The sperm need all the help they can get."

"Darling, my boys know which way to swim, trust me."

"Oh really? What makes you so sure?" I said, rubbing my leg grumpily.

James paused, then said, smiling smugly, "Because I inherited them from my father and his obviously knew which way to go. Henry and I are proof of that. Now, get back into bed so I can kiss your leg better."

* * *

I woke up the next day with a large bruise on my right leg. I was booked to do a wedding. I didn't really like doing wedding makeup because the brides—but more particularly their mothers—tended to be uptight and demanding. The upside was that weddings paid well, so I found it hard to turn them down.

I had met the eighteen-year-old bride-to-be, Jacinta Foley, two months ago and—how can I put this delicately?—she made Pamela Anderson look elegant. Dressed from head to toe in Burberry, with Burberry bag, scarf, wallet, key ring and shoes to match, six-inch false nails and masses of dark hair extensions, she came in clutching a picture of Posh Spice and told me that she wanted to look like her on her wedding day. She said she didn't care how much it cost because her father was "fuckin' loaded." Fine by me.

We did a trial run, during which she demanded more eyeliner, longer false lashes and darker foundation. "I want to look really tanned," she said, as I piled on another layer. Eventually, when she looked like a Jamaican cabaret star, she was happy.

Having met Jacinta, I knew her family was bound to be colorful too. It was going to be an interesting day. Her father had booked out Luttrellstown Castle—the same castle Posh and Becks got married in—and they had invited two hundred of their closest friends.

When I arrived, I was ushered to the bridal suite by a strung-out wedding planner. "They're all mad," she whispered to me. "No amount of money is worth the abuse I've had to take. No amount."

Jacinta was on the phone when I walked in. "I don't give a toss about your fat fuck of a sister. She is not singin' in the church and that's tha'." She hung up and sighed. "Sorry about tha'. It was me fella. His stupid sister wants to sing 'Careless Whispers' in the church. I don't fuckin' t'ink so. It's so tacky."

Jacinta had obviously been a bit heavy-handed with the Fake Bake self-tanner. She was a dark shade of tangerine. Her sister came out of the bathroom and Jacinta introduced us. "Anita, this is me makeup girl. She's going to make us into supermodels."

"Howzit going?"

Anita was small, very thin, had peroxided hair with the mandatory extensions and must have had shares in Fake Bake because she was even darker than her sister. She was wearing a tiger-print dressing gown. "Will you have a glass of champagne?" she asked.

"Thanks, but I think I'll wait till I've finished the makeup."

"Wha'? Are you mad? Get it into you. It's the real t'ing. It's fuckin' lovely."

"Okay, maybe just half a glass." There was no way I was going to get into an argument with this lot. I'd end up in traction.

I had just begun to do Jacinta's makeup when her father came storming into the room. "What the fuck is going on?"

"Wha'?"

"I've just had a call from me credit card company to check if I'd spent ten fuckin' grand on a holiday in Barbados. I could buy the fuckin' country for ten grand. Is that useless fucker not payin' for anyt'ing?"

Ten thousand euro. My God, where was she staying? She must be flying first class. I was dying to know what her father did for a living.

"Don't call Spike a useless fucker. He's just a bit skint at the minute, so I said you'd pay for the honeymoon," said the orange bride-to-be.

"A bit skint? He has so far paid for sweet fuck-all—and he ran up a bar bill of three hundred euro last night."

"Look, if you're too scabby to pay for me honeymoon, fine, we'll cancel the fuckin' t'ing. I'll be the only girl to have ever got married and not go on honeymoon because her father was too fuckin' tight to pay for it."

"Ah, now, don't be like tha'. I don't mind helpin' yiz out, but I'm not a fuckin' bank Link machine. He needs to get a proper job and support you."

"He has got a proper job. He's a musician. It takes time to be discovered, you know."

"Musician, my arse. Did it ever occur to you tha' he might be no shaggin' good? Tha' he and his band are shite? I'm givin' him six more months and then he's comin' to work for me."

"Thanks a lot, comin' in here upsettin' me on me fuckin' weddin' day. Some father you are. Me mother's probably turnin' in her grave at you roarin' at me," shouted Jacinta.

"Ah, now, Jacinta, don't start cryin'. I'll say no more about it for today and I'll pay for the honeymoon. But I'm warnin' you, tha' fella is to get a real job soon. Go on now, get ready and enjoy yourself. I'll see you later. We'll have a great day. Order another bottle of champagne."

As a significantly poorer Mr. Foley closed the door, Anita shook her head in disbelief. "You chancer! I can't believe you got him to fork out ten grand for the honeymoon. There'll be no fuckin' money left for me at this rate."

My sentiments exactly, Anita. Between Jacinta and the useless, talentless Spike, it seemed to me that Mr. Foley was being bled dry. I was dying to know what he did for a crust.

"So what does your dad do?" I asked, trying to sound casual rather than nosy.

"He owns SuperBurger and Tits "R" Us," said Jacinta, pouring herself another glass of champagne.

Well, that explained it. SuperBurger was the most popular fast-food chain in Ireland and Tits "R" Us was the most popular strip club in Dublin. They were queuing 'round the block to get into it, and rumor had it that when the police went in to check that there was no "funny business" going on in the back rooms, they were shown such a good time that they were now the place's best customers.

"Oh my God, Jacinta, look at this!" gasped Anita, who was staring out the window.

Jacinta rushed over. She clearly didn't like what she saw. "I don't fuckin' believe it. I'll kill him."

I looked down and saw a Tits "R" Us minivan pull up and ten buxom strippers in nonexistent minidresses climb out. Jacinta picked up the phone and roared into it. "I told you, Da, I don't want those fuckin' slappers at me weddin'."

Even people twenty miles away could have heard him bellowing down the phone: "THOSE FUCKIN' SLAPPERS ARE PAYIN' FOR YOUR FUCKIN' WEDDIN'. NOW BELT UP AND GET READY!"

I buried my face in my makeup bag so they wouldn't see me laughing. They cursed their father and lamented the fact that he was lowering the tone of the wedding.

"Fuckin' disgrace is wha' that is," said Jacinta, glaring out the window.

"Here, have a drink; it'll make you feel better," said her ever-helpful, underage, alcohol-swigging sister.

The girls proceeded to polish off a second bottle of champagne and eventually calmed down about the strippers ruining Jacinta's wedding, by which stage they were fairly sloshed.

I was panicking about time: we only had an hour to go and it normally took at least forty-five minutes to make up a bride—and that was a sober, low-maintenance bride. I finally managed to persuade Jacinta to stop drinking and sit down beside the window so I could apply her makeup in natural light.

Her face was a dark shade of orange with darker patches along her eyebrows and ears. I set to work, toning down the fake tan, trying to blend it and make it look a little more natural, but she was staring into a mirror and freaked. "Wha' are you doin', Emma? You're makin' me look all pasty. I want more bronze, just like we did in the trial run. Get out the bronzer and lash it on."

There was no point in fighting it—this bride was never going to be persuaded to tone anything down. I fished around in my makeup bag and found a very strong bronzer—a shade I had only ever used on very dark-skinned clients—and brushed it on.

Jacinta was delighted. "Deadly," she said, smiling at herself in the mirror. "That's more like it. Now do me eyes. I have the lashes here."

She handed me the false eyelashes. They were two inches long, with little diamanté studs dotted along each individual lash. They would have looked over the top on Liza Minnelli in *Cabaret*.

"Are you sure about these?" I asked, in a last-ditch attempt to salvage any credibility I'd have left after this job. "I have some plain black ones here that would look more natural."

"Fuck natural. I want to look like a movie star."

Fair enough! I stuck them on, then started working on her lips. I was using a nude color to try to counter the dramatic eyes.

"Hold on, I've changed me mind about me lips. I want them scarlet."

"What?" Was she completely insane? She'd look like a hooker! "I really think you should keep your lips nude with just some colorless gloss, Jacinta. Your eyes are the dramatic part of your makeup, so you need to keep your lips neutral."

"No, I don't want tha' colorless shite. I want scarlet. Show me what you have in there."

I sighed and produced an array of ruby red lipsticks and glosses. She chose the brightest red gloss. When her lips were done she turned to her sister for approval. Anita shook her head. Jesus, what now? I thought.

"You're still too pale. You need more of tha' bronzer," said Anita. "Tha' pale look is crap. I t'ink tha' Nicole Kidman looks a fuckin' state. She looks like a ghost. Why don't her mates tell her to slap on some tan? It's very fuckin' sad. All tha' money and she goes out lookin' snow white."

"I know, and she's Australian. Sure it's fuckin' roastin' over there," said Jacinta, shaking her head at the thought of poor pale Nicole.

I added yet another layer of bronzer to her cheeks and finally— although she now looked like a Las Vegas stripper—Jacinta was pleased.

I had to do Anita's makeup in a hurry. She demanded the same color scheme as Jacinta, so I put away the muted beige and brown eye shadows, the powder pinks and creamy peach blushers, the gently tinted lip glosses and natural-tone foundations.

When Anita was five shades darker, with equally scarlet lips, I helped them into their dresses. Anita's bridesmaid dress was a skin-tight, red satin Chinese-style minidress. The bride wore a skintight, white, full length, satin halter-neck backless dress encrusted with large crystals. It had a slit up the front that left little to the imagination. The Tits "R" Us ladies had some stiff competition here.

They looked at each other and beamed.

"You're a ride. All the fellas will be chasin' you," said Jacinta.

"Thanks. You're a fuckin' ride yourself. You look better than Posh on her wedding day."

"Ah, stop."

"No, I mean it. Better."

Jacinta looked thrilled. For her, there was no better compliment.

As they were leaving I wished them good luck and they assured me that they would tell all their friends to book me for their weddings. I was "fuckin' brilliant."

As I watched Mr. Foley proudly helping Jacinta into the car, fixing her veil for her and kissing her forehead as she beamed up at him, I felt a lump in my throat. I hoped we'd have a daughter so that James could walk her up the aisle. I imagined him all gray-haired and debonair, escorting our beautiful girl up the center of the church as I smiled from the top—looking stunning myself, of course—dabbing tears of pride from the corners of my eyes, while my tall, dark, handsome son squeezed my arm. . . .

FOUR

$\mathcal{S}$hit. Shit. Shit. Not pregnant again. Damn. I was sure I would be. We had sex on days twelve, thirteen, fourteen and fifteen to be on the safe side. What the hell was wrong with me? I rang James to tell him but Donal answered his phone.

"Hello."

"James?"

"No, Donal here, is that Olga?"

"No, it's Emma. Who the hell is Olga?"

"I know it's you, Olga Korbut, Olympic gold medalist. Come on, now, don't be shy."

"Donal, put me on to James."

"Lookit, Olga, I'm a huge fan. I used to love the way you somersaulted around on that beam and don't even get me started on the parallel bars. I believe you've come out of retirement recently. I'm delighted to hear it."

"Hilarious, Donal. You're a real comedian, now put James on to me."

I willed myself to sound calm. I was furious. How dare James tell Donal about my handstands? How dare he? That was private information. I'd kill him. I could hear Donal shouting to James that Olga Korbut was on the phone.

"Hi, what's up?" said James, trying to sound nonchalant as

Donal roared laughing in the background. He knew he was in trouble.

"Judas!"

"Pardon?"

"Judas, your thirty pieces of silver will be waiting for you when you get home. I suppose you think it's funny telling the lads about my handstands."

"Hold on, Emma—"

"Oh, yeah, I'm sure you all just sat around the locker room and had a good old laugh at my expense. Well, that is just charming. Thanks a lot, James. Some husband you are."

"Emma, relax, it's not that big a deal. I didn't tell them all about it. Donal was asking me if we were going to have kids and I said we hoped to and then he said that his sister had gone a bit mad when she was trying to get pregnant and had ended up going to India to see some healer and then I may have mentioned the handstands, but only in passing."

"Oh, well, if it was only in passing, sure that's fine. I feel so much better now. Don't give it another thought. Any other private information you'd like to divulge in passing is fine by me. Well, I won't keep you because I'm sure you have a few more gems to mention, in passing, to Donal. 'Bye for now."

I slammed down the phone. I was seething. How could he be so insensitive and disloyal? I pictured them all having a right old laugh at my expense. The mad wife. I hate all that macho bullshit. Each guy trying to outdo the other guy with his "my bird's madder than yours" stories.

You hear them going on: "My bird went to the supermarket in her pajamas last week . . . ," "My bird's making me do tango lessons . . . ," and on and on they go in some weird competitive ritual.

But my pet hate is the "I have to go home or my bird will kill me" routine. The guy is out with his friends, he looks at his watch, it's ten o'clock, he's tired, has had enough and wants to go home. So you'd think he'd say, "See you, guys, I'm off. I fancy an early night." Don't be ridiculous: he can't do that; it wouldn't look good, so he says, "I'd better phone the missus to tell her I'll be late."

Then he calls you and before you've even had the chance to say hello, he starts this strange monologue with himself. "I'm staying out with the lads. What's that? Ah, I know I said I'd be back early but we're having a laugh here. What? Oh, you've cooked dinner already. Oh, right, well, then, I suppose. Yeah. Okay. Well, I'll just finish this one and come home then. Relax, don't get your knickers in a twist, I won't be long, I'm on my way." Before you can tell him that you're going out to the cinema with a friend, there's no dinner of any description in any oven and he can stay out as long as he wants, you couldn't care less what time he comes home—he hangs up.

As I was standing in the kitchen thinking how annoying the phrase "don't get your knickers in a twist" is, and still fuming at James, the phone rang.

"*What?*" I shouted, expecting it to be James groveling.

"Emma?"

Oh, great. Fanfuckingtastic. It was Imogen. I was going to pretend I was a Russian housekeeper with no English, but while I was trying to get the accent right in my head, she said, "Emma, hello, are you there? It's Imogen."

Damn, too late now.

"Oh, hello, Imogen, sorry about that. I was just in the middle of something. How are you?"

"Very well, actually. Bit of news to tell you. I'm preggers again. Yep, Henry and I are expecting. And it's twins this time. Fancy that, and we weren't even trying, it just happened. Bit sorry that I won't be able to ride for a few months, but there you go. Still, it'll be maaahvelous to have some company for Thomas."

I felt physically sick. Lucky cow. Twins. That would be so perfect. What was wrong with me? I must have no eggs, or only little shriveled city ones. Bloody Imogen and her big, horsey, fertile, country eggs.

"Congratulations, that's amazing news," I said, trying to muster some enthusiasm and failing miserably.

Elephant-skinned Imogen, however, was oblivious to this. "Yes, it is, rather. Thanks. So how about you? Any sign of a cousin for Thomas?"

Sod Thomas, snotty little shit. I didn't want any child of mine hanging out with him. "No."

"Well, chop-chop, Emma. You need to set to. James would be a maaahvelous father."

Oh yeah, and what did she mean by that? What about me being a maaahvelous mother? God, she got up my nose.

"I'm sure we'll get around to it in our own good time," I said, trying desperately not to lose my temper.

"Well, you don't want to leave it much longer, Emma—you're not getting any younger. You may not feel maternal now, but once you have a baby, you will. Everyone does, even the least likely people. Motherhood is such a wonderful thing. The love between a mother and her child is like no other love."

Unbelievable. Now she was implying that I had no maternal instinct.

"Yeah, so I've heard."

"You really should try it, Emma. I'm sure even you would take to it. Going to fancy parties and restaurants is all very well, but it becomes a bit hollow after a while, don't you think?"

I had to do something drastic. I had to get her off the phone before I lost my temper and told her exactly what I thought of her. I yanked the phone from the kitchen to the front door. The cord was stretched so far that I thought it would pop out of the socket, but I didn't care. I opened the front door as quietly as I could and rang the bell loudly. "Oh, sorry, Imogen, have to dash—it's my mother. 'Bye now."

I was so angry that I didn't know what to do with myself, so I jumped up and down shouting "patronizing bitch" for five minutes until I was out of breath and my feet hurt. Some women swear by slapping on the Marigolds and giving the kitchen floor a good scrub in times of anger, but I think they're all depraved. Cleaning the kitchen floor definitely would not do it for me.

After jumping up and down I took out a tub of Häagen-Dazs vanilla chocolate fudge and ate my way through my anger. But then I felt guilty about the eight thousand calories I'd just consumed so I dragged myself to the gym.

I hated the gym. There was something so unnatural about a group of women in Spandex thongs jumping around like monkeys to cheesy seventies disco music. So I never went to classes, I just went down and watched *EastEnders* while "power walking" on the treadmill, or read *Hello!* on the StairMaster.

The *Hello!* was gone when I got there, but there was an old *Cosmopolitan* left in the stack so I took that. It had an article about masturbation and how men masturbated all the time and the effect this could have on fertility. If men were "slapping the salami" every day—*Cosmo*'s words, not mine—they might not have much sperm left for reproductive purposes.

I'd have to tackle James on that later. I had him on the back foot for telling Donal about my handstands so he'd have to listen to me whether he liked it or not . . . and, let's face it, James was not going to be too thrilled about discussing his masturbation timetable.

When I got home I noticed that the formerly bouncy, curly telephone cord now hung in a limp, straight line down to the kitchen floor. Great—every time I looked at it, it'd remind me of Imogen.

Twins. Lucky her. Maybe if I got James to stop masturbating, we'd have triplets and then I'd never have to get pregnant again. Hurrah. If Henry could produce twins, I didn't see why James couldn't manage triplets. I could picture it now. Two girls and a boy—Holly, Sophie and Ben. Two pink Babygros and a blue one. All sleeping sweetly in their cots side by side. Everyone would know the Hamilton triplets. They'd bring a smile to people's faces as they passed by. The girls looked like little Shirley Temples and the boy looked like the cute little kid in *Jerry Maguire*. Aww, they were gorgeous.

As I steamed the vegetables for dinner I imagined little Ben playing rugby for Ireland as his father watched proudly from the sidelines, although James would probably want him to play for England. Mmm, hadn't thought of that. It might be less complicated if he played tennis. Yes, tennis was better. We could go to Wimbledon and sit in the posh box where the families sit and cheer him on as he wins the tournament. Then, in an emotional acceptance speech, he'll thank his parents, but especially his wonderful mother for her support and encouragement throughout his formative years. I was clapping and wiping away tears when James walked in.

Obviously feeling bad about the Olga Korbut palaver, he had bought me flowers. He saw me in tears and came over to hug me. "I'm sorry, Emma. I didn't mean to upset you."

There was no point in trying to explain that I was crying with pride at our son's nail-biting, Wimbledon-final five-set victory, so I said nothing. He handed me the flowers and I put them in a vase. They were lovely, but I was going to make him sweat it out for a bit.

"I really am sorry, darling. I promise, no more indiscretions."

"Well, there'd better not be, James. That's private stuff, not for the locker room. I don't want the whole team laughing at me. You know what Dublin's like, the whole city will know about it. I'll be a laughingstock."

"You won't. I only said it to Donal and he swore he hadn't said it to anyone else."

"Oh really, and you believe him, do you? I'd hardly describe Donal as the soul of discretion."

"He is, actually. He plays up the gruff-rugby-player thing, but he's a really good guy."

"Okay, enough of the eulogy. You'll be telling me he's in touch with his feminine side next. Besides, I have something more important to talk to you about."

"Oh? What's that?" James looked at me warily.

"Masturbation."

"Emma!"

"I need to know how often you masturbate. There's no point looking appalled: it's a well-known fact that men masturbate regularly, I just need to know how regularly."

"Emma, there are some things that a guy needs to keep to himself and that's one of them."

"Oh, for goodness' sake, I don't want to watch, I just want to know. It's important."

"Why?"

"Because apparently if you're cleaning your pipe—or whatever the expression is—every day there'll be none left for when we have sex. We need nice full loads of sperm, not the measly leftovers from your earlier activities. So come on, tell me—how often, James? Every day? Twice a day? Couple of times a week?"

"I don't know. It depends."

"On what?"

"On lots of things."

"Like what?"

"Stuff."

"Like what?"

"Like how I'm feeling, what I'm thinking about, if I have an urge, stuff like that," said James, looking increasingly uncomfortable.

"Really? What kind of urge?"

"Well, if I woke up with an erection or saw a steamy film or something. Look, can we please change the subject? I really don't want to discuss this with you."

"Okay, but where do you do it? In the shower? Down the loo?"

"Well, I don't know, I suppose in the shower mostly."

"Well, at least it gets washed away there. Anyway, the thing is you have to stop it. I need you to save up all the swimmers for me. Keep them all inside so that when they're finally let loose they're champing at the bit and raring to go. That way they'll charge up and hunt down my eggs. It makes sense if you think about it. The less those sperm get out into the fresh air the more eager they'll be."

"Fine. Now can we please talk about something else?"

"Not yet, you haven't promised to stop masturbating."

"I promise."

"But how can you promise when all men seem to have to do it? It's like a basic need or something."

"I'll manage. I have incredible self-control. *Now* can we please change the subject?"

"Just one more thing, would you be thinking about me or Halle Berry when you do it?"

"Halle, in the James Bond bikini, of course."

FIVE

I went to meet Lucy for a drink and a moan. I've known Lucy since I was six. We moved in together after college with high hopes of finding fame and fortune. Neither of us found fame. I found James and Lucy found money—she earned shed-loads of cash as a management consultant, but worked all the hours in the day.

"Hi, sorry I'm late, last-minute crisis at work," said Lucy, as she plonked herself down on the couch beside me.

As usual she looked really well. She had long, slim legs that went on forever. She also had long, thick, shiny black hair and green eyes—if I didn't love her so much I'd hate her. "No worries. You look great. New suit?"

"Yeah, I treated myself to it last week. Cost a fortune, but what the hell? Us single girls have to look our best at all times. It's dog-eat-dog out there."

Lucy had been single for two years and was becoming increasingly cynical about love and meeting Mr. Right.

"How was Saturday night? I'm dying to hear all the gories," I asked, hoping it had gone well, though judging by the "dog-eat-dog" comment, it didn't look too good.

Lucy had been at a singles party organized by a friend from work. It was all very *Sex and the City.* Each of the ten girls invited had to bring a platonic straight single male friend, a bottle of champagne and a bottle of spirits. Lucy had taken Stephen, a friend of ours from college who had recently been dumped by his girlfriend of five years.

"God, it was awful. I should never have brought Stephen. Initially it was fine, everyone was a bit nervous so the drinks were going down like rockets. You'd swear we'd never seen alcohol before. Anyway, I was chatting to this cute doctor when Stephen came over and pulled me outside. He said some girl had just tried to snog him and he realized that it was a bad idea to have come because it was too soon and he was too raw and blah-blah-blah. I mean, he even squeezed out a few tears!"

"Poor Stephen."

"Fuck Stephen! Poor me. I got stuck counseling him for an hour and by the time we finally went back inside my cute doctor was rolling around on the couch with some brain-dead blonde Aussie. Stephen, having offloaded all his woes, bounced over to the girl who'd tried to snog him and shoved his tongue down her throat. The bloody Comeback Kid wasn't in it. By that stage I was freezing from standing outside for so long, sober and extremely pissed off. So I left, went home and ate a full bag of Reese's Peanut Butter Cups."

"Oh God, Lucy, what a nightmare. I can't believe you spent your night comforting Stephen."

"Tell me about it. I give up. I'm so sick of trying to meet someone. I spent ages getting ready, I looked about as well as I'm going to look, I clicked with a cute doctor and then it all went horribly wrong. Story of my bloody life."

"Come on, Lucy, you're stunning and loads of guys fancy you."

"Like who?"

"Like all the guys we were in college with."

"They're all married, Emma! They all ended up marrying the square-bear girls who never got drunk and made fools of themselves. It's the tinsel versus the calm scenario. They all married the calm ones."

She had a point: they did all marry the calm ones. Lucy and I had this theory—Tinsel and Calm. It was based on a Christmas party we had gone to in college when neither of us had snogged the guys we fancied and they had gone off with two boring girls. The problem—we discovered after hours of analysis—was that we had spent far too much time wrapping the decorations and tinsel from the Christmas tree around ourselves and leaping about the dancefloor like maniacs while throwing back neat vodkas. We were much too busy having a laugh, and had lost focus. Meanwhile the calm girls, who wouldn't dream of wearing tinsel as it didn't match their outfits, looked on from the edge of the dancefloor, sipping their red wine, smiling and shaking their heads at us as though we were the hired entertainment.

The guys we fancied joined in our fun and laughed and leaped with us until about midnight, when they—never ones to lose focus for long—went in search of Calm. They'd had their fun and now they wanted to score with minimal effort.

Tinsel girls were too much trouble. A guy would need buckets of energy to keep up with one, excellent negotiation skills and a rugby tackle or two to tear her away from the Christmas tree decorations for a snog. Tinsel girls won't laugh at a guy's joke if it isn't funny. They drink more, talk more and know more about music, politics and sports than a guy. Calm is by far the easier option: she will titter at all his crappy jokes, tell him that all his boring lads-on-tour stories are interesting and say she wishes she could drink more but she's so petite that alcohol goes straight to her head.

Tinsel wakes up the next day fully clothed, tongue stuck to the roof of her mouth, eyes molded shut with mascara, alcohol stains all over her clothes, Santa decorations hanging from her ears and layers of tinsel wrapped around her. She is, unsurprisingly, alone. Meanwhile Calm is up, showered, dressed in her smart-casual day clothes—neatly ironed jeans and a baby pink cashmere sweater—cooking breakfast for her new man.

Lucy sighed and took a slug of wine. I decided to help her out. That's what best friends are for. So I suggested a blind date.

"With who? I know all your male friends," Lucy said suspiciously.

"With Donal from James's rugby team." I knew Donal wasn't quite her type, but opposites often attract. Besides, the guys she usually went for never worked out, so it was probably time she tried something new.

"Is he the big ugly-looking yoke from the country?"

"Well, yeah—he's tall, but he's not ugly. He's actually very attractive and he has a brilliant personality. He's hilarious company. I'm telling you, loads of girls fancy him. You should see them after the matches, they're all over him."

Okay, I admit I was exaggerating slightly. But he was tall, he wasn't traditionally good-looking but you wouldn't call him ugly, and girls did seem to find his insane sense of humor entertaining. I also knew that if I said other girls fancied him Lucy's competitive streak would be aroused. I spent the best part of an hour singing Donal's praises until she finally agreed.

"I dunno. He's no looker. But I suppose there's no harm giving him a tryout. I've snogged everyone else in Dublin, so I have to look for bogmen now. My bloody biological clock is about to pack it in, so go ahead and set it up. I'm game."

"Great, I'll get James on the case. Drink?"

"Yeah, vodder and Diet Coke, please."

I ordered the drinks and sat back down. "Speaking of biological clocks, bloody Imogen's pregnant and she's expecting twins."

"Oh, shit, Emma, what a nightmare."

"Tell me about it. She rang last week to tell me and started having a go at me for not having babies myself. Stupid, insensitive wench. She even accused me of not being maternal."

"What? How dare she? You *are* maternal. What the hell would she know?"

One of the things I loved most about Lucy was her unswerving loyalty. If someone was mean to you, she'd hate them out of solidarity.

"Don't let that cow put you down. On the bright side, at least it means you could have twins too. Wouldn't that be perfect? You'd have a ready-made family in one go!"

"I was thinking that myself, actually," I confessed. "Triplets would be totally ideal. I've always wanted three kids, so that would be perfect."

"Remember that woman in England who had the sextuplets? That could be you."

"I'd settle for one. I really hope it happens soon. The thought of having to listen to Imogen for six more months is doing my head in."

"Don't worry, Emma, it'll happen for you. I know it will. And you'll be a brilliant mum," said Lucy, squeezing my hand.

"Thanks," I said, choking back tears. She was right: I would be a brilliant mum. Sod Imogen.

James was a bit dubious when I told him of my great plan to match up Donal and Lucy. In fact, he looked at me as if I was deranged and recently escaped from a mental institution. "Lucy and Donal? Have you lost your mind? They'll kill each other."

"What do you mean? Why?"

"Donal thinks women should be barefoot and in the kitchen, and somehow I doubt that Lucy would agree. She's a career woman."

"Just because she has a good job doesn't mean she wants to be working fifteen hours a day for the rest of her life, James. That's the whole point. She wants to meet a guy, settle down and have a family."

"That's all very well, but I just don't think Donal's the man for her. He's a great guy, but he's a man's man. I don't think he's Lucy's type."

"Well, what is Lucy's type?"

"I don't know, a city-type guy with a college degree, a successful job and a flash car, not a professional rugby player from Ballydrum."

"You're wrong. She's gone out with successful businessmen and it hasn't worked out. I think it's time she tried someone completely different, which Donal is."

"Okay, well, I'll talk to Donal."

"Call him now."

"I'll see him tomorrow and ask him then."

"No, call him now. Come on, I want to hear you selling Lucy properly. I want you to tell him how gorgeous and fabulous and clever and funny and great she is. Come on, James, call him now," I said, handing him the phone.

"Okay, okay, I'll do it now," said James, sighing.

He dialed Donal's number and I pressed up close to listen in. I wanted to make sure he said the right things about Lucy.

"Hi, Donal. How do you fancy going on a blind date with Emma's friend Lucy?"

"What's wrong with her?"

"Nothing, she's a bit of a looker."

"Would you do her?"

"Yeah, I would, actually, she's tasty."

I gave James a dead arm at this point.

"No limbs missing?"

"None."

"Okay, so."

"Great. See you tomorrow."

The next morning, as James was taking his shower, I decided to time him—fifteen minutes. In that time I could shower, moisturize, put on my makeup, get dressed and eat breakfast. What was he doing in there? I opened the door and shouted over the noise of the water: "What are you doing in there?"

"What?"

"What are you doing in there? You've been in there for fifteen minutes."

"So?"

"So, I want to know if you're masturbating. I thought we had an agreement. No more pipe-cleaning in the shower."

The shower door opened and a very red-faced James glared out at me. Shampoo was dripping into his eyes and he looked really cheesed off. "What I do and how long I spend in the shower is my own business. Jesus Christ, a man needs some privacy. I will not have you standing over me like some psychotic sergeant major, accusing me of masturbating every time I take a shower. It's eight o'clock in the bloody morning, now get out of here before I come over there and strangle you."

Yikes! James very rarely lost his temper, but when he did he was a bit scary. I'd have to trust him not to jerk off in the shower and not give him the third degree. I decided to cook him breakfast and apologize. He said it was fine, but that I needed to calm down about the whole masturbation issue and he didn't want it mentioned again. Some things were sacred.

SIX

I rang Lucy to tell her that Donal was keen for the date. She said she had seen a picture of him in the paper scoring a try and was having second thoughts. "He's desperate looking, Emma."

"No, he isn't. That's a bad photo and, come on, he was covered in mud and sweat. No one looks good when they are all mucky."

"Yeah, nice try. He's a fierce-looking yoke, but I said I'd go out with him so I will. Okay, what's the plan?"

"Well, he said he'd pick you up after the game this Saturday to go out for dinner."

"Where's he taking me? What'll I wear?"

"Uhm, I'm not sure, actually, but he's not short of cash, so I'm sure he'll bring you somewhere nice. The little black dress should do the trick."

"Yeah, it's not too dressy and not too casual. I'll wear it with my new Jimmys."

"Oooh, did you get Jimmy Choos?"

"Yeah, they're to die for. Black with really pointy toes and killer six-inch heels."

"Wow! Poor old Donal won't be able to keep his hands off you."

"Mmm, on second thoughts," she said, giggling, "after seeing that photo, maybe I should wear a tracksuit and runners."

I had no idea where Donal was taking her. He wasn't the most sophisticated guy in the world, but I was hoping he'd pull out the stops. I had told James to tell him that Lucy was a bit of a high flyer and was used to going to nice places. I hoped he wouldn't blow it.

When James came in I quizzed him as he made himself some toast. "You know the date with Donal?"

"What date?" he said, stuffing a slice of bread in his mouth.

"James! The date with Lucy."

"Oh yeah. What about it?"

"Where's he taking her?"

"No idea. Why?"

"Because she wants to know what to wear."

"Birds!"

"It's perfectly reasonable to want to know where you're going on a blind date. Where do you think he'll take her?"

"Knowing Donal, probably Burger King and the Black Hole," said James, finding himself very amusing.

"Hilarious. Look, I want you to tell him to take her somewhere nice. Blind dates are bad enough without being taken to some grotty pub."

"Okay, I'll mention it."

"You won't forget now, will you?"

"Remind me tomorrow."

"James!"

"I'm joking. I'll tell him tomorrow."

Suffice it to say that things didn't go according to plan. On the day of the date, Donal got a kick in the head in the last five minutes of the game and was stretchered off with his face covered in blood.

When they'd cleaned him up on the sideline, it was clear that he needed quite a few stitches and might have a slight concussion, so the physiotherapist took him to the hospital.

Three hours later he emerged with eight stitches down the side of his now very swollen right eye. Being Donal, he didn't decide to call Lucy, explain what had happened and go home and get cleaned up. Instead he threw on an old rugby jersey and tracksuit bottoms he found in the trunk of his car and turned up at her apartment half an hour late with one side of his face covered in stitches and dried blood. He rang the bell.

Lucy opened the door, screamed and slammed it shut.

"Hello? Lucy?"

Jesus Christ, how did this tinker with the mad eye know her name? Was he some kind of stalker? Or ax murderer? Lucy looked out the peephole. He didn't seem to have any weapons, but then again his tracksuit was quite baggy so he might be harboring a knife or a gun. There was something strangely familiar about him. She had definitely seen him before. Maybe he'd been stalking her for a while.

"Go away, I'm calling the police!" she roared through the letterbox.

"Are you Lucy Hogan?"

"How the hell do you know my name?" said Lucy, trying to sound brave as she dialed 999, her hands shaking.

"It's Donal. Donal Brady. Are you all right?"

What? Donal? Lucy looked out the peephole again. Oh God, it *was* him. She opened the door. "What the hell—"

"Howrya. What's going on? Are you okay?"

"Your face!"

"Oh yeah," said Donal, reaching up to his eye. "I forgot. I must look a right state. I got a kick in the head in the game today. No permanent damage done. Did I give you a fright?"

"Well, yes, you did. I thought you were some kind of mad rapist or something."

"Sorry about that. Come on, we both need a drink. Are you ready to go?"

"Uhm, yeah, I suppose so," said Lucy, looking from her tight little black dress and Jimmy Choos to his tracksuit and runners. "Where are we off to?"

"I know a great pub so why don't we go there for a few and see how we go?" said Donal, as cool as you like.

Lucy was a bit taken aback. "See how we go"—what the hell did that mean? Was this pub some kind of initiation ceremony where, if he didn't like her after a few pints, he'd cancel the dinner and save himself a few quid?

As she sat fuming in the car, Donal howled along to the radio, turning every few minutes to wink at her with his one good eye. They drove to a rundown part of town and Donal rammed the car up on the curb outside a pub called the Black Hole. Lucy had never heard of it and had only ever been in this part of town once before, when she got lost on her way to the airport.

"Is this it?" she asked, in shock.

"Yep. The best pint of Guinness in Dublin. It's owned by a fella from my hometown. It's a great spot. Come on."

Donal marched in ahead of her, greeted the barman with a roar and a slap on the back and ordered a pint of Guinness. The pub was a dingy dump with no windows, sawdust on the floor and Christy Moore's greatest hits belting out from the speakers. When her eyes got used to the dark, Lucy could make out four other people. The barman, and three customers sitting up at the bar. An old guy, an older guy and a guy who was so old he should have been dead. They all turned to stare at her.

When she asked for a white wine spritzer, Donal and the barman laughed for five minutes and she ended up with a pint of Harp. Lucy hadn't had Harp since she was fifteen and drinking it from cans outside the local disco.

Donal chatted to the barman while Lucy sat down at a grubby table and wiped the sawdust off her Jimmy Choos. A few minutes later Donal strolled over with her pint and four packets of dry-roasted peanuts. "I thought you might be hungry," said Sir Galahad.

"I am, actually. I thought we were going out for dinner."

"Ah, sure we'll see how we go. I'm in need of a drink after that kick in the head."

Over the next hour, Donal bored Lucy rigid with a blow-by-blow account of his rugby career to date, while Hoovering up four pints of Guinness. Lucy, meanwhile, sat and listened while she munched her way through three packets of dry-roasted peanuts (about a zillion calories in each pack, but she was too hungry to care) and tried to drink her Harp. She decided to give him an hour to prove he wasn't as much of an oaf as he appeared.

With five minutes left to prove himself, the blissfully thick-skinned Donal passed out at the table. The pints of Guinness combined with the kick in the head had proven too much even for him. Lucy couldn't believe it. This had to be a setup, she thought. Come on, someone's having me on. *Candid Camera, You've Been Framed!* . . . something? But when Jeremy Beadle didn't appear she leaned over and shook Donal. Nothing. He was snoring. She shook him again, a little harder this time. Nothing. So she poured her pint of Harp over his head.

"What the fuck?"

"Oh, hello. Nice of you to wake up. I think I'm the one who should be asleep—did you manage to bore yourself into a coma? Well, much as I'd love to stay and listen to some more of your mind-numbing rugby stories, I have to go home and stick a red-hot poker into my eye. This has been a real eye-opener for me. I actually believed that man had come a long way from the cave and you, Donal, in one evening have proved me wrong. Well, I must dash, the poker awaits me."

"Ah, come on, now, relax. We'll go and get some food. The kick in the head must have knocked me out."

"No, thanks, I'm leaving."

"Don't be so uptight," said Donal, stumbling to his feet.

"How dare you call me uptight? You don't know anything about me. All you've done is ramble on all night about your boring rugby career."

"Well, you weren't saying anything so I had to talk. You've had a look on your face all night as if you'd smelt something nasty. Like you had shit on your stupid-looking shoes," said Donal, pointing unsteadily at them. "You're like some spoilt princess who was brought up with a silver spoon in her mouth. I'm obviously not good enough for you because I don't drive a flash car and wear suits."

"You arrogant shit. I don't give a damn what car you drive. I do, however, object to being collected by somebody with blood all over his face in a filthy tracksuit. I would have been quite happy to wait an extra half an hour for you if you had called and explained. As for your choice of venue! No, I don't like smelly, dingy pubs. I never have and I never will. I drank Harp when I was fifteen and have spent the last eighteen years of my life working my ass off to make damn sure I never have to drink that shit again. And in my world, a conversation is an activity that necessitates the participation of two people. Not a coma-inducing monologue about your prowess on the rugby pitch. Maybe in your backward little town men behave like pigs and women find it attractive, but in my world a pig is a pig," said Lucy, standing up and grabbing her coat.

"I'd say you're fantastic in bed," Donal said, grinning at her. "I like my women feisty."

"Yeah? Well, how's this for feisty?" said Lucy. She slapped him across the good side of his face and stormed out.

The next morning I spent two hours on the phone with her. She ranted and raved about what a dreadful night it had been, how awful Donal was, how she was never going on a blind date again, how all men were bastards, even the ugly ones, and how she'd rather spend the rest of her life alone than have to go through another date like that. She thought the city guys she dated were bad, but this guy was pure caveman. How could James be friendly with someone like him? He was awful.

"Look, I know Donal can be a bit rugby-guyish, but he's really nice underneath it. In fairness to him the kick in the head and the alcohol must have made him behave out of character."

"How do you know he's such a nice guy? What has he ever done that's so nice?"

"Well, you know James met Donal when he was still living in England playing for the Titans and then Donal decided he wanted to move home to Ireland and play for Leinster and persuaded James to come with him?"

"Yes."

"Well, the reason Donal suddenly decided to move back is because his sister Paula and her husband were killed in a car crash and they had named him as his niece Annie's legal guardian. His parents are pretty old so he had to bring her up. He came back to look after her shortly after the crash."

"Oh my God."

"I know. Paula and her husband were killed outright and Annie was really traumatized. She was only ten at the time. She's thirteen now and she's in boarding school. Donal goes to all her hockey matches and to her parent-teacher meetings and all that stuff. James said he's brilliant to her and she worships him."

"My God, Emma, why didn't you tell me this before the date?"

"Because I wanted you to like him without the sympathy vote."

"Well, it doesn't really change anything, anyway. He may be a great uncle and I'm sorry about his sister dying, but it still doesn't take away from the fact that he was a creature last night."

"I'm sure he'll be mortified today. Honestly, I've never seen him behave that badly."

"Well, I have Harp and sawdust all over my Jimmy Choos to prove it. Anyway, I think I've chewed your ear off sufficiently for the time being. Let me know what he says to James about the date. Let's see if he has any remorse!"

"Will do. I'll call you when I find out."

I told James what had happened and he found it all hilarious. Especially the part where Donal fell asleep at the table, he loved that bit. He promised he'd get the lowdown from Donal at training.

When James called later that day he was laughing so much he could hardly speak.

"Well, what did he say?"

"He said—ha-ha—he said—ha-ha-ha—he said—ha-ha-ha—"

"James! What did he say?" I said, beginning to giggle myself.

"He said he thinks she's fantastic and he's mad about her."

"What?"

"He said he thought she was very good-looking but a complete pain in the neck for most of the date, but when she poured the pint over his head and read him the riot act he totally fell for her. He's going to call her and ask her out."

"Oh my God," I said, laughing, "is he insane? Does he not realize that she thinks he's the devil himself?"

"Donal reckons she's mad about him. He said she got far too hot and bothered for someone who wasn't into him and he reckons she's gagging for it," said James.

My God, the man was certifiable.

SEVEN

$\mathcal{I}$ decided it was time for some medical aids to this pregnancy lark. I didn't want to waste another month guessing when I was ovulating. I had heard someone talk about an ovulation test at a dinner party James and I had gone to at my friends Jess and Tony's house a few weeks earlier.

Of the five couples invited, we were the only ones who didn't have kids. As we were just a few months into trying, it didn't bother me too much, but I was surprised by how boring the women were and how one-dimensional. The conversation was all about babies, and if you didn't have one—tough.

Jess had met them at her antenatal classes so they all had eight-month-old babies. The conversation revolved around cracked nipples—lots of winking, wincing, laughing and in-jokes about cracked nipples. I didn't see anything remotely funny about it, but then I never particularly enjoyed discussing period pains either. I always thought girls who sat around talking about periods were very odd. Why waste time on something you have no control over, can do little about and will have to go through every month for decades to come?

After the hilarious cracked-nipple chat, they then had a competition over who'd had the most stitches. Some weirdo called Alison was delighted to announce that she had undergone such a dreadful birth and ended up with so many internal and external stitches (internal—this was news to me!) that her doctor refused to tell her the number for fear of upsetting her, so she won. Judy, who had been in the lead with thirty stitches, was not happy at being relegated to second place.

But the pièce de résistance was the conversation about who was having postbaby sex and who wasn't. They all said they were, but I reckoned Judy was lying because she still seemed to be having trouble sitting down comfortably and her husband spent the night leering at my boobs—even James noticed—so I don't think he was getting any.

Meanwhile the men were having a whale of a time discussing the latest political scandal to hit the papers: the leader of the opposition had been outed in a kiss-and-tell scoop by his mistress, Amanda Nolan, who hosted a daytime chat show. I was particularly interested in the story because I had done her makeup for *Afternoon with Amanda* a number of times, and had a great laugh with her. She was a real character and always regaled me with juicy gossip about well-known Irish figures.

James called me over to tell the others about Amanda, and I had a great time with the men gossiping and arguing about the affair and its consequences for John Bradley's political career, not to mention his twenty-five-year marriage. I could see that the mothers were none too happy for me to be laughing and joking with their husbands. I was a "traitor" of sorts. But having escaped from the "which nursery is best?" conversation, I had no intention of going back.

On the way home I said to James that when we had kids, if I ever turned into a boring old fart who talked about cracked nipples on a Saturday night, he was to shoot me on the spot.

*　　*　　*

When I rang Jess to thank her the next day, she said she could see I'd found all the baby talk a bit boring, but that once I had my own I'd understand.

"Do you always talk about that stuff when you meet up or do you talk about other things as well?" I had to ask. I refused to believe that Jess found it as interesting as she was making out.

"Well, we met at antenatal classes, Emma, so obviously our common bond is our children," said Jess defensively.

"Of course, I understand. It's just that you never really talk about that stuff with me, so I just wondered if I was being selfish by not asking you about it. I just never really thought of it, to be honest."

"Well, of course you didn't. You don't have a baby so how could you know? It's not interesting unless you've gone through it."

"Is it really that interesting—talking about stitches for an hour?"

This was Jess, with whom I'd had my wildest nights. Jess, who could do twelve shots of tequila in a row without passing out or throwing up. Jess, who loved nothing better than a good gossip and a laugh about old boyfriends and disastrous dates. Jess, who had married Tony who was as mad as she was. Jess and Tony had been the most fun couple I knew. And now she was telling me that she liked hanging out with these grannies. In days gone by she would have been the first to slag them off.

Did having a baby mean leaving your personality in the hospital? Did your conversation have to turn to nappies and nurseries? Did you not have any interest in anything outside your child? It was scary to see someone change as much as Jess had. Tony hadn't changed—granted, he'd calmed down a bit, but then we all had. But Jess was like a different person. She hadn't left the house in months except to go to baby groups. You couldn't have a conversation with her because she spent half the time cooing to little Sally or talking to her in that annoying baby voice people use when speaking to small children, and her concentration span was about ten seconds long. Then again, I thought, if you were at home all day with a baby, it probably would be all-consuming. I'd have to be careful not to turn into a boring old housewife when I had mine.

"No, it isn't that interesting, really," admitted Jess. "You know, I woke up this morning and realized how boring it must have been for you to have to listen to. In fact, I was bored myself. When I'm with the girls on my own we always seem to revert back to baby chat so I'm used to it. But seeing them through your eyes—well, they are a bit dull. I need to get out more. I think I'm turning into a granny. I haven't worn anything but a baggy tracksuit in six months. I've forgotten how to put on makeup. I talk to no one all day and then by eight o'clock I'm in bed exhausted. I used to be really good fun and full of beans. Now I'm just knackered all the time. God, Emma, I need to get out and get my personality back!"

"Hey, you're not boring and I'll give you a top makeup lesson to get you back on track. Besides, I didn't mean to insult your new friends. They were all very nice. I was just the odd one out, so naturally I found the conversation a bit one-sided. Anyway, look, let's meet up for a slap-up dinner and lots of wine."

"I'd love that. Let's do it soon!"

"Great. I'll call you next week."

I felt relieved: at least Jess was thinking about leaving the house. And if we met in a restaurant, she could concentrate on having a proper conversation. I'd get Lucy to come too. She got on well with Jess, although she was a bit cheesed off as she hadn't heard from her since Sally was born, despite having called in with presents after the birth and talking regularly to her answering machine.

I decided not to call Jess and ask her about the ovulation test because then she'd know I was trying and she'd be looking at my stomach the whole time trying to figure out if I was pregnant or not. It had happened straightaway for her. She had actually conceived on honeymoon, and I knew she'd be eager to help me out in her very sweet way, but I didn't want any added pressure.

I took myself to Boots and scoured the shelves of the family-planning section. There was a selection of brands. I opted for a five-pack of First Response ovulation sticks. Bloody expensive too—thirty euro for five measly sticks. I nearly put them back on the shelf, but then I remembered I'd spent sixty euro the day before on a funky long-sleeved T-shirt. Priorities, I reminded myself, priorities.

When I got home, I opened the pack and took out the instructions. First Response claimed to predict the two days when you were most likely to become pregnant. Excellent, I liked that. It sounded very positive, very confident. I should have bought these sooner.

Right, instructions:

If you are having difficulty becoming pregnant it could be that you are not making love in the two days when you are most fertile, around the time of the ovulation.

Mmm, yes, that was probably what we were doing wrong. Not getting the precise days right. Okay, what did I need to do?

The test will measure luteinizing hormone (LH), which is always present in your urine and increases just before your most fertile day of the month. This increase, or surge, in LH triggers ovulation, which is the release of an egg from an ovary.

Oh, come on, we all knew that eggs were produced at ovulation; get to the point.

The appearance of two easy-to-read purple lines in the test's result window indicates your LH surge prior to ovulation. Most women will ovulate within 24 to 36 hours after the LH surge is detected. Predicting ovulation in advance is important because the egg can be fertilized only 6 to 24 hours after ovulation.

Yikes, I had no idea you had only six hours. That was absurd. How the hell did anyone get pregnant? Six hours—come on, give a girl a chance.

Your two most fertile days begin with the LH surge. You are most likely to become pregnant if you have intercourse within 24 to 36 hours after you detect the LH surge.

What? But it said six hours and then it said twenty-four to thirty-six hours, so which was it? Not so bloody straightforward, after all. I decided to get on with the test.

How to perform the test: holding the stick by the thumb grip, with the absorbent tip pointing downward and the result window facing away from your body, place the absorbent tip in your urine stream for five seconds only.

The "five seconds only" was underlined. Jesus, I hadn't thought I'd need a stopwatch.

With the absorbent tip still pointing downward, replace the overcap and lay the stick on a flat surface with the result window facing up.

I took off my watch and placed it on the sink. I was so busy staring at it to make sure I didn't go over the five seconds that I ended up peeing all over my hand. Yuck. I washed my hands, laid the soggy stick flat, as instructed and waited.

While I was waiting for the results to show up, the phone rang. My mother left a message on the machine: "Are you there, Emma? Are you screening this call? Well, call me tomorrow. I need to talk to you about that sister of yours. She is out of control. Not to mention your useless father, who refuses to come into town shopping for a new jacket for his own party. I saw something for myself today in that nice boutique, Lillie's, in town, and they've put it aside for me until tomorrow. I need you to come with me to tell me if it's nice. It costs an arm and a leg, so I need to get a second opinion, but it's very stylish. Are you there, Emma? Okay, well, I might pop in later to describe it to you. Call me when you get this message."

Shoot, I'd forgotten to call the caterers about Dad's sixtieth. I'd have to do it first thing in the morning. I also needed to call my brother Sean in London to see if he was going to bring anyone home for the party. I'd call him later. . . .

Shit, now I'd lost my train of thought. What was I supposed to be looking for? I grabbed the instructions.

Reading the results—two similar purple lines mean that you have detected your LH surge, you should ovulate within the next 24 to 36 hours. A purple reference line and a light purple test line mean that you have not yet reached your LH surge. You should continue with daily testing until the two lines are the same purple color.

Bloody hell, this was daylight robbery. I'd be broke if I had to pee on these stupid sticks every day. I looked at the stick. There was only one purple line. What on earth did that mean?

I looked down at the instructions.

If only one purple reference line appears, you have not reached your LH surge. You should continue with daily testing.

Yes, but what if I'd passed it? What if I'd missed the ovulation day? Then I'd just be peeing on the sticks every day for two weeks for no good reason.

Straightforward—my arse.

I wondered if there was another way of finding out when you ovulated—an easier way. I decided to check it out on the Internet.

I logged on and typed in "ovulation." It came up with 331,000 matches. I needed to narrow it down. I typed in "ovulation testing"—aha, only 39,900 matches, that was more like it. I found a site that offered a fact sheet on natural methods of testing for ovulation. It said the key was to check the elasticity of your mucus. I wasn't sure what mucus was, but I had a horrible feeling it might be related to vaginal discharge—gross. It was simply not fair: women should not have to go through this. I sighed and looked at the suggestions:

Be prepared to check your cervical mucus (CM) consistency several times every day during each cycle. Using white tissue paper, wipe vaginal opening to obtain CM specimen, or insert one clean finger into vagina as far up as the cervix, and then remove finger.

Hold on a minute. How the hell was I supposed to know when I was as far up as my cervix? I should have paid more attention in biology classes. I racked my brains. The nuns probably omitted the chapter on reproduction in case we got any ideas. So where the hell did my cervix begin? I decided to read on and maybe I'd have a poke around later. Hopefully I'd find it.

CM should be observable on fingertip. If using tissue, apply a fingertip to collected CM and then pull gently away to test elasticity. If using finger, test CM elasticity by closing and again opening finger with thumb. Note the following: elasticity of CM: (a) sticky and breaks easily or (b) slippery and stretches like raw egg white.

Oh my God, this was unbelievable. It was horrendous. I'd never be able to eat meringues again. Egg whites would never have the same appeal.

As fertility approaches, CM should gradually change from dry to wet, from sticky to slippery, and from white to transparent. The most fertile CM is very thin and very slippery, often referred to as EW CM (egg white cervical mucus). If you observe several different types of CM during one day, record the observation with the more fertile characteristics.

How the hell were you supposed to tell the difference between slippery and sticky? Why, in God's name, was I supposed to write it all down in some sort of diary? What for? To read about in my old age?

The last day on which fertile CM (EW CM) is observed is considered peak fertility day. Also note days on which sexual intercourse occurs and any bodily discomforts such as cramping, twinges, etc. These are important indicators if you see a specialist.

Jesus Christ, at this rate I'd never get pregnant. The choice was to pee on my hand or fiddle about with my elusive cervical goo . . . AAARGH!

EIGHT

The next day I called Sean. He was a typical brother and never rang. I was lucky to get the odd email as he worked forty thousand hours a week. He lived in London, where he had moved ten years ago after graduating from university, to work as a junior lawyer in Brown and Hodder. It was a prestigious law firm and we were all terribly proud when he was made a partner a week after his thirtieth birthday. There were only eighteen months between us and we had always been close.

"Hello, it's your sister, remember me?"

"Hey, sis."

"Hello, stranger. Thanks for all the emails, I'm worn out reading them."

"Ha-ha. Sorry, I've just been—"

"Up to your eyes, I know, I know. How's it all going?"

"Very well, actually. There are some great perks to being a partner, the best one being your own space to park your Porsche Boxter."

"You didn't!"

"I certainly did."

"*Coooool.* I'd say the birds are throwing themselves at you. Flash car, loaded, successful, gorgeous."

"I may be successful but I still look the same."

Sean was a redhead too. We were both suspicious of Babs's true parentage because she had long blonde hair. Granted, it had gotten darker over the years before it got lighter again with the help of copious highlights, but there was no red at all. She was also eleven years younger than Sean. . . . I'm not accusing my mother of any wrongdoing, you understand, I'm just saying it was a little strange and the red definitely came from my father's side.

Anyway, Sean had also gotten lumbered with the gray-blue skin and the big orange freckles—which thankfully I'd managed to avoid—so he had never been very confident about his looks. He also had the misfortune—or maybe stupidity (he should have picked a guy with buck teeth and a hunchback)—to have a best friend, Jack, who looked like Brad Pitt. Girls were always befriending Sean to get to Jack, which didn't help his self-confidence. Sean is such a nice guy—I know I'm biased, but he really is—that I knew he'd meet someone fantastic eventually.

"I'm ringing about Dad's party on the twenty-fourth. We're just finalizing the numbers and I'm checking to see if you're planning to bring someone. Mate, girlfriend, girl-you-fancy . . . whatever."

"Actually, I'm going to bring a date."

"Oooh, great. Who?"

I was delighted to hear this. In ten years he had never brought anyone home. Whoever she was, he must like her.

"Her name's Amy, she's twenty-two, Irish and absolutely gorgeous."

"Wow, Sean, you sound smitten."

"Yeah, I am, actually. But let's keep it to ourselves. I don't want Mum rushing out and buying a hat just yet."

"What does she do?"

"She's between jobs at the moment. She wants to be an actress so she was temping in my firm for a few weeks to keep her ticking over while she went to auditions. She's really pretty, Emma, a real looker, and she's really talented."

Wannabe actress—sounded a bit dodgy to me.

"So she did study drama?"

"Well, she traveled for a few years and then she did some drama course over here. She nearly got a part in *EastEnders,* but they said she was too good-looking. That happens a lot, she often gets turned down for dramatic roles because she's too pretty."

Well, that's the best excuse I ever heard: "I'm too good-looking to get parts." I didn't like the sound of this girl. She sounded a complete idiot. Why couldn't she make herself look ugly for the auditions if she was that good an actress?

"Wow, well, that's a good problem to have—being too pretty."

"Yeah, I know. I'm dying for you to meet her. I know you'll get on really well with her. She reminds me a lot of you. Things she says and does."

"Oh really, like what?"

"Oh, you know, she gives as good as she gets and doesn't let me get away with anything. And she says it like it is, very direct. I love that about her."

A bully. Sean was saying his bully girlfriend reminded him of me. Charmed, I'm sure.

"I'm not direct. I'm very sensitive and subtle."

"Ha-ha. Come on, Emma, you're the most direct person I know. It's a great trait and it's the reason I know you and Amy will get on so well."

I decided to let it go. I knew I wasn't going to like Amy one bit, but I'd make an effort for Sean's sake and I'd be subtle and indirect about it.

"Okay, well, I'm looking forward to meeting her. She'll be thrown in at the deep end—all the uncles and aunties are coming and the Devlins and the O'Connors, so she'll get to meet everyone."

"She'll be well able for them all. Okay, I'd better go, I have a conference call. See you in two weeks."

When James came home I asked him if he thought I was direct. He looked at me suspiciously. "Is this a trick question?"

"No. Am I?"

"Yes."

"What? No, I'm not."

"Yes, you are. But it's a good kind of direct, not a bad kind." James was becoming a real pro at this.

"In what way am I direct?"

"You don't beat around the bush. You just say what's on your mind."

"But not in an aggressive, bullish type of way?"

"No, absolutely not."

"In what kind of a way?"

"In a subtle kind of way."

"James, how can I be direct and subtle?"

"Because, darling, you are a very special person with amazing communication skills."

"Yeah, right. Anyway, Sean's bringing his new girlfriend back to Dad's party. She's a wannabe actress and apparently a stunner."

"Excellent, always nice to have some eye candy at family parties."

"Easy, tiger. A wannabe actress, though. She sounds a bit flighty."

"Emma, as long as Sean's happy, what does it matter what job she has?"

"Or doesn't have—apparently she can't get work because she's too pretty."

"Good old Sean. You should be happy for him."

"I am. I just want him to be with someone as nice as he is. She sounds a bit hard."

"I'll tell you what," said James, putting on Sky Sports and settling down to watch some football match, "why don't you ring your mum and discuss it with her for a few hours? She's much better at this than I am."

"No, James, I want to analyze it with you."

"Emma, I need to relax before the big game tomorrow, and no offense, but talking about some bird neither of us has ever met is not my idea of chilling out."

"Fair enough, I'll leave you alone, but only because of your big match. We can discuss it further after that. So who is this?" I said, snuggling down beside him, feigning interest in the football.

"Real Madrid and Chelsea."

"Is Beckham playing?"

"Yes."

"Oooh, good, I'll watch it too."

"Okay, but no talking, watch the game."

"Okay . . . just one thing—do you think I should wear my red dress to Dad's party?"

"Yes, absolutely."

"Not the black one?"

"Emma!"

The next day, James's team was playing its big match so I decided to go down and support him. He had only been the Leinster head coach for two months, having been promoted from assistant when

Johnnie Mooney resigned over a pay-raise dispute midseason. I was delighted when Johnnie left as it gave James the opportunity to step out of his shadow. Since then, all the papers had said that James was an excellent coach and so far the team had been doing well under his leadership. He was really nervous about this match, though, so I knew it must be a big one and I wanted to show an interest. He said that if they won this game, they'd be in the quarter finals of some big European league. I might not know a lot about rugby, but I knew this league was important. I was determined to go and cheer them on.

I had a photo shoot for Spirits—the top hairdressing salon in Dublin—that morning: they had asked me to make up the models for their new ad campaign. The money was good and it'd keep me in ovulation sticks for a while. The shoot dragged on into the late afternoon, but I managed to wrap it up and make it to the match for the second half.

The big stadium was jammed full of people. I had never seen such a big crowd at any of James's games before. I managed to squeeze through and stood near James who was running up and down the sideline, roaring instructions at the team. He looked really serious and quite sexy in his team tracksuit. I tried to catch his eye to wave at him, but he was far too engrossed in the match to notice me.

It was a close game and I was swept away with the atmosphere. It was electric. The man beside me told me that this was the best Leinster side he'd seen in years and that English fella coaching them was a genius. My heart swelled with pride. With five minutes to go Leinster was three points behind. We needed a try, my new friend told me. "Come on, Leinster," I roared.

One minute to go and Leinster had a lineout on the opposition's twenty-two yard line. The hooker threw the ball in; Donal jumped ten feet in the air, caught it and took off like a bullet to-ward the opposition's line. He mowed the other players down as he thundered forward and then he scored! Donal scored the winning try! The crowd went berserk. James jumped up and down and hugged the players. Then he saw me waving frantically at him and jogged over to hug me too. My new friend looked at me in awe and then I introduced him to the genius coach—my husband, James.

We had drinks in the clubhouse after the match and I was thrilled to see James basking in his well-deserved glory. He was chuffed that I had been there to cheer him on and I vowed to go to all the matches from then on.

Later that evening I got a chance to corner Donal and grill him about Lucy.

"So, you big oaf, have you called Lucy yet to apologize?"

"I called her at work, but she hung up on me."

"Well, do you blame her? You fell asleep, Donal."

"I know, I know, I feel bad about it. But seeing as how she won't talk to me, I've come up with a plan B."

"Oh yeah, what?"

"All will be revealed tomorrow," said Donal, and winked at me.

God, I hoped he wasn't going to do anything too insane. I quizzed James, but he had no idea.

Lucy was sitting at work the next day when she got a call from a giddy receptionist to say there was a delivery for her. The girl could hardly speak, she was laughing so much.

"Well, just send it up to Sarah," said Lucy, annoyed at being in-terrupted for something so trivial. Her secretary—Sarah—handled that kind of thing.

A few minutes later she heard squealing and giggling outside her office. Then she heard Sarah asking someone in a very loud voice, to gales of laughter, "Do you have an appointment, sir?"

Lucy was walking toward the door to see what the hell was going on when it burst open and Donal marched into her office dressed as a caveman. He was wearing a leopard-print tunic with Moses sandals and carrying a spear. Colleagues appeared from nowhere to see what was going on. Quite a crowd had gathered.

For once, Lucy was speechless. What was this nutter doing making a spectacle of himself in her office? Donal began to beat his chest and howl like a werewolf. He got down on bended knee and asked Lucy to forgive him for having behaved like a caveman and to give him another chance.

Lucy found her voice: "Get out, you lunatic. You're making a holy show of me, not to mind yourself. This is my workplace, not a zoo," she hissed, as her boss Ross Brophy stormed through the door looking extremely annoyed.

"What the hell is going on here, Lucy? I have important clients in my office who are asking me what the howling noises coming from next door are."

Donal stood up. "Sorry, it's my fault. I'm trying to get Lucy to go out with me."

"Well, can you please do it somewhere . . . Donal? Donal Brady?"

"That's right."

"My God, I was at the match yesterday—that was some try you pulled off," said Ross, shaking Donal's hand, suddenly oblivious to the fact that Donal was naked but for an animal-print rug. "What a game."

"They were tough opponents, all right, but we felt we had the edge on them up front and we just kept plugging away," said Fred Flintstone.

"That drive at the end to score the try was spectacular," said Ross. "Listen, my clients next door are big rugby fans. You wouldn't come in and say hello, would you?"

"Only if Lucy here agrees to go on a date with me," said Donal, grinning at Lucy.

"Lucy, if you don't go out with Donal, you're fired," said Ross.

Lucy shrugged. She didn't know whether to laugh or cry. "Well, okay, then, but I choose the venue this time."

NINE

I spent the next day with my mother in Lillie's boutique while she tried on every stitch in the shop, finally opting for a beige dress with chocolate brown velvet trimming. She looked lovely in it, but I said I thought Dad would have a heart attack when he saw the bill. Big mistake. Huge.

My mother launched into a dramatic monologue—was it too much to ask for a little treat after thirty-five years of marriage? Hadn't she supported and encouraged my father throughout his career, entertaining all his boring accountancy colleagues, and look at him now, partner in the firm? She had stood by him through thick and thin and all she wanted was to look nice for his birthday and now I was making her feel guilty about it. Could she not buy a frock without a big song and dance being made of it?

I had to stop her before she moved on to the "no one appreciates me" speech so I distracted her by pointing out that she now needed a matching bag and shoes, and she should get really nice ones as she deserved it, and it was important that she look her best as she was hosting the party. This sent her into a frenzy and we spent another two hours trudging from shop to shop to find the perfect match. Thankfully the shoes were procured before my patience ran out and I strangled her.

As we were driving home she turned to me and asked, "Now, what are you going to wear?"

"No idea, I haven't thought about it."

"Well, don't wear anything too racy and, whatever you do, do not attempt to wear that black dress with the plunging neckline. It makes you look cheap. And no animal prints either—they're so common. Wear a nice trouser suit with a nice crisp white shirt or a nice long skirt or—"

"Mum! I'm thirty-three. I think I know how to dress. Now, go home, put your feet up, have a nice long bath and relax. I'll call you later," I said, pulling up in front of the house.

"Well, all right, but promise me you won't wear that black dress," she said, hauling the shopping bags out of the back of the car.

"I promise."

"And you'll come over early to do my makeup?"

"Yes, of course."

"Okay, well, I'll see you on Saturday. Be here by five so we have plenty of time."

"I will."

"Okay—you don't think the shoes are too high?"

"No, they're perfect."

"Because I'll be standing all night and I don't want to be uncomfortable. I'm not used to such high heels. Maybe I should change them for the lower ones with the straps in that other shop."

"Mum, the shoes are lovely. Stop fussing."

"Well, it's all very well, but I'm not as young as I used to be and I can't wear such high shoes anymore. Maybe I should change them."

"*Mum!* The shoes are fine."

"I don't want to look like mutton dressed up as lamb. I think I'll change them. You shouldn't have let me buy them, Emma, they're too high."

"Fine, change them. Wear Wellington boots and a housecoat. I don't care anymore. I'll see you on Saturday," I said, and drove off at top speed before I stabbed her with the high-heeled shoes.

When I got home James was finishing a telephone interview with the *Irish Times*. "Yes, I'm confident that we'll beat Perpignan next week . . . no, I'm not daunted by playing them on their home turf, we're looking forward to the challenge . . . I think our front row is the best in Europe . . . Donal Brady is a great asset to the team and an excellent captain. He's a great motivator . . . well, let's win this match first before we start talking about the semifinal . . . okay, Gary, see you in France next week."

James hung up and kissed me. "Good day with your mother?"

"Nightmare. She was like a lunatic. James, what did you mean there, 'see you in France next week'?"

"It was Gary Brown from the *Times*. He's coming to cover the match next Saturday in Perpignan."

"I thought your match was here."

"No, it's an away match."

"Well, you can't go."

"Sorry?"

"You can't go. It's day fourteen."

"Oh, you mean your dad's party. No, of course I'm here for that. The match is next week."

Jesus, did I have to spell it out? "No, James, it's day fourteen of my cycle. We have to have sex on that day so you can't be in France."

"Emma, it's the quarter final of the European Cup."

"I know, but we can't skip a month. It's been five months already and nothing. I don't want to miss one. At this rate I'll never get pregnant. Can't you just go for the day?"

"No, I can't. We're going for five days. We need to train out there for a few days before the match. I'm sorry, darling, but this is nonnegotiable."

"Well, maybe you could leave some sperm behind and I could use a turkey baster or something." I'd read about the turkey baster in some old novel. I realize it was a desperate measure, but I was beginning to panic. James would be gone from day twelve to day sixteen. It was a disaster. The months were slipping by and my biological clock was ticking away. I'd never get pregnant at this rate.

"Emma, calm down. It's just one month. It's no big deal. We'll focus next month, I promise," James said, laughing at the turkey baster idea. I knew it was silly, but I could feel myself getting really hot and bothered. I wanted to do everything I could to get pregnant and those were key days.

"I'm coming with you."

"What?"

"I'm going to come to France."

"But, Emma, I won't have any spare time. I have to be totally focused. This is the biggest match of my career. If we win this it'll be the furthest Leinster have ever got. It's a really big deal and I can't be distracted. It's all about training and team bonding."

"I don't care, I'm coming. I'm sure you can spare me fifteen minutes a day. I know it's a really important match and I won't distract you, but I'm coming."

"It'll be really boring for you. I won't have a spare minute."

"James, I'm only looking for a few minutes of your precious time. Come on, it's not going to kill you or wear you out, and I promise not to get in your way."

The problem with baby-making was that it had pretty much wiped out the spontaneous rip-your-clothes-off sex we were used to. Now it was all about timing and dates, whereas before we had just hopped on each other whenever the mood took us. The focus had changed from pleasure to which-is-the-best-position-to-help-the-sperm-reach-the-egg-quickly sex. Still, if that was what it took, then that was what we had to do.

I could see James was not happy about the prospect of me tagging along to France. He was really nervous about the match and he wanted to be there for the team one hundred percent. But I wasn't going to distract him. I just needed his sperm once a day.

"I really don't think it's a great idea, but if you promise not to get annoyed when you're left on your own all day and not wake me up in the middle of the night for chats because you can't sleep, then I suppose it's okay. I'll allocate you two minutes and twenty-five seconds of my very precious time."

"Very generous of you to allocate two minutes for foreplay," I said, grinning. "I promise not to pester you when you're coaching. In fact, you won't even know I'm there," I said.

"Somehow, Emma, I doubt it."

That Saturday I went to my parents' house at five to do my mother's makeup. I had organized caterers to serve the food and set up a bar so that Mum and Dad could enjoy the party without having to worry about people's glasses being empty, or them not having enough to eat.

When I arrived, Dad was skulking around in his new suit, looking harassed. "Thank God you're here," he said, rolling his eyes. "Your mother's like a lunatic. I'm going to hide out in the study. I've had to change my tie three times already. Good luck!" he said, and scampered off.

I went upstairs to my mother, who was sitting in her bathrobe, hair in curlers, on the phone to my auntie Pam. "No, I'm just wearing an old dress I have from years ago. Nothing fancy at all.

Okay, well, Emma has just arrived so I'll go. I'll see you later, Pam. 'Bye now."

"An old dress from years ago?" I said, shaking my head. "What are you like?"

"Emma, people don't need to know your business. As I've said to you before, keep yourself to yourself. Now, what's this about Sean bringing a girl? He called me this morning to say he's bringing someone and that he told you last week, and you never said a word to me. What's going on? Who is she? Is it serious?"

"Well, Mum, I was just keeping myself to myself."

"Stop that nonsense. Now, who is she?"

"Her name is Amy, she's Irish and he seems to like her, but it's early days so don't be getting too excited."

"Oh, lovely, an Irish girl. What does she do?"

"She's an actress."

"An actress?"

"Yes."

"Oh." My mother was suddenly less enthusiastic. "What does she act in?"

"Who?" said Babs, strolling in midconversation and throwing herself onto the bed.

"Sean's new girlfriend. He's bringing her to the party tonight," I said, filling her in. "Apparently she has been having great difficulty getting parts because she's too pretty."

"What?" they both said.

"Too good-looking? What a load of bollocks," said Babs.

"Barbara, there is no need for foul language. What do you mean, she's too pretty? I thought that would be an advantage."

"I agree. Look, I'm just telling you what Sean told me. We can ask her ourselves when we meet her. Sean said she's a stunner."

"Compared to who? Gwen McKenna, the dog he was snogging

at Christmas?" Babs sniggered, flicking her blonde hair back over her shoulder. She was a real head turner—tall, thin and blonde—and she knew it. Her face was actually not her best feature; she had inherited Dad's rather large nose and square jaw, but she had nice blue eyes and lovely long, thick, very blonde (bleached) hair and a knockout figure. She ate like a pig and was stick thin, but she was only twenty—in a few years she'd have to work at it; everyone did. I was looking forward to the day when she'd have to go to the gym like the rest of us mere mortals to keep the blubber at bay.

"Babs, don't be so mean. Gwen is attractive in her own way." In fairness Gwen was very unattractive, God love her, but Babs was far too dismissive of people for her own good.

"Oh, get over yourself, Mother Teresa. She's a dog. Anyway, I'm off to have my shower."

"Barbara?" said my mother, looking very serious all of a sudden. "I'm warning you now. You are to wear something respectable this evening. It's your father's sixtieth birthday, not a nightclub. I'm not having you showing us up in front of the relations. Do you hear me?"

"Yeah, yeah. Relax, I'll dress like a nun."

Two hours later—having made up my mother, who complained that I was being heavy-handed, and Babs, who complained I was putting on far too little—we were ready. I was wearing a red wrap-around dress—which, surprisingly, didn't clash with my hair. Thankfully, it had gotten darker as I got older so it was now more auburn than ginger. Babs was wearing skintight, very low-cut (of the almost-exposing-her-pubic-hair variety) snakeskin trousers and a beige boob tube. She came down only after Sean had arrived with Amy so Mum couldn't cause a scene.

Amy was very pretty—stunning face, beautiful porcelain skin,

great smile—and had short, blonde hair. She was, however, small
and a touch—shall we say—curvy? For some unknown reason she
was dressed like someone who didn't have a mirror at home. Lucy
and I called girls like her "friends-and-family girls." As in, how the
hell could their friends and family let them go out dressed like
that? Surely if any good friend saw you wearing something that really didn't flatter you, they'd mention it. Or, at least, your mother
would. . . . Well, mine certainly would.

Amy was wearing a tight backless silver dress that did nothing
for her curves. Her neck was covered in a silver choker, with GUCCI
emblazoned across the front—handy for those who wanted to
know where she had bought it but were too shy to ask.

Sean was standing with his arm 'round her, looking like the cat
that got the cream. He was delighted with her and, in fairness, I
could see why. She was by far the best-looking girl he had ever been
with. James was clearly impressed too. "Very nice to meet you,
Amy. Great dress," he said.

"Thanks, I got it in Harrods. That's the great thing about London—the choice of shops is so good. Dublin's such a backwater
when it comes to fashion. And the social life in London is so much
better, there's no comparison. Why on earth did you come to live
here?" asked Amy, turning up her delicate little nose at the
thought.

"To be honest, I think London's full of tossers, present company
excluded, of course," said James, smiling at Sean. "Anyway, it's a
well-known fact that redheads are fantastic in bed," he added,
winking at me. "Now, who needs a refill?"

The doorbell rang, and for the next hour my uncles and aunts
and friends of my parents flowed through the door. The men all
made a beeline for James to congratulate him on winning the
match and to quiz him about his plans for the quarter final. They

huddled in the corner, analyzing the players, trying to outdo each other with statistics and rugby trivia. Everyone had an opinion on how Leinster should approach the game in Perpignan and they all wanted to voice it.

Meanwhile, in the other corner, Amy was holding court. She was telling my aunties how wonderful London was, as if they were hillbillies who'd never been farther than the local barn dance. ". . . The restaurants are so superior to the ones here and the bars are so cool. My agent is always taking me to these new places—he's really well connected so we get tables at all the top restaurants."

"Your agent, did you say?" said my auntie Tara.

"Yes, I'm an actress."

"Oh, how exciting. What parts have you played?"

"Well, I nearly got a part in *EastEnders,* but they said I was too good-looking," said our future Hollywood star.

"So have you actually acted in anything?" asked Babs.

"Well, I'm doing auditions at the moment, and if I don't get a part soon, I'll probably go to Hollywood. My agent thinks I should go straight into movies. The American market is more open to hiring good-looking women."

"Would you ever think of coming back to Dublin and trying your luck here?" I asked, a bit fed up with listening to her pie-eyed fantasies.

"Come back here? Are you mad? The best thing I ever did was getting out of this dump. If you want to be successful you can't sit around Dublin waiting to be discovered. London and New York are where it's at."

"What auditions are you going for?" asked Babs.

"I'm currently preparing for an audition for a part in the new Barclays ad."

"Barclays Bank?" I asked.

"Yes, it's a new ad campaign they're running for their new branding, so it's a really big deal."

Okay, come on. She had to be joking. An ad for a bank was a really big deal and involved preparation? Give me a break. It's not exactly Shakespeare. I decided to try to be open-minded for Sean's sake. Maybe this ad was going to break the mold and be like a mini-movie or something.

"So what does it entail?"

"Well, I'm going for the bank manager's part. I have ten lines of fairly complex dialogue and it has to be delivered in a friendly but professional manner. It's very difficult to get the tone exactly right, but my acting coach and Sean have been helping me out," she said, smiling over at Sean.

Acting coach? For a Mickey Mouse part in some crappy bank advert?

"So when's the big audition?" asked Babs, who I could see was trying not to laugh.

"Next week, so I have a few more days to go over my lines with my coach. My agent says this could be my big break. The coverage would be huge. It will air after every prime-time show on TV and my face will be on all the billboards around London. You can't buy that kind of publicity. It will make my career."

"Wow! I had no idea bank ads were such a springboard for success," said Babs, still managing somehow to keep a straight face.

"Well, a bank ad here in Ireland obviously wouldn't be any good, but an English one being watched by millions of people could make you famous overnight."

"Well, I hope you get the part," I said.

"Oh, I'm sure I will; my coach says I'm word perfect," said the shy, retiring Amy.

I had to get up and move away. This girl was an idiot and a

delusional one at that. Granted, she had a lovely face, but she was no movie star in the making and she talked a lot of crap. I was pouring myself a large vodka when my auntie Pam came up and dug her bony fingers into my arm. Pam was a real nosy-parker—of the curtain-twitching variety—and drove us all mad. She was my father's youngest sister and even he wasn't too keen on her.

"Well, Emma, how's married life?" she asked.

"Great, thanks, Pam," I said, throwing back a glug of vodka.

"I see you've put on a bit of weight since I saw you last? Have you news for us? Is Dan about to be a granddad?"

Oh, great. Just what I needed—some annoying old bag telling me I looked fat and reminding me that I wasn't pregnant.

"No, Pam, he isn't."

"Oh, now, I know you young ones don't like to say anything till after the first three months. My Julie was the same. Don't worry, your secret is safe with me," said the biggest mouth in Ireland, winking at me.

"No, Pam," I said firmly. "I'm not pregnant. There is no baby on the way." I wanted to make it crystal clear so she couldn't misinterpret it in any way and cause more embarrassment by telling everyone Dad was about to be a grandfather.

"Oh, well, now. You'd want to get on with it. Aren't you married over a year? Your mother would love a little grandchild. She sees how fond I am of mine and has often said she'd love some of her own. You don't want to leave it too late, Emma, you're not a slip of a thing anymore."

"Yes, thanks for reminding me, Pam." God, the woman was maddening. Just because her daughter had sprouted five kids in seven years didn't mean the rest of us wanted to. Now I felt fat and barren.

By the end of the night I had been asked by my auntie Tara if I was feeling broody, my auntie Aisling if there was a pitter-patter of tiny feet on the way any time soon and my auntie Doreen if I was going to bring up my children in the Catholic faith.

Fifteen years ago, at the time of the moving statues in Ireland, Doreen had gone down to stand in a field with thousands of others to stare at a statue of Our Lady that was said to have moved and spoken to one of the local girls. After five hours in the field, Doreen was convinced she saw it move—my father claimed it was because Doreen was swaying from exhaustion after standing still for so long. From that day forth, Doreen had given up drinking and smoking and now attended Mass every single day, without fail. She was always preaching to her wayward relations and was particularly keen to convert James—who, thus far, had managed to dodge her.

Doreen spent her holidays in Fatima, Lourdes and Medjugorje with all the other pilgrims. She told me she was very concerned that I might bring up my children as Protestants and they would never know the true wonder of Our Lady. "The Catholic faith has brought me great joy, Emma. I hope you'll give your children the chance to be brought up in this wonderful religion."

I was a lapsed Catholic who hadn't been to Mass in ten years, but I was planning on bringing up the children I was trying to conceive as Catholics. Although I might not have seen the inside of a church in a while, all those years spent in the school chapel had rubbed off on me—once a Catholic, always a Catholic. James said that as long as our children didn't become priests or nuns he was quite happy for them to be brought up Catholic. It made sense as we lived in a predominantly Catholic country, he said, and as he had no ties to the Church of England, he was okay with it.

Unfortunately Doreen got me toward the end of the evening— I had had enough of the baby torment and was watching James having a great time huddled in the corner, still analyzing rugby with the men. I had to get away from Doreen, so I landed James in it. I told her that he was insisting on bringing up our children as Protestants and I needed her to go over and work on bringing him 'round. She scooted over to him and got him in a headlock.

Sean came over to me, laughing. "Poor old James, should I save him?"

"No, let him sweat it out a bit, I've had enough of our aunties for one night. Jesus, if one more person asks me if I'm pregnant or when I'm going to have kids, I'll hit them."

"Oh dear, that bad?"

"Yes! Do I look fat in this dress?"

"Yep, huge. You look like you're carrying twins."

"Hilarious, you're nearly as funny as James."

"So—what do you think?" asked Sean.

"About what?"

"About Amy?"

"Oh, of course, sorry. She seems lovely and I see what you mean about her being so pretty. You seem very keen."

"Yeah, I am. I think this could be it for me, Emma. I really do."

Jesus, not her! I didn't want Sean marrying her: she was an idiot. I looked at his face as he caught her eye and called her over. He was besotted—oh God, he really was keen—I'd have to try again. Maybe she was one of those people who grew on you. I decided to be supernice.

"Hi, Pooh Bear," she said, kissing him.

What a ridiculous thing to call someone. It was pathetic. I looked at Sean—it was the kind of cutesy name he would normally have scorned, but he was beaming at her. He was definitely in love.

"So how have you found tonight? Not too stressful, I hope?" I said, in super-friendly mode.

"Yeah, it's been fine. I always find coming back to Dublin a bit depressing, though. Everyone's so parochial. It's like living in a goldfish bowl. Nothing exciting happens here. I mean, I was in the Ivy recently with my agent and we were sitting two tables down from Liz Hurley. That would never happen here. London is so glamorous. Aren't you tempted to move there with James?"

No, you stupid cow, I am not. People like you—lepers who go to London and think they're hot chili peppers because they sat two seats down from some B-list celeb in a posh restaurant—are just sad. "No, I'm not tempted at all. James loves it here too, so we're happy to stay put," I said. "I think I can live without seeing Liz Hurley."

"Well, maybe when you get older and married and have kids and stuff you want a more boring life," said Amy, endearing herself to me with every syllable. "But I could think of nothing worse, could you, Pooh Bear?"

Pooh Bear decided to sit on the fence—as bears do.

"I think there are pros and cons to both. Hey, James, you managed to escape Doreen's clutches," said Sean, as James joined us.

"Yes, I did, no thanks to my wife," he said, glaring at me. "She seems to be under the illusion that I'm a staunch Prod who's demanding to bring up the children I don't have as Protestants. Where did she get this notion, Emma?"

I began to laugh. "Sorry, James, she was doing my head in so I fobbed her off on you."

"Well, you owe me. The woman had me saying decades of the rosary. Christ, it was awful."

Sean and I laughed at the thought, but the humorless Amy piped up, "Well, James, if you lived in London you wouldn't have to put up with any of this backward Irish Catholicism. It's so embarrassing."

"What's embarrassing?" said Babs, barging into the middle of the conversation.

"Doreen's been trying to convert James," said Sean.

"Ha-ha, I was wondering what she was doing with the rosary beads out. That's not embarrassing, it's hilarious."

"Hilarious for you, maybe, not so much fun for me. My conversation went from tactical kicking to the wonder that is the Virgin Mary," said James, beginning to laugh too.

"Well, in London people don't behave like that. I'm so glad we're going back tomorrow, Pooh Bear."

"What?" squealed Babs. "Did she just call you 'Pooh Bear,' Sean? Now, that's what I call embarrassing."

"Barbara, for once in your life, shut up," snapped Sean.

"Okay, Pooh Bear, I will. Would Pooey-Wooey like a dwinky-winky?"

I grabbed her by the arm and pulled her into the kitchen—before Sean lost his temper—where we dissolved into fits of giggles.

"We have to get rid of her," said Babs.

"Yeah, but he really likes her. It's going to be difficult."

"She's such a leper."

"I know. I wish she'd fuck off back to bloody London and leave us and Pooh Bear in peace."

TEN

A few days later I was on the plane with James and the Leinster squad. I was the only woman among thirty men and James had been slagged mercilessly about it. They all wanted to know why I was coming when their respective girlfriends and wives were flying in on the morning of the match. James had banned them from coming out any sooner because they would be a distraction and, in his infinite wisdom, had made up some story about me needing cheering up. I discovered this when Donal slapped me on the back as we were checking into the hotel and said, "I hope you're feeling better. You're far too young and good-looking to be depressed."

I looked over at James, who was handing out the room keys and studiously ignoring me. When we got to our room I pounced. "Why does Donal think I'm depressed?"

"No idea."

"You have no idea? None at all?"

James turned 'round and sighed. "Okay, well, everyone wanted to know why you were coming with me so I said you needed cheering up—I couldn't think of anything else on the spot and I was hardly going to tell them that you were coming out for the sex."

"But what did you tell them I needed cheering up for?" I demanded, none too happy about being thought of as a looper by the squad.

"I didn't specify, I just said you were a bit down so I thought it best to bring you with me."

"In case I stuck my head in the oven?"

"Don't be silly."

"Why couldn't you just say you wanted me here to support you?"

"Because, Emma, none of the other boys have their partners here, remember? Because I banned them from coming over before the game in case they were a distraction. So it doesn't look too good that I have you with me."

"Yeah, but why did you have to say I was depressed? Do you think I'm depressed?"

"No, and I didn't say 'depressed.' I said 'needed cheering up.'"

"But why did you say it? Do you think I'm depressed about the baby stuff?"

"No, but maybe a little tense."

"What do you mean, 'tense'?"

"Emma, you insisted on coming with me because of dates, refusing to wait until next month, putting me in an awkward position with the team, so I said you were a bit down, okay?"

"Well, if one of us doesn't track my fertile days, we'll never have a baby. I don't think that's uptight, I think that's common sense. If I could get pregnant on my own, believe me, I wouldn't have trekked out here with you and thirty smelly rugby players. I can think of much better ways to spend my time. And I'm sorry I'm cramping your style, but you're the coach, so you can do what you want. I bet you Alex Ferguson brings Mrs. Ferguson on trips to Manchester United matches and doesn't give a toss what the players say."

"Have you ever seen Lady Ferguson on the sidelines?"

"No," I admitted grumpily. "But I bet if Roy Keane's wife wanted to go away with him, he wouldn't tell the whole team she was certifiable."

There was a knock on the door. It was Dave Carney, the assistant coach. He was coming to tell James the bus was there to take them to the training ground.

"Now? You're going already? But we've only just arrived."

"I told you it was going to be nonstop."

"Well, what time will you be back at?"

"I should be here for a quick shower before dinner at seven," James said, grabbing his sports bag and heading out the door as fast as he could.

"Well, if anyone asks, you can tell them your depressed wife is feeling better."

"Okay."

"And don't join in any of the play, just stick to the sidelines. I don't want you having any injuries."

"Fine. I have to go now, they're waiting. I'll see you later."

I sat on the bed and sighed. This baby lark was really getting to me. Did all women go through this? Trail around after their husbands waiting for them to spare them a few minutes so they could procreate? Where was the fun in having sex on set dates and times? Why did the women have to do all the work? Why did God make the women have the eggs? Why did the onus have to be on us? Why couldn't it be men who had to check their penile discharge and pee on sticks and drag their wives to bed for unspontaneous sex? It wasn't fair. The more I thought about it, the angrier I got. I could feel my blood pressure going through the roof. I needed to calm down so I decided to go for a walk.

As I wandered around the pretty town of Perpignan, all I could see were mothers with babies and pregnant women. It was like a Stephen King horror movie—every mother and child in the town must have been out on that sunny Wednesday. They were coming at me with their prams and bumps from every angle. The midday heat wasn't helping my mood either, so when I passed a church, I decided to pop in, cool down and light a candle.

Since I had become a lapsed Catholic, the only time I ever went into a church was to light a candle for a special request. The last time had been when I wanted to lose weight for my wedding. The Slim Fast milkshakes just weren't doing it for me, so I resorted to divine intervention. In the end, Lucy got me twelve sessions with a personal trainer as an early wedding present and it worked a treat.

I had been religious in the past though. When I was at school—a good old-fashioned Catholic convent run by slightly barmy nuns—I had gone through a very religious phase. I was twelve and my teacher was a very holy woman called Mrs. Butler. We said a decade of the rosary first thing in the morning and then we had a collection for her brother, Father Brian, who was working in Peru as a missionary. After lunch we had another decade of the rosary and then another before we went home.

I adored Mrs. Butler and thought she was absolutely wonderful. That year she went to Jerusalem for Easter week and didn't her husband drop dead on the way to communion in the holiest church in the Holy Land on the holiest day of the year—Easter Sunday. Well, poor old Mrs. Butler was distraught, as was I. In fact, I think I might have cried even more than Mrs. Butler at the death of her husband—whom I had never set eyes on.

Mrs. Butler looked to her faith to find solace and I joined her. I prayed every night after school, kneeling down in front of the statue of Our Lady that we had on the table in the hall. I would spend hours on my knees—rosary beads in my hands—praying for Mr. Butler's soul, Father Brian's mission, the starving children in Africa, peace in Northern Ireland, that Johnny Logan would win the Eurovision song contest. . . .

My parents were at a loss. They didn't think it was right to discourage me from praying, but they were concerned at the intensity of it. Whenever they wanted to use the phone, they had to do so with me kneeling beside them in the hall praying silently. It got on their nerves, but they weren't sure how to handle it.

When I announced at dinner one night that I wanted to become a nun and go out to the mission to help Father Brian bring God to the indigenous people of Peru, my parents decided to speak to me. Later that night they came into my room and sat on the side of my bed. This was always a bad sign. If one came in and sat on your bed you knew you were in trouble, but if they both came in you were in deep shit.

"What are you reading there, kiddo?" asked my father, trying to be all jokey to ease the tension.

"The life of Saint Bernadette," I said, not looking up from my book, which I was truly engrossed in. Saint Bernadette was my new hero. John Taylor from Duran Duran was out; Saint Bernadette was in!

"Pet, why are you spending so much time praying? Is there something troubling you, apart from poor Mr. Butler, of course?" my mother asked, much more in tune with what was going on.

"I'm praying for God to give me a vocation," I told them in all sincerity.

My mother took my hand. "Sweetheart, there are lots of things you can do when you're older to help people. You don't have to be a nun to be a good person. You could be a doctor and save people's lives, or you could be a lawyer and defend people who have been wrongly accused, or—"

"Mum," I said, looking at her with pity, "there's no greater way to serve God than to be a nun and not get distracted by material goods."

"But you won't be able to have children if you're a nun."

"The children of Peru will be my children." I had an answer for everything.

My mother looked at my father and shrugged. He gave it one last shot. "Emma, nuns can't do tap dancing, you know."

I faltered. Tap dancing was my favorite out-of-school activity. I loved it and fancied myself as a bit of a Ginger Rogers. But I rallied well. "God sets us all little challenges, Dad. My sacrifice will be tap dancing—it's a small price to pay compared to what other people have to forgo."

I was so pious that the pope himself would have looked like a sinner compared to me. It lasted three months. In June I said a tearful farewell to Mrs. Butler and went on a family camping holiday to France where I met Jean-Christophe, fell madly in love and had my first snog. The rosary beads were out and tanned French guys with fluff on their upper lips were in.

The church in Perpignan was cool inside and very quiet. I felt calmer instantly. I had spent so much time in churches growing up that there was always a feeling of familiarity when I entered one, wherever I was. I went over to the side, lit a candle and wished for a baby. "Dear God," I prayed, "please make me pregnant soon."

I then spent a leisurely afternoon checking out the makeup counters in Perpignan looking for new products and drinking cups of frothy café au lait on sun-drenched terraces, trying to order in my rusty school French as the garçons glared at me impatiently.

By eight o'clock that evening, I was worried. James was still not back and I'd left five messages on his mobile, which was switched off. Eventually at half past eight he staggered in the door, assisted by two players.

"Oh my God, what's wrong?"

"Ow, ouch, ow," cried James dramatically, collapsing on the bed.

"What's going on?" I demanded.

"Groin strain," grunted Paddy O'Toole, the number three on the team.

"*What?*" I wasn't sure what a groin strain was, but I was pretty sure it was not conducive to having lots of sex.

The two players backed out the door and I was left with the patient, who was writhing in pain on the bed. "James, what exactly is going on?"

"Oh God, Emma, I'm in agony. Can you get me some ice, please? The physio said I needed to put ice on it."

"I'll get you ice in a minute. What happened?"

"I was showing Donal how to jump higher in the line-outs and I landed badly and—oh God, the pain . . ."

I was trying to stay calm. Maybe it wasn't as bad as he was making out—James was not a good patient. "So what's wrong exactly? Where does it hurt?"

"I'm in agony."

"Yeah, I know, but where exactly?"

"My upper thigh—for Christ's sake, Emma, what does it matter? Will you please get me some ice? I'm dying here."

I stormed out of the room counting to ten, then twenty, and by the time I got to fifty, I was no calmer. I got a bucket full of ice from the bar and came back in.

"Oh, thank God," said James, when he saw the ice. "Can you wrap some in a towel and hand it to me?"

"How bad is it?" I asked, fetching a towel from the bathroom and filling it with ice.

"Well, we won't know until tomorrow for sure. If the swelling is bad, I'll be in pain for weeks. But hopefully the ice will help," he said, taking it from me and placing it against his inner thigh.

"Can you have sex?"

"What?"

"You heard me."

"Jesus, Emma, I'm in agony, I can barely walk and all you can think about is sex."

"Oh, I'm sorry, was I bothering you there? How selfish of me, thinking only of myself and the baby I want and you obviously have no interest in or you wouldn't have gone out and behaved like some stupid irresponsible teenager and ended up in this ridiculous state, thus rendering my journey here completely *futile!*"

"Would you please keep your voice down," James hissed from the bed, shaking his homemade ice pack at me. "This is not about selfishness, this is about me trying to make my team better so we can win on Saturday. Do you really think I did this on purpose? Do you think I enjoy pain?"

"No, James, I am well aware of your extremely low pain threshold."

"Believe me, Emma, if you had this injury you wouldn't be so flippant."

"Fine. So is sex out of the question? I mean, it's not your penis you injured, is it?"

"No, but it's right beside it. Sex would be excruciating."

"How do you know? If you have a black eye, would that stop you snogging? No, and that's right next to your mouth." I was clutching at straws, but I didn't want to waste any time and James was prone to being delicate about his health.

"Emma, this is not a black eye. It is a very severe groin injury."

"Let me see."

"No."

"James, let me see it." I pulled away the ice pack and could see nothing. No swelling, no bruising—nothing. "There's nothing there."

"The swelling can take twelve hours to show up. It may not look bad, but it feels bad."

"How about if you lie back and think of England and I gently lie on top, being very careful not to lean on your sore side?"

"*No!*"

"Let's just try it out."

"Emma."

I lay on top of him carefully, putting all my weight on my hands, but then I lost my balance and fell, kneeing him in the groin. He howled like a banshee. "Get off me, you lunatic. Jesus Christ, are you *insane?*"

"I'm sorry, I lost my balance. There's no need to raise the dead."

"Emma," James ground out, "I would greatly appreciate it if you left me in peace before I really lose my temper."

"Drama queen," I shouted, and slammed the bathroom door, then locked myself in to have a long, hot soak in the bath to calm down. Tomorrow was day fourteen. I prayed that the swelling would not be bad and that he'd be feeling better—because even if I had to tie him to the bed and gag him, we were having sex.

ELEVEN

The next morning James's groin was only very slightly swollen. Needless to say, he believed the dig I had accidentally given him with my knee hadn't helped matters. But I knew he was feeling better because whenever he thought I wasn't looking, he walked normally—without the exaggerated limp.

We had an intimate breakfast—just the two of us and the thirty squad members—and then they all headed off for strategy meetings and training sessions.

"What time will I see you later?" I asked.

"Same as yesterday, I guess," answered the grumpy gaffer.

"Are you feeling better?"

"Marginally."

"Look, James, I didn't mean to—"

"Well, well, if it isn't the screamers," said Donal, interrupting us. "Declan said you were very noisy last night, howling like werewolves, he couldn't get a wink of sleep. Fair play to you, James, with the groin strain and everything. You're all man, I'll say that for you. Anyway, can you keep it down tonight? Poor old Declan needs his kip." Donal slapped James on the back and roared laughing as he walked away.

I looked at James, who was smiling for the first time in eighteen hours. He leaned in and whispered in my ear, "We'll have to give them something to really talk about tonight. I'll see you later and, yes, I promise to stay on the sidelines today. Sorry for being such a grump. I'm a bit tense about the match."

"Will you be able to?"

"Oh, I think I'll manage. See you later."

I was delighted. Now I wouldn't have to jump him when he came in and tie him to the bed, or give him a sleeping pill and hop on him that way—the other alternative I had come up with the night before. I wondered if I could go to prison for that. Surely not. An all-female jury would totally understand, wouldn't they? Anyway, it wasn't an issue now. I decided to go into town and get some hot underwear to help raise the sail, as it were.

I bought some sexy red lingerie and went back to the hotel to pee on my ovulation stick to double-check. It was definitely day fourteen in my cycle, but I wanted to check the ovulation status. I peed and waited. One line was thin and a bit blurry and the other was thick and strong. I suddenly realized I didn't know which was the reference line and which the test line. Damn, I hadn't brought the instructions with me. Which was which? I couldn't remember. I began to panic. I needed to know—after all, I had traveled over for this. I had to make sure.

I decided to go to the pharmacy I had seen near the hotel and get some new sticks. My French wasn't great, but reference was *référence* in French and test was probably *test* so it would be easy to figure out from the diagrams on the instructions.

I walked into the *pharmacie* and looked around. The shelves were packed with *médicaments*. I wandered down the aisles, looking for anything resembling an ovulation test, but couldn't see any. The woman in the white coat was clocking my every move. When I approached the counter she sighed and said, *"Oui, Madame?"* in that dismissive way French people have when they know they're dealing with a tourist.

"Bonjour, parlez-vous anglais?"

"Non."

Shit. Okay, now I'd have to play the pidgin-French-plus-sign-language game. I took a deep breath and launched.

"Je chercher le sticks *pour le bébé,"* I said, pointing to my stomach.

"Pardon?" said the unimpressed pharmacist, looking at me as if I was some kind of retard.

"Je chercher le test *pour le bébé?"* I tried again, raising my voice this time in some lame hope that shouting would make it clearer.

By this stage, there was another woman in the *pharmacie* who was waiting behind me and decided to join in. "You have the sick baby?" she said, in strongly accented English. Isn't it amazing how wonderful it sounds when a French person speaks English and how utterly wretched it sounds when I try to speak French?

I turned to face her. "No, not a sick baby. I'm needing the test so I can make the baby," I said, resorting to pidgin English and doing so with a French accent. I sounded like Peter Sellers's Inspector Clouseau.

She looked puzzled and spoke in French to the pharmacist, who shook her head. They turned back to me and shrugged. I was trying desperately to think of another way to explain. I took a nail file from the counter, straddled it, crouched down and pretended to pee on it, making *sssss* noises so they'd understand, and then said, "To check for *le bébé,"* and rubbed my stomach again.

"Mon Dieu!" said the pharmacist, staring at me in shock. I could picture her telling her friends over dinner about the mad foreigner who had come into her *pharmacie* and performed doggie impressions.

"Ah, oui, j'ai compris," said the customer, smiling at me, and laughing as she explained it to the pharmacist.

"Ah, d'accord," said the pharmacist, looking relieved that there was a sane explanation for my behavior.

I smiled gratefully at the customer; she nodded and smiled at me. The pharmacist handed me a pregnancy test—I could tell by the drawing.

"Oh, no. *Non,"* I said. *"Pas le bébé,* uhm, it's for before *le bébé."* I was desperately trying to think of the word for "before" in French.

The two ladies, meanwhile, were looking peeved. They thought they had cracked my code.

I took a deep breath and pointed to the test. *"Non,"* I said, *"le bébé* is not possible, I need to make the *bébé."* I looked around for inspiration and I saw a calendar. I pointed to it and the pharmacist handed it to me.

"Regardez," I ordered the two women. I pointed to day fourteen. *"Très important pour le bébé,"* I said. *"Le test pour le bébé— ici,"* and I tapped on day fourteen. They still looked puzzled.

Damn. I was getting really hot and bothered now. My face was purple with effort and embarrassment. Half of me just wanted to leg it out the door, but I decided to give it one last go. So I pointed to day fourteen and, making a hole with my thumb and index finger, poked my other index finger in and out, miming sex, and said, *"Le sexe, ici pour le bébé. Je* need *le* test *pour* checking the eggs. Ah, yes, *les oeufs."* Hurrah, I had remembered the word for "eggs"; I was in the home stretch.

"Je need to *faire le* test *pour* checking *les oeufs pour le sexe pour le bébé."*

The two women looked at each other and then the penny dropped. *"Ah, oui, Madame, vous cherchez le test d'ovulation,"* said the pharmacist.

And there it was—"ovulation" was the same in French. We all

nodded and laughed. I paid the formerly stern-faced pharmacist, who patted my arm and wished me *"bonne chance."* We were all women. We understood. It was tough out there.

I skipped back to the hotel, put on my new red underwear and waited for James. He hobbled into the room and collapsed on the bed. I took a deep breath and asked him what was wrong. He said the groin strain had gotten much worse during the day and he was in agony. I tried not to cry with frustration.

"Could you help me with my shoes, please?" asked Hopalong Cassidy, in a particularly whiny voice.

"Fine," I said grumpily.

As I reached down to untie his laces, James grabbed me, swung me back onto the bed and kissed me. "Just kidding, darling, I'm feeling fit, healthy and raring to go. Now, let's get these sexy red lacy bits off."

The next day was final training and motivation-building day. James was up at the crack of dawn and didn't get back to the hotel till late that night. When he did arrive, he looked very grim. The prop forward Dave McCarthy's shoulder injury had not cleared up. He was out of the game and, as a key player, would be sorely missed. I could see James was really worried, but he was putting on a brave face for the team.

For the next three hours his phone rang constantly as everyone we knew called to wish him luck and journalists hounded him for last-minute prematch comments. I felt really nervous for him. After dinner that night, everyone was very subdued—jitters were setting in, so they all went to bed early to get a good night's sleep before the big game.

I woke up in the middle of the night to find the bed empty.

James was sitting in the corner of the room, staring at a piece of paper, pen in hand.

"Can you not sleep?"

"Not a wink," he said, looking up.

"What are you doing?"

"Trying to write a speech to give the boys tomorrow in the locker room. I want it to be really motivational, but I can't get it quite right. I'm nearly there—I just need to tweak it a bit."

He looked like a little boy sitting there with his hair all ruffled and the pen in his mouth, frowning down at the paper. On the floor beside him was a book of Churchill's greatest speeches.

"Just speak from your heart, James. They trust you and look up to you. Whatever you say will motivate them," I said, in supportive-wife mode.

"It has to be good, Emma. With Dave out of the game, Perpignan has the advantage. I want them to go out there tomorrow and win. I need to give them a really rousing speech."

"Let's see what you've written," I said, picking up the pad. James's speech was largely made up of quotes from Churchill's broadcasts during the Second World War. It was totally over the top—he might just about have gotten away with it if he was speaking to fighter pilots on a mission to bomb enemy territory or something, but this was a Leinster rugby team. Come on—know your audience.

We have before us an ordeal of the most grievous kind. . . . You ask, what is our aim? I can answer in one word: "Victory—victory—at all costs, victory, in spite of all terror, victory, however long and hard the road may be. . . ." But I take up my task with buoyancy and hope. I feel sure that our cause will not be suffered to fail among men. At this time I feel entitled to claim the aid of all, and I say, "Come, then, let us go forward together with our united strength."

I tried to tread carefully so as not to hurt his feelings. "James, I really don't think you need to quote Churchill. Just use your own words."

"Darling, Churchill is considered by many to be the most motivational speaker of all time. Mayor Giuliani quoted Churchill when he spoke after the September eleventh attacks to great effect. I'm sure these quotes will get the boys going."

"James, Giuliani was speaking to a city under terrorist attack. This is a rugby team you're talking to. The match tomorrow is hardly an 'ordeal of the most grievous kind'—it's a rugby match, for goodness' sake. They're looking for a slap on the back and a few whoops."

James looked down at his notes. "Well, what about this bit? 'In the bitter and increasingly exacting conflict which lies before us, we are resolved to keep nothing back, and not to be outstripped by any in service to the common cause.'"

"James, I just don't think it's hitting the right mark. It's a bit stuffy for a bunch of Irish rugby players." I had to make him see this was madness. There was a time and a place for Churchill's war speeches and it most certainly was not a smelly dressing room.

"You mean to say that you don't think Donal and the lads would appreciate 'Victory—victory—at all costs, victory, in spite of all terror, victory, however long and hard the road may be . . .'?" he said, smiling despite himself.

"Nope."

"What about JFK's 'Ask not what your country can do for you but what you can do for your country'?"

I shook my head.

"You think I should just say something more straightforward?"

"Yes, use your own words. It'll be much more effective. Now, come back to bed and try to get some sleep. I want you looking your best for the front-page pictures on the Irish papers when you whip Perpignan's ass tomorrow."

"Quick, give me my pen. I must take that eloquent motivational line down."

The next morning I kissed James good luck and he headed off with the team to the ground for some warm-up training. Meanwhile the wives, girlfriends and families were arriving at the hotel. I had been charged with helping them check in and giving them directions to the stadium. Paddy O'Toole's wife was first in. She complained about the heat, the flight, the rude taxi drivers. . . . I plastered a smile on my face, handed her a pile of photocopies with directions to the stadium and legged it out the door. I wanted to be there early to get a good seat and I had no intention of listening to her moaning in my ear throughout the game.

By kickoff the stadium was jammed. About a third of the stands was filled with die-hard Leinster supporters who had traveled over for the game. They were all singing "Molly Malone" and waving banners. The atmosphere was fantastic.

I don't know what James said to the team in the locker room that day, but they came out with all guns blazing. From kickoff, Leinster was hungrier, more aggressive in attack and more solid in defense. There was no contest, Perpignan was beaten 23 to 6 and all hell broke loose. When the final whistle blew the stadium erupted. I sobbed and hugged the two big supporters beside me. The fans rushed the pitch and Donal and James were carried shoulder high to the clubhouse where the celebrations kicked in.

Later that day after copious drinks, toasts and cheers, James and I finally got a moment to ourselves and I spent a good ten minutes telling him how proud I was of him. He hugged me and said, "I'm proud of you too, darling."

"For what?"

"For being so dedicated to having a family. I think you'll be a wonderful mother and I know it's frustrating, but I also know that you'll be pregnant soon. It'll happen, Emma, I promise it will."

"Thanks. You'll be a wonderful father too," I said, sniffling into his shoulder. "I know I'm a bit hyper about it, I don't mean to be a pain. I'm just finding it all very frustrating."

"You're fine."

"Thanks, but let's be honest here—I stalked you to France, forced you to have sex with me while injured and two days ago I squatted in a French chemist, pretending to pee like a dog. I am definitely losing the plot."

We both laughed.

"Well, okay, maybe you are a little insane, but I like that you're passionate about things—it's who you are."

"Yeah, well, believe me, passion and obsession are an exhausting combination. I feel about a hundred and forty."

"Maybe we should forget it for a while and just let nature take its course?"

"I've tried to, James, but I can't—I'm obsessed."

"Well, can we at least cut out the après-sex gymnastics? I'm worried you're going to break something and I don't fancy having to explain it to the doctor in Casualty. 'And how did this happen, Mr. Hamilton?' 'Well, you see, my wife was cartwheeling around the bed after sex, as she does, to stimulate my sperm. . . .' "

"Ha-ha. Well, okay, I'll keep it to sticking my legs up in the air and shaking them about."

TWELVE

*L*ucy thought long and hard about where to take Donal on their second date. She wanted it to be something memorable for him and when she saw an ad for *The Vagina Monologues* she knew she had found the perfect solution.

She called Donal, told him they were going to the theater and he was to pick her up on Friday night—sober, uninjured, wearing normal clothes and on time.

Donal wasn't too keen on the theater: at six foot four he always ended up sitting with his legs wrapped 'round his neck, staring at his watch and praying for it to be over. Movies, he liked—plenty of leg room, popcorn, nachos covered with melted cheese and usually a skimpily clad starlet to look at. Theater, he found dull. The last girl he had gone out with, Cathy, had dragged him to *Waiting for Godot.* It was the longest, most ridiculous load of old rubbish he had ever seen and he fell asleep halfway through.

When Cathy had poked him in the ribs to wake him up and glared at him, he had whispered loudly, "That fecker Godot isn't going to turn up, so can we please just go home?" much to her embarrassment. The relationship ended shortly after.

Still, he owed Lucy a decent date after the last fiasco, so he said it sounded like a great idea and made sure he was on time and looking smart.

Lucy stared at him. "No iron, then?"

"What?"

"The state of your clothes, you look like you slept in them."

"These are my good clothes, I'll have you know. I dressed up for tonight—it's the first time I've been out of a tracksuit in weeks. I like your skirt, nice and short. Come on, let's go before I pull it off you. You shouldn't look so sexy—I'll never be able to concentrate on the play now."

Lucy smiled. "Oh, I think you'll manage."

"So what are we going to see?" Donal asked, praying that it wasn't another Beckett play or, God forbid, a musical. Who in their right mind wanted to go and watch a bunch of people—old enough to know better—prancing about, swinging their arms in the air and singing about love and death? Maybe he'd be lucky and it'd be a comedy, something nice and light, not some heavy meaning-of-life crap: he liked to be entertained, not depressed.

"It's a modern play by a woman called Eve Ensler. It's supposed to be really funny."

Great, thought Donal, this sounds good. Funny was good.

"Thank God—I thought you might drag me to *The Miserables* or one of those dreadful musicals where they all howl about the injustice of life."

"No, I think you'll like this. I hear it's supposed to be very lively," said Lucy, beaming at him.

They went for a drink first and just as the play was about to start—Lucy had timed it all to perfection—they ran 'round to the theater and slid into their seats. Donal hadn't had a chance to see the billboards outside so he had no idea what the play was called—or about.

He looked around as the lights went down and was surprised to find that he was the only male in the audience. He turned 'round to see if all the men were down the back, but no—there was only him. The theater was very small and they were sitting four rows from the front. He began to feel uncomfortable—where were all the men?

A very good-looking woman came out and sat on a stool in the middle of the stage. Donal recognized her from TV. She was an actress in some comedy show. He began to relax. It was obviously some comedy stand-up thing.

The actress began to speak—about her vagina. At first, Donal thought he was hearing things, but then he realized that no, this woman was actually talking about her vagina being lonely and needing friends or something. Jesus Christ, he thought, had he walked into a madhouse? What the hell was this? Some lesbian arty-farty play? Was Lucy a closet lesbian? Did she swing both ways? He looked over at her: she was staring straight ahead, smiling.

The actress began to shout now. She was roaring at the top of her voice, telling them all that her vagina was angry. Apparently it was fed up having things shoved up it. When she mentioned tampons, the audience giggled. Donal thought he'd die of embarrassment—he was not one to be sitting around with a bunch of women talking about Tampax. He hated that sort of thing.

Donal squirmed in his chair while the rest of the audience roared with laughter and whooped along as the actress ranted on about her angry vagina. Lucy had tears running down her face she was laughing so much—all the more amused by Donal's discomfort. Jesus, this was awful—shouting about tampons in a fake American accent. He hoped it was a short play.

But worse was to come. The madwoman began to describe the smell of her vagina. She said she liked it smelling of fish, just the way God had intended it. Mother of Christ, thought Donal. How did I end up here listening to women talking about the smell of their privates? He looked around for the exit door. He'd never get out without causing a scene. Lucy had made sure he was sitting in the middle of the row—surrounded by laughing women.

Donal was shocked, and he would normally consider himself fairly unshockable. He really didn't need to hear this. He had no wish to know about this stuff. Jesus, had women gone mad? The actress got up and walked off the stage to rapturous applause. Thank God for that, thought Donal. It's over. He hoped they'd stop clapping—he didn't want her to come back on for an encore. He just wanted to get the hell out of there.

He grabbed his jacket, but Lucy put her hand on his arm. "Not over yet. Lots more to come!" she said, winking at him.

"Jesus Christ, Lucy, what the hell is this?" he hissed. "It's like some kind of cult outing."

Lucy smiled at him, and before she could respond a small, squat, aggressive-looking actress came onstage to replace the younger one. This one told them all to go out, spread their legs, get a mirror and have a good long look at their vaginas. Donal prayed she didn't have a box of mirrors with her, because if they all started stripping down he was out of there. After tonight, he never wanted to hear the word "vagina" again. In fact, he was beginning to think he never wanted to see one again. This play was one sure way of pushing a man toward a life of celibacy.

"Ladies, I recommend that you all go home and examine your vaginas tonight," said the actress. "When I was offered a part in this play, I decided I'd better look at mine and see what all the fuss was about, and I can tell you, it was an incredibly liberating experience." She looked around. "Ah, I see we have a brave man among us," she said, spotting Donal—he was hard to miss, being the tallest person in the theater by a good seven inches. "Well done, sir.

You're the only man here tonight. Very brave of you to come. I think you should be applauded for it."

All the women turned to stare at Donal, who was purple with embarrassment. They clapped and cheered him. It was the longest two minutes of his life. And just when he thought things couldn't get any worse, they did.

The actress who liked to look at her vagina now told them all to stand up and shout out the word "cunt." She demanded that they stand up and "reclaim" the word.

"Come on—one, two, three—shout it out," she roared.

The women in the audience started giggling and saying it quietly, then it got louder and louder and soon they were all shouting "cunt" at the top of their voices. Donal looked around the room in horror—they were like a bunch of wild animals. Lucy was doubled over, her shoulders shaking.

"Come on, brave man, you too," said the actress, looking at Donal. "Don't be shy, come on now: cunt!"

Everyone was looking at Donal and laughing and shouting "cunt." He gritted his teeth and said it too. God, this was the worst night of his life—shouting "cunt" in a room full of lunatic women.

When the play finally ended and the lights went up, Donal grabbed his jacket and shot out the door like a bullet. He didn't fancy being congratulated by a hundred liberated women for coming along to their "vagina show."

Lucy found him lurking 'round the corner by the side of the theater.

"Drink. I need a stiff drink," said Donal, grabbing her arm and diving into the nearest pub. She sat down and he went to the bar.

"Pint of Guinness, white wine spritzer and give me a stiff whiskey straightaway, will you?"

The barman nodded. "Just been to see that vagina show, then?" he said, smiling.

"Jesus, have you seen it?"

"God, no, are you mad? You'd never find me in there. But I've seen a few lads coming out of it and they all look like you do now. Here you go, get that into you," he said, handing Donal the whiskey, which he proceeded to down in one. When he came over with the drinks, Lucy was still laughing.

"Oh yeah, laugh away. You certainly exacted your revenge. That was, without a shadow of a doubt, the worst night of my life," said Donal.

"I'm sorry, but the sight of you shouting 'cunt' was the funniest thing I've ever seen. I wish Emma and James could have seen you."

"Jesus, Lucy, if this gets out I'll never be able to show my head in the club again. You have to keep this to yourself. I'd be the laughingstock of the dressing room—don't do it to me. God, I can see it now: 'Donal Brady, vagina man,' " he said, beginning to see the funny side, after sinking his second drink. "What exactly was that? I mean, a play about vaginas talking! Is it a lesbian thing or what?"

"Typical," said Lucy. "Typical male response. Just because a group of women go to watch a play that talks openly about vaginas, suddenly we're all lesbians. If a group of guys went to see a play that talked about penises, would they be gay?"

"If they were all standing up, shouting 'cock cock cock,' then, yeah, they probably would be. It's not very macho."

"Well, I bet you that most of the women there were heterosexual. It's nice to go out and talk about subjects that are taboo in day-to-day life. It's funny and liberating."

"Did she have to go into such detail, though? Some of it was a bit over the top."

"You mean you didn't enjoy the bit about the Tampax, and not washing your vagina with shower gel—letting the fishy smell flow," said Lucy, grinning at him. "That was my favorite part."

"Please, stop, no more. Can we talk about something else? Too much information can be a bad thing. I'd like to keep a little mystery going when it comes to women's privates, and I can assure you that all guys prefer the smell of soap to the smell of fish."

"Come on, Donal, you can say it—cunt!" laughed Lucy.

"Stop. Enough. What do you want to drink? Same again?"

"Nothing for me, thanks, I'm going to head home. I need to get my mirror out and examine my vagina. I want some of that 'vaginal wonder' she was talking about. I'll give you a call and let you know what I find!"

THIRTEEN

After Perpignan, I was convinced I was pregnant. I felt tired all the time and my boobs hurt—mind you, that could have had something to do with the fact that I was constantly poking them to see if they were tender. Also, when I went to Marks & Spencer to buy food and stood by the fish counter, I definitely felt a little queasy.

I began to get excited. We'd have to give the baby a French name as it was conceived in France. A little Jacques or Delphine. We'd take them to France on holiday and they'd grow up bilingual. It was July now, so I'd be giving birth in March. Maybe I'd give birth on St. Patrick's Day and we'd have to call him or her Patrick or Patricia. I'd take the summer off and spend warm sunny days bonding with the baby. I'd be able to take it on long walks to get fit again. We'd stroll by the sea and chat to other mothers and their infants; it would be fantastic.

As the due date of my period grew closer, I poked my boobs regularly, just to make sure they were still sore. I also stuck my nose into a plate of smoked salmon and definitely felt a twinge of nausea. I took naps between makeup jobs—after all, I needed my rest. Two days to go, one day, due day . . . nothing. Hurrah, I was pregnant. I rushed down to Boots to get a pregnancy test, and on my way back I felt it. My period had arrived. I was devastated.

When James came in that evening I greeted him from the couch, blotchy-faced and surrounded by tissues. He said all the right things, then went out and got me my favorite takeaway Thai dinner and watched *Love Story* with me—even though I had subjected him to it already and he thought it was a load of rubbish.

"Love means never having to say you're sorry," I mouthed along with Ali McGraw, as I sniffled into my Kleenex and James stifled a yawn.

Two days later, James told me that he had made an appointment with our GP Dr. Murphy to talk to him about fertility and see if there was anything we should be doing that we weren't. "I hate seeing you so upset, so I think we should talk to the professionals and sort this out," he said.

I felt a bit strange going to Dr. Murphy about fertility. He had been my doctor throughout my childhood, but when I had needed prescriptions for the pill and smears, I had gone to the Well Woman Center. I was too embarrassed to go to Dr. Murphy and ruin his nice innocent view of me. Dr. Murphy was there for when you had the flu or tonsillitis or the measles, not for anything that implied you might be having sex. Still, it was nice that James was making an effort, and he was right, we did need medical advice, so we went along.

Dr. Murphy greeted me like a long-lost friend and sat us both down. "Now, my dears, what can I do for you?"

"Well, Doctor," said James, and cleared his throat, "Emma and I have decided to try for a family. We are now in our midthirties and feel that it's time we began to look at the possibility of conceiving. . . ."

I decided to jump in: James was being far too long-winded and waffly. "The thing is, I've been trying to get pregnant for seven months and so far nothing's happening. So I'm a bit fed up."

"I see," said Dr. Murphy. "How old are you now, Emma?"

"Thirty-three and a half."

"And you, James?"

"Thirty-five."

"Well, I have to say first of all that you both have youth on your side. I'm quite sure that there's nothing wrong with either of you—these things don't happen overnight. When you've been on the pill for any length of time and then come off it, it usually takes the body a good six months to adapt. I have no doubt it'll happen for you very soon. The important thing is not to get too stressed about it. Just relax and enjoy yourselves and it'll all come together."

"Is there something we should be doing or taking that could help speed things up?" I asked.

"Well, ovulation tests can be helpful in narrowing down your most fertile days and, of course, a healthy lifestyle helps. Maybe you could cut down a bit on caffeine and alcohol and try to exercise a couple of times a week. But everything in moderation is fine. Don't be stressing yourselves out unnecessarily."

"But what if something's wrong and we don't know about it? What if I have endometriosis or uterine fibroids?" I asked. I had spent a few hours that morning on the babycentre.com/fertilityproblems website and I wanted concrete reassurance. I wanted answers, tests, results.

"The likelihood of you having either of those problems is very slim, but if you like we could do some preliminary tests. A sperm sample test and some blood tests to check your hormone levels and a smear might be worth looking at."

"Yes, I want to have those," I said, jumping at the chance to do something. "I really want to move forward on this, Doctor."

Dr. Murphy looked at me and smiled. He could see my frustration, desperation and impatience.

"Okay, well, I'll set up an appointment with a gynecologist colleague of mine, Dr. Philips. He's very good, I know you'll like him."

A week later, and James was giving his sperm sample at a private clinic recommended by Dr. Murphy. I went with him for moral support, although he said he didn't need any. The clinic was very plush and the waiting room was full of couples whispering to each other. All the men looked fairly tense. James was a bit grumpy about me tagging along. "You really didn't have to come, Emma. I don't need hand-holding," he whispered.

"Yes, but what if you can't manage to give a sample and you need some help?" I whispered back. "I don't want some saucy nurse having to go in and finish off the job for you. I'd rather be on hand to help you out."

"In fairness, I think I can manage a sample on my own, thank you."

"Well, just in case, I brought you this," I said, handing him a picture.

"What on earth . . . ?"

"It's Halle Berry in the James Bond bikini. You told me you found it a turn-on, so I tore it out of a magazine in the hairdresser's yesterday."

"Very thoughtful of you, darling. Didn't the hairdresser mind you ripping pages out of her magazines?" said James, shaking his head and smiling at me.

"Not when I explained what it was for. In fact, she told me she thought I was very open-minded and understanding."

"Great, so everyone in the hairdresser's now knows what I'm up to today. Anyone else in on it?"

"No, believe it or not, I didn't take out an ad in the *Times.*"

The nurse came out and called James. I went up with him. She handed him a small cup and told him to place his sample in it. "And we have provided some material to help you. We know it can be difficult for men to give samples on demand, so there are some magazines and a video if you need to use them."

"Yes, right, thank you, Nurse," said James, blushing furiously as he strode toward the door.

I sat down and tried not to laugh.

Twenty minutes later James came out and handed the nurse his sample.

"How did it go?" I asked.

"Not here," he hissed, as he frog-marched me out of the clinic. When we got outside I asked again.

"It was fine. A bit slow to start, but I got there in the end."

"You were in there for ages. What type of porn did they have? *Playboy* or what? What was the film? *Debbie Does Dallas?* Was Halle's picture helpful?" I asked, giggling.

"Well, I must say the magazines were pretty hard-core— *Mayfair, Hustler,* that kind of thing, and the film option was *Shakespeare in Lust,*" said James, laughing now too.

"Did you watch it?"

"No, the magazines did the trick."

"Were they new or old?"

"Old."

"Gross. Were the pages stuck together?"

"Well, no. If the pages were stuck together the guy wouldn't have been aiming in the cup, now, would he?"

"Was it hard to get it into the cup?"

"It was a bit on the small side, but I managed."

"I wish they gave women something to look at when they're having smears. It would make the process a lot more pleasant."

"Maybe you should suggest it to Dr. Philips tomorrow."

I decided not to bring porn to my appointment with Dr. Philips. He was a sweet man in his midfifties, and I think he would have passed out at the mere suggestion.

He took a smear, then some blood for tests. He asked me questions about my periods—were they regular? Heavy? Painful? Long? Was there cramping? Sweating? Light-headedness? Severe mood swings?

When we had ruled out most of those things, he suggested that I go for an ultrasound to check that my womb looked healthy and to look for any signs of polycystic ovaries. He booked me an appointment for the next day. I was to eat nothing and drink two liters of water at least an hour before my appointment and under no circumstances was I to pee—I had to be nice and bloated for the ultrasound.

The next day I woke up and poured myself a glass of water. After one glass I felt I needed to pee. After fifteen I thought I would burst. I got into the car and drove to the clinic. Every bump in the road was torture. I thought I was going to pee in the car. It was awful. When I got to the clinic, the receptionist said the radiologist was a bit behind and she was afraid I'd have to wait forty minutes for my appointment. She was right to be afraid, I thought grimly, as I sat down and crossed my legs. Very soon she'd need a pair of goggles and a swimming cap behind that desk—my bladder couldn't take much more of this: it was begging to be set free and I wasn't sure how much longer I could control it.

Forty torturous minutes later I was lying back on the bed, legs akimbo, while the radiologist tut-tutted. "Did Dr. Philips not make it clear that you needed to drink two liters of water before coming here today?" she snapped.

"Yes, he did, and I have drunk the water. I'm about to burst there's so much water inside me," I said, through gritted teeth.

She sighed. "Well, you obviously didn't drink enough. It's no use. We'll have to do an internal. Go and empty your bladder and come back straightaway."

Joy . . . freedom. I leaped off the bed and hurled myself into the toilet. The relief was wonderful. Why the hell hadn't they told me I could have an internal ultrasound? I would have opted for that any day.

I went back in, climbed onto the bed and assumed the position. The sour-faced radiologist came toward me, holding a large stick with a round head that looked remarkably like a giant vibrator. I had a sneaking suspicion, however, that this monster would provide none of the pleasure of its smaller cousin. It was unceremoniously shoved in, where she proceeded to swish it about roughly from right to left, staring at a screen and muttering under her breath. She kept clicking on the mouse and dragging lines across from one side to the other. I'm one of those people who like to be informed about what's going on, particularly when someone is staring at my innards on a TV screen.

"So what do you see? Does it look normal?" I asked, squirming with discomfort as she shoved the camera to the far left of my womb.

"Dunno, hard to say," she mumbled, as she continued to click and measure lines across the black fuzzy screen.

"Well, does anything look really abnormal?" I tried, desperate for reassurance.

"I can't say until I've studied the printouts. Dr. Philips will explain it all to you."

"Well, can you tell me if you see anything that looks like it could be a big problem?"

"Nothing stands out, but as I said, I'll have to study the results," said the witch in the white coat, as she yanked the camera out. "You can get dressed now."

I wanted to grab her by the hair and scream at her. I wanted to beat her over the head with the vibratorlike camera, but I was putting all my energy into not crying. Why was she being such a bitch? Didn't she realize how awful and humiliating this was? Why the hell had she become a radiologist if she hated people so much? She should have gone into research. She was only fit to deal with lab rats. I was furious and upset. I stormed out of the room and when I got to the safety of my car I bawled. I was sore, and feeling very sorry for myself.

When I went to see Dr. Philips—three weeks and one further blood test later—my upset had turned into fury. I told him I thought his choice of radiologist extremely poor and I was raging at the way in which I had been treated. He checked the name on the report and said it must have been a temp as the radiologist he normally used was charming. He apologized profusely and said he would make sure I never had to deal with a stand-in again.

He then told me that everything looked normal. The blood tests taken on day four of my cycle had shown that my hormone levels were normal.

"We checked your FSH to confirm that sufficient quantities are being produced to trigger the follicles within your ovaries to begin preparing an egg for release. High levels of FSH are often taken to be an indicator that egg reserves are running low. We also checked your LH, which controls the development of the egg. Levels surge to trigger release at ovulation. However, consistently high levels can prevent such a spurt, and can be an indicator of PCOS, but your levels are normal. Also your prolactin levels were normal. Prolactin is a stress hormone released by the pituitary. High levels can inhibit the release of FSH and LH. It is also the hormone that will eventually stimulate breast milk."

Normal stress levels? Was he trying to wind me up? I was totally strung out. The way things were going, if the stress hormones were the ones that stimulated the breast milk, my baby would be sucking on empty. I'd be a basket case by the time I got pregnant.

"And finally, the blood test we did on day twenty-one of your cycle was to check your progesterone levels. The body increases its production of this hormone after releasing an egg, so the test confirms ovulation is taking place. It would appear that you're a very healthy young lady who ovulates regularly," said Dr. Philips.

I knew FSH was follicle stimulating hormone and I recognized LH as the luteinizing hormone from my ovulation-stick instructions, but he had lost me on the PCOS. Still, I got the gist of it—I was producing eggs. I appeared to be normal.

"So what do I do now?" I asked.

"Go home, my dear, and lead a normal life. Try to be healthy and, most importantly, try to relax and enjoy a normal sex life. Regular sex around the midstage of your cycle is advisable, but don't get too tied down with dates and times. The more relaxed you are, the more likely it is that you will fall pregnant. I have no doubt you will succeed in the very near future. The best of luck to you," said Dr. Philips, shaking my hand.

I wanted to hug him and thank him for being so nice, but I was feeling too emotional so I just mumbled, "Thank you for your help," and went home to tell James the good news. Along with his healthy sperm, I had healthy eggs. We were good to go.

FOURTEEN

$\mathcal{L}$einster lost the semifinal—21 to 14—and James was gutted. They played really well, but the team from Toulouse out-played them with their superior scrummaging (well, that's what Gary Brown of the *Irish Times* wrote anyway). All the papers praised James for having taken Leinster all the way to the semifinal and predicted that he had a great career as a coach ahead of him.

I reminded him of this as he sat staring gloomily out the window a week later, stirring his coffee. "I really thought we were going to win it. I really did," he said, for the zillionth time that week.

"Look, James, no one's dead. I know you're upset, but everyone thinks you're a hero for getting so far. Look at the positives. You're being hailed as the best coach Leinster has ever had, you've just been given a big pay raise and a three-year contract. Come on, it's not the end of the world."

James sighed and looked at me. "It is to me."

I was losing patience with the dramatics. He had been moping around the house for a week, watching a video of the match over and over again. He needed to snap out of it.

"For goodness' sake, it's not as if you were fired. You lost a game, next year you'll win the league."

"It's a cup, Emma. It's the European *Cup,*" he snapped. "Is it too much to ask for a little sympathy after I've lost the most important game of my career?"

"I've given you buckets of sympathy. I've spent the last week dancing around, telling you how great you are and trying to cheer you up. Come on, James, it's not that dramatic. Look on the bright side—at least you have healthy sperm."

"Emma, can you please, just for once, not bring sperm, babies or reproduction into the conversation? It's doing my head in. This is about my career and has nothing whatsoever to do with baby-making. It may come as a shock to you to know that not everything in the world revolves around *fertility*. Now I'm going to have a long, hot shower and I would really appreciate it if you refrained from following me into the bathroom to check if I'm masturbating," he said, and stormed out the door.

While James was in the shower, Donal rang. "Howrya, is he there?"

"No, he's having a shower."

"How's he doing?"

"Jesus, you'd swear he'd just had his leg amputated. He's so touchy and grumpy."

"Ah, but we came so close."

"Oh God, not you too. Look, take him out and get him drunk or something. I've tried everything, but he won't cheer up."

"The lads have organized a surprise for him tonight. We'll cheer him up for you."

"Good."

"Okay, well, just tell him I called and I'll see him down at the club at seven."

"Will do. Oh, by the way, Donal, I hear you're a liberated man."

"What?"

"Cunt cunt cunt cunt cunt," I said, laughing, as I hung up.

I left James a note on the kitchen table:

Donal called. You are to be in the clubhouse at seven.
P.S. You can shake it till it falls off, for all I care.

At three o'clock that morning, James staggered into the bedroom wearing a Superman outfit—red knickers and all. He leaped on top of me and kissed me. "Darling, I jusht wanna say that you're the besht wife in whole world and I'm shorry for shouting at you. Alsho, if I shay sho myshelf, I am the besht coach in Europe. The lads shaid I was top bloke and they promised to win the cup for me nexsht near. Now come on, let'sh make babiesh," he said, pulling off his cape. But his feet got tangled in the red knickers and he ended up falling off the bed and passing out on the floor.

I pulled him back onto the bed and covered him with the duvet. My very own superhero . . .

With James having regained his positive outlook on life, I decided I should do something to make me feel better about myself. I needed to be distracted and to stop wallowing in my pregnancy obsession and driving my husband insane. I reasoned that it was time for me to give something back to society. I was also secretly hoping that if I did some good work I'd get a break on the pregnancy front. "What goes around comes around" and all that. I narrowed it down to three options—Amnesty International, prison visits or the Samaritans, the helpline for suicidal people.

First I went to an Amnesty meeting. Of the four people there, I was the only one not wearing a poncho and Moses sandals. My dressing down had consisted of Miss Sixty jeans and a D&G T-shirt. Suffice it to say that I didn't exactly blend.

I sat down beside Simon, an earnest young man with long, dirty-looking dreadlocks and an apparent aversion to personal hygiene. Suzanne, the Amnesty representative—wearing the "must-have" poncho, jeans and a pair of open-toe Birkenstocks—explained what Amnesty was about and pointed out that they had no time for do-gooders who joined for three months, then drifted away. They needed passionate people, active members, who would go on marches, write protest letters, participate in night vigils outside embassies and be available twenty-four/seven as committed members of the organization. At this stage the poncho-clad recruits were nodding vigorously and clapping.

Then Suzanne asked us all to explain why we had come to Amnesty and what we felt we could contribute. Simon gave an impassioned speech about having spent a month on the West Bank, seeing firsthand the Israeli brutality toward the Palestinians. "They are living like dogs, in subhuman conditions. We have to increase the pressure on the government to do something. We need to hit the streets."

Christ, what the hell was I going to say? By the time my turn came, I'd decided honesty was the best policy. I told Suzanne that I knew Amnesty had a shop, as it was quite near where I lived, and perhaps I could work there for a couple of hours on Sunday afternoons. . . . Thus ended my blink-and-you'll-miss-it career with Amnesty.

I met up with Lucy after the Amnesty fiasco to discuss my options. She said I'd be mad even to consider prison visits. She pointed out that you could get landed with a serial killer–type inmate who, on his release, would hunt you down and murder you. I pointed out that serial killers were probably not first in line for friendly prison visits. Still and all, better safe than sorry, said Lucy. After all, that Harold Shipman had seemed like a nice old family doctor and look what he'd gotten up to. She said the Samaritans sounded like a much better option. Better to be on the end of a telephone with a suicidal teenager than face-to-face in prison with a murderer. She had a point and I was very fond of the phone, so I'd probably be a natural.

The Samaritans it was. I had seen endless ads crying out for recruits, so they were obviously desperate. I spent a long time deciding what to wear to the initial meeting and finally opted for dungarees, a pair of sandals that I bought in Scholl (luckily I didn't bump into anyone I knew in there—I'd never live that one down) and tied a red bandanna 'round my head in the manner of Leroy in *Fame*.

When I arrived at my local Samaritan center, the place was heaving with men and women dressed in smart suits, including the lady from the Samaritans. I felt like a complete idiot—I looked like a caricature lesbian, not a married do-gooder. The meeting went quite well as, thankfully, we didn't have to "care and share" or give impassioned presentations on what talents we had to offer. I decided to sign up for the training. It couldn't be that bad—could it? After all, I spent hours listening to my friends moaning, so I was quite confident I'd be a whiz on the phones.

The training—which took place over a six-week period, every Wednesday night and all day Sundays (I'd better have twins at this rate of do-gooderness)—proved intense. The team leaders kept asking us how we felt about death and losing people close to us. Everyone was nodding and staring at their feet, remembering lost loved ones. Well, I've never lost someone close to me except Garfield—if you can count a cat. I tried to remember how sad I was when he got run over by a car, but it was so long ago that I couldn't even picture what he looked like and kept imagining the cartoon cat, which made me want to laugh.

Then we had to discuss topics like abortion, euthanasia, crime and anorexia. It was all a bit stressful. None of my group seemed to have a sense of humor. When I said that my father prayed for euthanasia to be legalized so he could suffocate my granny in her sleep and save the rest of us from her constant moaning, there was a deathly silence.

Later, when we discussed abortion, I got a bit hot under the collar. I said I thought it was very selfish of women to abort their babies when there were so many couples having trouble getting pregnant. Why couldn't they just have the babies and give them up for adoption? That way everyone would be happy. It was only when I stopped talking that I realized I'd gone bright red and was shaking my fist in the air like some fanatical pro-lifer. The other volunteers were all staring at me in horror. I quickly added that, of course, it was each woman's prerogative to make her own choice. But it was too little too late. I had been black-marked.

The team leader took me aside and asked me if I really thought the Samaritans was for me, and explained—as if to a three-year-old child—that while it was great to have a sense of humor in life, euthanasia was no laughing matter, and that the Samaritans were not there to judge people's choices so I'd need to consider my feelings on abortion very carefully.

After tea break we did our first role-play where you had to pretend to be a Samaritan and deal with the caller's problem. Darryl, a very intense middle-aged volunteer from Belfast, was playing my caller. He was pretending to be a woman who was a victim of physical abuse.

"Samaritans, can I help you?" I said, in my most sympathetic voice. I decided to imitate Marilyn Monroe's nice soft voice so I sounded a bit American.

Darryl looked at me strangely. "Yes, hello. I'm in a terrible state. I don't know what to do. You see, my husband—"

"Mmm, I see, so you're married, then?"

"Em, yes, I am, actually. Anyway, my husband—"

"Where did you two meet?"

"Well, in university. Anyway, the thing is he beats me and I just don't—"

"Do you mean to say he's beaten you more than once?"

"Well, yes, that's why I'm calling," hissed Darryl, glaring at me. "I'm a victim of abuse and I'm feeling so depressed. I think I just want to end it all."

"Well, I don't blame you, that's dreadful. But you should never have let him thump you twice. Next time he does it, get out a baseball bat and give that son of a bitch a belt over the head with it that he'll never forget," I said, now sounding a lot more Rocky Balboa than Marilyn.

Darryl glared at me, mumbled "pathetic" under his breath and stomped out of the room. The team leader took me aside and reminded me of the Samaritans' golden rules, most of which I had broken: never give advice, never interrupt, never judge. Then she asked me to go home and have a nice long think about why I wanted to be a Samaritan and maybe to look at other forms of community service.

After much reflection on the short journey home, I decided not to continue with the Samaritans but to use the listening skills I had learned during the training in my everyday life. I would become an excellent, nonjudgmental listener so that all my friends and family would come to me first with their problems and, hopefully, that would be do-gooderish enough.

FIFTEEN

A few weeks later Henry called us to say that Imogen had given birth to healthy twin girls. He was over the moon, as were James's parents. I forced myself to be enthusiastic, congratulated Henry, told him how wonderful it was to have two beautiful daughters and how I couldn't wait to see them. James then spoke to Henry again and all I could hear was, "Of course we'll come, we wouldn't dream of not being there . . . we'll come for a long weekend . . . it'll be great to see everyone . . . what's that? . . . oh, wow, Henry, that's really nice of you, she'll be thrilled. Hold on, I'll put Emma back on now." He handed me the phone. "Henry wants to ask you something," he said, smiling at me.

"Emma," said Henry, sounding all formal, "Imogen and I would like you to be godmother to little Sophie."

My heart sank. I felt sick. The last thing in the world I wanted was to be godmother to Imogen's kid. Besides, I knew they were only asking me because we had no kids and they felt sorry for me. "Oh, Henry, that is so nice, but I'm sure Imogen has friends she'd much rather ask."

James poked me and mouthed, "What are you doing?" I slapped his hand away.

"Not at all, Emma, it's you we want," said Henry.

"Okay, then, I'd be delighted. Thanks for asking me. It's really sweet of you."

"Excellent. We'll see you in a few weeks' time for the christening."

"Super."

I hung up and sat down on the couch. I thought I was going to throw up. The last place in the world I wanted to be was at a christening.

"Emma, it was a bit rude of you to refuse at first," said James. "It was really thoughtful of Henry and Imogen to ask you to be godmother. I thought you'd be chuffed."

I looked at him. He just didn't get it. He tried to and he was really supportive, but he just didn't really get it. "James, why on earth would someone desperately trying to have a baby want to be godmother to someone else's child, especially when it's someone they don't really get on with?"

"You get on well with Henry and I thought Imogen was growing on you. Besides, it'll be nice for you to be involved in the christening."

"I'd rather set fire to myself."

"Emma!"

"No, I really mean that. I can think of nothing worse than having to go to the christening and stand there while everyone coos over the two beautiful twins and tells their parents how lovely they are and analyzes who they look like and says how wonderful it is for Thomas to have two sisters and how you never know the true meaning of the word 'love' until you have a child and how your life is not really full or complete until you experience the joy of motherhood. And then they'll all stare at me and ask when I'm going to have children—you know, James, for some mad reason I just don't really fancy that."

"Oh, come on, stop exaggerating. It won't be that bad and people don't go on like that."

"That's where you're wrong. Men don't go on like that to other men, but men and women go on like that to other women. We get the brunt of it, believe me. It's just like when you're single and people in relationships go on about the joy of finding your soul mate and the special bond that marriage brings and how they can't imagine being alone and then say things like, 'Don't worry, I'm sure you'll meet someone soon . . . plenty of fish in the sea' or 'How do you have the energy to go out all the time, we prefer to stay in. . . .' and you want to scream, 'I'm fucking exhausted! I'm sick of going to nightclubs, but if I stay in, alone, I'll probably slit my wrists.' "

James shook his head. "How did we get from you being godmother to slitting your wrists because you're alone on a Saturday night?"

"Because I'm trying to explain to you how difficult it can be. You're tormented when you're single, then if you get married, you're constantly quizzed about having a baby, and then if you're lucky enough to have one child, you're asked if you're going to have another and if, God forbid, you have two children of the same sex you'll be asked if you're going to try for another child in the hope that it will be a different sex, and if it isn't, everyone will look at you with pity and say, 'Ah, well, maybe you'll go again.' That's what I'm trying to explain to you, because that's what it's like."

"Well, next time anyone asks you if you're planning to have kids, tell them to fuck off."

"Oh yeah, sure. I can just see myself telling Imogen's mother to fuck off at the christening. It's not that easy."

"She's a bit of a battle-ax, it wouldn't be that difficult. I'm sure you could manage it."

"It's not funny, James. I really don't want to go to the christening and now it's a million times worse because I'm godmother. Why the hell did they have to ask me?"

"They were trying to be nice, Emma, wanting you to feel included. It's a pretty big honor to be asked to be godmother, you know," James said, and before I could answer, he added quickly, "I can see that a christening is not your ideal day out right now, but you just need to calm down. It'll be fine," he said, and turned on the TV. He clearly didn't want to continue this conversation.

There was no point in arguing any further. James didn't really understand why I was freaking out and I didn't want him to think I was totally ungrateful to his brother for asking me to be godmother. I had a sneaking suspicion that James had told Henry we were trying for a baby and that was why I'd been asked. It was a pity ask. There was only one thing for it: I'd have to look sensational so that no one would be tempted to feel sorry for me. I didn't want anyone's pity. Besides, I thought, in a lame attempt to cheer myself up, it was weeks away. I might be pregnant by then but I needed to relax, like Dr. Philips had said, and stop getting so wound up.

I woke up the next day and had a stern talk with myself. Getting het up was bad for me. I had to force myself to be calmer and more Zen-like. I decided to try yoga. Lucy swore by it—mind you, she never seemed that chilled out herself. Still, all the magazines and health columns raved about it so it was worth a shot.

I went down to the gym to see what they had to offer. *Astanga* yoga, *hatha* yoga, *iyengar* yoga, *sivananda* yoga and Pilates. I had only heard of *astanga* and Pilates and there happened to be an *astanga* class beginning five minutes later, so I opted for that.

A tall, lithe woman of about fifty was taking it. There were ten other people in the room and they all seemed to know each other. There was lots of "Are you going on the *astanga* weekend in

Kerry?" and "How's that knee injury?" The teacher introduced herself as Anna and asked if there were any beginners. No one put up their hand so I didn't either. I just wanted to sit at the back of the class and try to blend in.

"And we begin with *samasthiti,* the first stage of *tadasan,*" said Anna.

I looked around and everyone was sweeping their arms up over their heads and staring at their thumbs. So far, so good.

". . . and swan dive into forward bend, nose toward your knees, fingers level with toes."

While the rest of the class bent their bodies effortlessly in half, my nose was parallel to my belly button and my fingers were gripping on to my knees. At least Anna was bent double and couldn't see my pathetic attempts.

". . . downward dog, tailbone reaches toward the ceiling, press hard into the hands—arms straight, shoulders working, chest drops between the armpits pressing toward the thighs, press the heels down to lengthen the hamstrings."

Everyone dived down—hands and feet flat on the mat with their bums sticking up in the air. I followed suit. A lot of very loud, raspy breathing ensued. It was very off-putting. They all sounded as if they were being strangled. I was going purple and gasping for air as the blood rushed to my head.

It was between the warrior and the upward-facing dog that Anna spotted me for the intruder I was. "You, in the pink top," she barked, as I collapsed from my pathetic attempt at the position, "how many times have you done yoga before?"

The class all turned from beneath their postures to glare at me. They sighed and shook their heads. Clearly a beginner was the scourge of this yoga class. I was now purple from embarrassment as well as blood rush.

"Oh, well . . . uhm, just once," I lied.

"You should have told me you were a beginner," she snapped, as she strode over and began twisting my body into positions that defied gravity and sanity. I was in agony, but too afraid of her to complain. She twisted my head one way, my shoulders the other, and my tailbone (I thought only animals had those) until I was sweating profusely and crying with pain. I thought the class would never end. When it finally did, I hobbled out the door and went straight home to soak in the bath. Relaxing—my arse! I had never been so humiliated or tortured in my life. Anna was a sadist and the class was a bunch of pompous yoga-ists. Never again. I'd have to find a less painful way to relax.

As I was watching *EastEnders* on the couch later that night, munching chocolate digestives, I felt very relaxed. Maybe this was my way of chilling out. It might not be healthy, good for the figure or stimulating to the mind, but it was a whole lot more fun than trying to salute the sun as a downward dog warrior.

SIXTEEN

*T*hree months and another phantom pregnancy after my visit to Dr. Philips, I still wasn't pregnant. I was feeling really despondent, on top of which the christening was looming. We were off in a couple of days and I was dreading it. I was feeling very sorry for myself when my mother called. "Hi, it's Mum, how are you?"

"Crap."

"Do you have to use that word? It's so common."

"Yes, I do."

"Oh, I can see you're in a mood. What's wrong with you?"

"What is wrong with me, Mother, is that I've been trying to get pregnant for ten months and have nothing to show for it."

"I told you it would take time."

"Can you, please, for once in your life, not do the I-told-you-so thing?"

"There's no need to take your anger out on me, young lady. I realize it must be frustrating, but these things take time. You can't rush it."

"Ten months is not rushing it."

"Well, getting yourself into a heap about it won't help. You have to keep busy and stop thinking about it all the time. Let nature take its course. Take on more work and keep your mind off it."

"Mum, I've been doing three weddings a week on top of my slot with Amanda Nolan on *Afternoon with Amanda*. I'm very busy."

"That brazen hussy ruining that poor man's political career," Mum said, referring to John Bradley's political demise after the story of his affair with Amanda broke. My mother was a staunch supporter of Bradley's party and had been devastated when he was forced to resign.

"He's the one who was married, Mum. He's the one who cheated on his wife. Amanda's single," I said, defending her. She was one of the few people I enjoyed spending time with anymore. She didn't have any children and had no interest in talking about them. She said she had seen far too many women changed by motherhood from fun-loving, interesting people to one-track obsessives, and decided it was not for her. She thought I was mad wanting to get pregnant and was constantly trying to change my mind. She was very funny about it, and always made me laugh. I liked her for being different: it made a nice change from hearing and reading that you're not complete as a person until you have a child.

"She's a well-known girl-about-town. John Bradley was a fine politician. The party's not the same since he left. That new fella, Finnegan, is useless."

"Well, Bradley should have kept his penis in his trousers, then, shouldn't he?"

"Emma! There's no need to be vulgar. You're being very contrary. I hope you're being nice to James. You'd want to be careful, Emma. You need to mind your man. If he comes home to a grumpy face every night he'll run off with a pretty young one with a spring in her step."

"Well, that's great. Thanks, Mum, just what I needed to hear.

Thanks for cheering me up by telling me my husband is going to run off with someone else. Jesus, is it too much to ask for a little sympathy for my predicament, particularly as I have this stupid bloody christening coming up?"

"Now, listen to me, Emma. You're to stop feeling sorry for yourself and go to that christening with a smile on your face. Nobody likes a whinger. I know it's not the ideal situation, but you've been asked to be godmother to that little girl and you've accepted, so you must go and be gracious and charming. Everyone has their own problems, you're not the only person to go through this and you won't be the last. So just try to buck up and think positively. Now, go and put some lipstick on and a nice skirt and welcome your husband home with a cheery smile. I'll call you before you go."

Aaaargh, my mother had the most amazing ability to wind me up. I was in a rage now. God, what century were we living in? "Go and put some lipstick on"—had she missed the whole feminist movement? Where had she been in the sixties? I glanced at my reflection in the hall mirror as I passed it. I stopped and stared down at my saggy tracksuit bottoms, oversize long-sleeved T-shirt and slippers. My hair was due a wash and I wasn't wearing any makeup. I looked a state. But I was enjoying looking like this. It suited my mood—foul. I stomped back to my horizontal position on the couch.

The next day, Babs called over after college. She only ever called over when she wanted to get her makeup done before going to a party or if she needed to borrow money. "Hi."

"Hi, how are you?"

"Exhausted. College life is tough going. There's always some party to go to and you can't not go in case you miss a good night," said Babs, yawning. "I'm also broke. Dad's allowance would be all right if we were living in the seventies, but it doesn't stretch very far."

"Why don't you get a part-time job?"

Babs looked at me as if I was mad. "A job? How the hell am I supposed to fit a job into my life? I haven't got the time. Speaking of money, any chance you could lend me a few quid?"

"Lend?"

"Okay—give."

"I had a funny feeling that was why you called in," I said, sighing.

"It isn't, actually, you big martyr. Mum told me to. She said you've gone a bit psycho about the kid thing. She told me to pop in and cheer you up."

"Did she say 'psycho'?"

"No, she said 'uptight'—same difference, as far as I'm concerned," said the ever-helpful Babs, throwing her bag on the floor and flopping down on the couch.

"Well, thanks for being so blunt. I feel much better now. You can go, your work is done."

"Oh, relax, you know what she's like. If she isn't worried about something she's not happy. So how are you, anyway?"

"Not great. It's been ten months and still nothing."

"Are you having loads of sex?"

"Yep."

"Well, what are you complaining about, then? Sounds good to me. Unless James is crap. Is he crap?"

"No, he isn't, he's great. It's just different when you're having sex to get pregnant. It's all a bit planned, it's not very spontaneous."

"Oh, right. Well, maybe you should get some sex toys to spice it up a bit. There's an amazing new vibrator you can get on the Internet—it's supposed to be incredible. I can order you one if you like."

"Thanks, but no thanks. I really don't need one."

"Fair enough. I'm getting one for myself so I'll tell you if it really is as good as they claim."

"Yeah. Okay. Whatever. Do you want tea?"

"Any chance of a beer?"

"No, sorry, don't have any."

"What? James always has beer in the fridge."

"Yeah, well, not anymore. We're on a health drive."

"Jesus, crap sex and no jar—no wonder you're a psycho."

"Tea?"

"Yeah, if that's the strongest thing you have."

I went into the kitchen, took some deep breaths and counted to a hundred and twenty. Babs could be a real handful at times. When I brought the tea in, she stared into her mug and made a face. "What's this?"

"It's green tea."

"Well, it's revolting. Since when do you drink this muck?"

"Since I read that green tea is incredibly good for you."

"Does it make you pregnant?"

"No, but it prevents cancer and is an antioxidant, which is brilliant for eliminating toxins and so it's really good for your skin."

"You don't have cancer and you couldn't have any toxins in you 'cos you've no alcohol in the house. So why are we drinking the muck?"

"Look, just drink it and shut up. You're a pain in the arse sometimes."

"Do you make James drink this shite as well?"

"He really likes it, actually," I lied. James thought the green tea was revolting and refused to touch it.

"Yeah, right . . . and Dolly Parton sleeps on her stomach. Well, can I at least have a biscuit to help me drink this?"

"No biscuits."

"What? No bickies? What's wrong with them? Do they attack sperm or something?"

"No, we've just decided to be more healthy. Eat less rubbish and more fruit and veg. I have prunes, if you want."

"No, thanks, I'd rather eat cow dung. You really need to lighten up, Emma. This living-like-those-Amish-people lark isn't doing you any good. Go out and have a few jars and a large Mac and fries—it'll make you feel better. This monk stuff won't last."

"Well, thanks for coming over and cheering me up. I feel a lot better now. You should think about a career in counseling, you've a real talent for it."

"Okay, fair enough. I can see I'm wasting my time here. Besides, I need to go and get ready for tonight. I'm going to a fancy dress. Pimps and tarts. Should be a good laugh. Remember that, Emma? Going to parties and having fun? For God's sake, you're not ninety, stop being such a granny."

As I watched her stroll down the road I started to cry. Maybe she was right. Maybe I was a sad cow. Were the green tea and boring lifestyle really making any difference? I was bored, boring and absolutely gagging for some chocolate and a bottle of wine. But I wanted a baby more. For once in my life I wanted to do things by the book. Not to take the easy way out. To be totally focused and do everything in my power to make it happen. I was always reading about how if you really want something you have to do everything in your power to make it happen. But I was miserable and I was probably making James miserable. Okay, I *was* making James miserable. I decided to call him.

"Hi."

"Hi."

"How are you?"

"Fine, what's up?"

"I've been thinking about this whole health drive I've been on."

"Yes," said James, sounding suspicious.

"Well, I'm calling you to tell you that I've decided the clean-living stuff is a load of old rubbish and it clearly isn't working. So I think we should go out tonight, get plastered and have some good old-fashioned sex for no reason."

"You mean I can go out and not be badgered into drinking tomato juice and green tea? I dunno, Emma, I was kind of getting into it."

"Very funny. Just make sure you're home early. And no fertility talk, I promise."

"What? But we'll have nothing to say to each other. It's our only topic of conversation."

"Am I that bad?"

"Just a tad obsessed and the healthy-lifestyle drive was becoming a real bore."

"God, I've been like a broken record, haven't I? Sorry, James, I promise not to mention it once tonight."

"This calls for a celebration. I'll book a table in La Poule. Alcohol, steak and normal sex. Whoo-hoo, I'll be home early, all right."

We got all dressed up and had a great time, eating fabulous French food and drinking gorgeous red wine. It was lovely. We giggled about the first time we met, talked about our families, school days, friends and, for once, did not mention babies. I was tempted at one point to bring it up, but I bit my tongue—I know, miracles do happen! It was just like old times, the two of us getting sloshed together and having a laugh. By the time we staggered home we were so drunk we passed out fully clothed on the bed—so much for the casual sex.

SEVENTEEN

Three days later James and I arrived in Sussex for the christening. I had spent a fortune on a sexy black dress with a plunging neckline and shoes with killer heels. I was determined to look my best. Thankfully, we were staying with James's parents, Mr. and Mrs. Hamilton. Imogen's mother—the dreaded Mrs. Gore-Grimes—was staying with Henry and Imogen. I had met the woman once and she was awful—really overbearing and tactless.

We had dinner with James's parents, who raved about the twins. It was really touching to see them so excited about their new grandchildren. I started to think about how excited my parents would be if we had a baby, and had to excuse myself from the table: tears were welling in my eyes as I imagined Dad cooing over a cot, looking all proud and chuffed.

It was ridiculous. I'd only been in the house twenty minutes and I was crying already. I told my reflection in the mirror to get a grip, dabbed my eyes and took some deep breaths. When I came back into the room, they were talking about the Leinster semifinal and Mr. Hamilton was saying how he had read all the Irish papers on the Internet praising James. He was congratulating his son on his new contract and his great success in his first year as coach.

As I looked at Mr. Hamilton's face, so full of pride at his son's achievements, I thought of how wonderful it would be for James to have that with his own son. I began to well up again and had to excuse myself. I pinched and cursed myself for being so pathetic. I knew I had to control my emotions or I would make a show of myself at the christening. A few deep breaths later and I went back in to sit down. James was busy describing the second half of the match to his father and Mrs. Hamilton was in the kitchen preparing supper.

The rest of the evening went smoothly. I managed to get a handle on my emotions and there was no more baby chat so it was fine. That is, until James got up and said, "Come on, Emma. We'd better go and see the twins now before it gets too late."

I had hoped that we'd just see them in the church. I hadn't planned on calling over the night before to coo at them and I knew, feeling the way I did that evening, it would be dangerous for me to be around children. But there was no getting out of it. I plastered a smile on my face and got into the car.

Once the doors were closed, I turned to James. "Look, I'm feeling a bit sensitive tonight. I don't know what's wrong with me. I keep wanting to cry. Can we make this a really quick visit?"

"Emma, I haven't seen Henry in ten months. I'm not going to charge out of his house after five minutes. Just relax, it'll be fine."

When we got there, Imogen was holding court in the drawing room, surrounded by her brood. Her dreadful mother was there, as was little Thomas. I smiled and kissed Imogen, Henry and the twins, and bent down to kiss Thomas, but he started to cry and scream, "No, get away, don't like you," which was just a tad embarrassing.

"Now, Thomas, don't be rude to your auntie Emma. She's trying to be nice," said Mrs. Gore-Grimes. "Go and give her a kiss."

"Don't want to," howled Thomas.

"Go on, a little kissy-wissy for Emma," said Granny Gore-Grimes, as I prayed for the floor to open up and swallow me.

"*No!*" he yelled, running away from me.

"Thomas, come back. . . ."

"Mrs. Gore-Grimes, really, it's quite all right," I said, as firmly as I could, hoping that someone would shove a soother in Thomas's mouth to shut him up.

Henry and James snuck out into the kitchen under the pretense of getting us all drinks and never came back. I was left with the incredible baby-making machine that was Imogen and her "delightful" mother.

"So," I said, as brightly as I could, "how are you feeling, Imogen? I must say you look great."

That was a lie. The only consoling thing in that room was Imogen's weight. She had whacked on a good two stone and looked very chunky. I know it was bitchy of me, but it made me feel just a little bit better about myself.

"Yah, well, I feel great. Having children is such a wonderful experience. I just love my two little princesses and Henry is totally besotted. It's true what they say about fathers and daughters. As for Thomas, well, he just loves his sisters, don't you, Tom-Tom?"

Thomas was glaring at his sisters with a look of pure hatred. He didn't look too enamored to me.

"Great," I said.

"Come on, then, Emma, come and hold Sophie. She's your goddaughter, after all," said Mrs. Gore-Grimes, thrusting Sophie into my arms.

I looked down at the tiny bundle. She opened her eyes and stared at me. My heart melted. She was beautiful. She was perfect and had that lovely baby smell—a mixture of talcum powder and baby lotion. I couldn't take my eyes off her. She sighed and then yawned, her little rosebud mouth making a perfect O. I was in a world of my own when I heard, "Well, well, Imogen, I think someone's getting broody."

I looked up and saw mother and daughter nodding and winking at each other.

"You can't have Sophie, I'm afraid, you'll have to have one of your own," added the old witch, taking Sophie from me to give her a bottle.

"You really should have a baby, Emma," said Imogen, joining in to torment me further. "I know James is keen to have children, he said as much to Henry."

"You don't want to leave it too late," said the fat lump's mother. "You modern gals are far too busy partying and focusing on your careers when you should be having children and staying at home to look after them. Mark my words, children and grandchildren are what it's all about," she said, beaming at her daughter. "Chop-chop, Emma. Give that nice husband of yours a child."

I was speechless. I couldn't believe that anyone could be so insensitive. My shirt was stuck to my back with sweat. I had to get out of there. As I stood up, Thomas came hurtling across the room, beaker of orange juice in hand. He tripped over my foot, drenching me and hitting his chin on the floor. He opened his big gob and screamed.

"Oh, poor Tom-Tom," said his grandmother, rushing over. "Did Auntie Emma trip you up? Mean Emma! Look, we'll smack her," she said, smacking me rather hard on the leg. "Mean, nasty Emma. Come on, Tom-Tom, we'll smack her again."

Thomas—who, I now realized, had inherited his violent streak from his grandmother—smacked my leg, then kicked me in the shins. Meanwhile, I was trying to wipe orange juice off my very expensive Joseph trousers. Henry, who had popped his head 'round the door to see who was torturing poor Thomas, saw him kick me. "Thomas," he said sternly, catching his son by the arm, "we do not kick people. Apologize to Emma."

Thank God one of them thought it was out of order for him to kick me. Thomas wriggled out of Henry's grasp and ran to Imogen, sniveling.

"Thomas," said Henry. "Apologize at once."

"Oh, leave him alone, Henry, he didn't mean anything by it. Emma tripped him up and he was just a bit angry."

"I don't care, Imogen. He's not allowed to kick people. He needs to learn that. Thomas, come over here at once."

"Honestly, Henry, it's fine, forget it," I said.

Christ, I just wanted to go home. Where the bloody hell was James? I mumbled about getting some tissues for the spill and darted out of the room. I found James sprawled on the couch in the TV room, beer in one hand, cigarette in the other, watching football.

"Where the hell have you been?" I hissed.

"Oh, hi. I've just been catching up with Henry," he said lamely, trying to hide the cigarette. I could see by his eyes that he was a little tipsy.

"I'd like to go home now," I said, my temper bubbling below the surface.

"We'll go in two minutes, I just want to see the end of this match," he said, turning back to the TV. "Go on, Giggs, shoot— oh, he missed again."

I leaned over and grabbed the keys of his father's car. "Well, I'm leaving, so if you want to walk home, by all means stay and watch your match," I said, and stalked out the door.

James followed me out after saying a quick good-bye to the others. He got into the car and slammed the door. I took off like a

158 / Sinead Moriarty

Formula One specialist, leaving skidmarks on Henry and Imogen's driveway.

"For God's sake, slow down. What the hell is wrong with you now? Why did we have to leave in such a hurry? I was enjoying catching up with Henry over a few beers."

"Oh, I'm sorry, James, did I interrupt your little tête-à-tête with Henry? How selfish of me, especially considering I was having such a jolly time myself."

James sighed and crossed his arms. "Okay, what happened this time? What evil, nasty remarks did they come out with in their continuing conspiracy to make your life hell? Go on, I'm dying to hear."

"You smug bastard!" I shouted, swerving dangerously across the road. "While you were having beers with Henry I was left in that room with those witches, telling me to get on with it and have a baby soon before I keel over and die of old age, and how selfish I was not to be pregnant already because my husband's going around telling everyone how fucking desperate he is to have kids and I'm such a selfish bitch that I'm holding out because I'm too busy partying. That's the conversation I was having," I said, thumping the steering wheel with rage.

"Oh for God's sake, it couldn't have been that bad. If someone looks at you sideways you think it's a personal affront these days. Imogen does something really sweet by asking you to be godmother to her baby and all you can do is bitch and moan about it. Everything is about you these days. Well—newsflash, Emma—the whole world is not out to get you. Will you please just calm down and stop getting so het up about every little thing that happens? It's really tiresome. Just chill out and stop taking everything so seriously. Where's your sense of humor gone? You said you wanted to stop drinking and eating all that healthy crap and get back to being the fun Emma you used to be—and for a few great days you were."

I felt as if my head were going to explode. I was so angry that I wanted to wrap the car around a tree out of spite. My hands shook as I gripped the steering wheel. "Well, I'm so sorry I've been such a pain to live with. I must be going mad because I thought we both wanted to have a baby so I was doing crazy stuff like following the doctor's orders and trying to be more healthy. Poor you, having to put up with someone who wants to have a family with you. Why don't you just divorce me and marry some fun, happy-go-lucky *bimbo?*"

"If you're going to be childish about it, there's no point in having this conversation. I want to have a child as much as you. But I do think you need to calm down and stop being so bloody obsessive. The doctor, whose instructions you're so eager to follow, said you needed to relax if you wanted to get pregnant. So could you please do us all a favor and try to lighten up? Stop being so grumpy and defensive."

I flung the car into the Hamiltons' driveway, rushed inside and locked myself in the bathroom where I cried myself sick. At one point James knocked on the door. "Emma, come on out, you're being silly."

"No," I said, sobbing extra loudly so he'd be sure to hear me.

But instead of talking to me and comforting me, he walked off and went to bed. I unlocked the door an hour later and found James fast asleep in the guest bedroom that Mrs. Hamilton had put us in. I couldn't sleep in another room and announce to the whole house that we were arguing, so I climbed in beside him and spent a fitful night tossing and turning. James, meanwhile, slept like a log, stinking of beer and snoring.

I got up early the next morning and went out for a long walk. My head was throbbing from lack of sleep and my eyes were stinging from crying. I was still really upset. James and I had fought before, but only silly fights, never ones where we said really horrible things to each other. I felt that he had overdone it last night—I knew he had been drinking, but he wasn't drunk. He had meant what he said and it had really hurt. I knew a lot of it was true, which was worse: I was obsessed, but no matter how hard I tried I couldn't control it. I thought about having a baby all the time. And everyone around me seemed to be getting pregnant on their honeymoon, or after their first attempt, like Imogen. What if I never got pregnant? What if there was something wrong with me that the doctors had missed? When I saw our friends with their children my heart ached. I wanted that for us. We'd be good parents, so why was it so bloody difficult? Well, one thing was for sure: I had to try to relax. In this state, not only would I never get pregnant, but I'd end up alone.

I stayed out all morning, only reappearing at lunchtime to get changed for the christening. When I got back, James was waiting for me. "Look, Emma, I'm sorry. I didn't mean to be so harsh. It was the beer talking. I'm sorry I upset you."

I shook my head sadly. "It wasn't the beer, James, it was the truth. I've been a pain and I've begun to get paranoid and a bit self-obsessed about it all. I just didn't realize you felt so strongly about it."

"I don't. Emma, look, I want a baby as much as you, and I know it's harder for you as the woman. I'm just worried that it's taking over your life completely. I hate seeing you so unhappy."

"I know. I'm going to try really hard to chill out about it all," I said. "Oh my God." I'd just caught a glimpse of myself in the mirror: I looked like a hag. Thank God I was a makeup artist: at least I could do something about my blotchy face. "Look at the state of me. Come on, help me get ready. I need to look sensational so fat Imogen can be jealous of me for a change."

Half an hour and layer upon layer of makeup later, I was ready. I looked at myself in the mirror—not bad: I scrubbed up well. I came downstairs and James whistled. He leaned over and whispered in my ear, "And by the way, I have no intention of running off with any bimbo, particularly when my wife looks this hot."

The christening passed without a hitch. Having vented my frustration the night before, by the time we got to the church I was feeling calm and serene—I know it's hard to believe, but I was, honestly!

My love affair with my goddaughter Sophie was complete when I saw her all dressed up in her christening gown. She looked like a tiny angel. Her other godmother, Gemma—an old school pal of Imogen's who was hugely pregnant and, thankfully, seemed happy to take a backseat—didn't get a look in. I was the one who proudly held Sophie as the vicar wetted her head, and she made my day by not uttering a sound. The other twin's godmother—Imogen's horsey friend Annabelle—struggled with a howling Luisa when the water hit her forehead.

My dress went down a treat, and as Henry's friends got drunker and drunker, they kept staring down my top and telling me that I was a "fine bit of totty." As I was the only woman there who hadn't given birth, the male attention was a welcome relief from the constant round of:

Wives: "So, how long have you been married?"
Me: "Nearly two years."
Them: "Any children?"
Me: "No, none."
They nod. I nod. We smile awkwardly.
Them: "Ah, well, no need to rush into it."
Me: "No . . . yeah . . . yeah . . . no . . . no need to rush."

Them (desperately looking to get away from me): "Oh, look, there's Victoria and Charles, I must go over and say hello, do excuse me."

Me (delighted to see the back of them): "Sure, no problem."

But the best part of the day was when I pulled aside Thomas— who had kicked me again during the meal—while no one was looking, and told him that if he ever kicked me again, I'd rip Tinky-Winky's legs and arms off and feed his torso to a pack of hungry wolves. Thankfully his speech was still basic and all he could muster as he cried in his grandmother's arms was, "Emma, mean, Tinky-Winky . . . arms . . . hungry," but a suspicious Mrs. Gore-Grimes kept a close eye on me for the rest of the afternoon.

EIGHTEEN

$\mathscr{A}$ couple of weeks later Lucy, Jess and I went out for dinner. We had been seeing a bit more of Jess in the last few months as Sally was in nursery school now two days a week and she was in much better form and less distracted. I had arranged the dinner to celebrate Lucy's recent promotion and pay raise. I wanted to make a fuss of her as she was always trotting out to congratulate everyone else on engagements, weddings and babies. It was time to focus on her for a change.

We met for drinks at seven. I ordered champagne and we toasted Lucy's new job. She was chuffed with the attention and we settled down to a good night of drinking and laughing—until I went to pour Jess a second glass of champagne and she stopped me, shaking her head. "Sorry, Emma. No more for me, I'm afraid." I looked at her. Her eyes welled up and she began to cry. "Yep, I'm pregnant again. I'm thrilled, really, just a bit emotional about it all," she said unconvincingly.

I saw Lucy's shoulders slump. Her night of fun and celebration was officially over, after fifteen minutes in the limelight. I felt really sorry for her. It wasn't fair of Jess to come in and start weeping about being pregnant. For God's sake, what the hell was wrong with her? She wanted kids, and she was clearly having no problem producing them, so why the glum face? Besides, if she had suddenly decided after Sally that she didn't want any more, why hadn't she gone back on the pill?

"Well, that's great, Jess," I said. "You must be thrilled. You always said you wanted a couple of kids."

"Yeah, I know. I'm rea-real-really happy," she said, sobbing into her tissue.

Lucy and I looked at each other in shock. Why was she so upset?

"Jess, it's perfectly obvious you're not happy at all. What's wrong?" asked Lucy, cutting straight to the point.

"I'm sorry, guys. I know I shouldn't complain, but I didn't want this to happen."

"Well, then, why didn't you prevent it?" said Lucy bluntly.

"Because I do want kids. I mean, everyone does. Right?"

Lucy shrugged, I nodded.

"And I don't want Sally to be an only child, so I suppose I was trying to get pregnant, and I don't know if I'm cut out for motherhood. I don't think I'm very good at it. I really don't like it very much."

I was shocked. Jess was always talking about Sally's first smile and Sally's first tooth. She was obsessed with the child. How could she think she wasn't good at it?

"But, Jess," I said, "you're always telling me stories about how much you love Sally and how proud you are when she does stuff for the first time. You're a brilliant mum. You're so into her and enthusiastic about her, it's lovely. You're a natural."

"But that's just it, Emma. I'm not. I say those things because I hear other mothers saying them. Don't get me wrong—I love Sally to bits and I'm really proud of her, it's just that I've had no life for a year and a half. Now she's in nursery and I was just getting my life back, but I'm pregnant again. I can't bear it. I want to be myself again."

"But you are yourself. Life changes when you have kids, everyone says that. You've just got different priorities," I said, trying to make her feel better. She looked like she was going to have a nervous breakdown and, to be honest, I only wanted to hear about the nice side of motherhood: I didn't want to be put off.

"It can't be that bad," said Lucy. "You've got a great husband and a healthy child. Come on, Jess, get some perspective, you're very lucky."

"I know I'm lucky," said Jess, frowning, "but you have no idea how bloody hard it is. I'm sorry, Lucy, but until you—"

"—go through it you can't understand. Yeah, yeah. I've heard it all before. Just try being single at thirty-four and see how shit that feels," snapped Lucy. "I'll take the nice husband and the kids and you can have my life for a while."

I have to say, she had a point. Jess was being self-pitying and she had ruined Lucy's night out.

Jess was angry now. "It must be difficult having a successful career, being respected and looked up to by your colleagues. Having a big fat salary with no one to spend it on but yourself. Buying designer clothes, going for facials at the drop of a hat. Traveling to New York on business and being chased 'round Dublin by a rugby star. Gee, Lucy, it must be really tough."

Lucy looked flushed, and angry too. "So that's how you see my life? Well, have you ever thought how your life seems to me? You sit around on your arse watching daytime TV or having lunches and coffees with other mothers. You spend time with a daughter you adore . . . you've got a great husband—there's always someone to cuddle up to at night. You've got someone to talk to after you've had a shit day. When I get home after a crappy day, all I have to keep me company are the four walls of the apartment I worked my ass off to pay for. Sometimes I wake up in the middle of the night and have panic attacks because I'm terrified of growing old alone, but that's a reality I have to accept and deal with. I watch my friends move on with their lives while I stay stuck in my single rut. I often have to force myself to go out when I'm so tired and depressed I just want to curl into a ball and scream. Why? Because I know if I stay in, there's no hope of meeting Mr. Right. God! You smug married people make me sick."

I was stunned. I had never heard Lucy talk so honestly about being single. Obviously I knew it got her down and that she was scared of ending up on her own, but I never grasped how awful that fear must be.

Jess shook her head. "Lucy, I'm sorry, I didn't mean to sound so harsh. It must be really difficult for you. All I'm trying to say is that it's not always sunny on this side either. I think I'm just overwhelmed by how hard being a mother is. No one tells you that your vagina's going to be ripped wide open and you're going to need internal and external stitches so that you can't sit down properly for weeks. The only respite you get is by cutting a hole in a cushion so that it's like sitting on a doughnut. No one tells you that going to the loo will be like pissing nails. If you even think about not breast-feeding, you're considered a freak of nature. The pressure is unbelievable, so you give in and walk around with cracked nipples and leaky boobs for months."

Mother of God, this was desperate stuff. Every orifice seemed to have been a no-go area for Jess postbirth. I wondered if she had a low pain threshold or was it really that bad.

"And as for the adoring husband," continued Jess, "he slopes off to the spare room every night because he has to work in the morning, leaving you with the baby to feed, and you don't have a clue what you're doing. You're just winging it. When Sally wakes up in the middle of the night I sometimes want to strangle her. The sleep deprivation is really what gets me down. The first time I bathed

Sally, I was so tired I dropped her in the water and thought I'd drowned her. I didn't stop shaking for days."

I had to interrupt her. I really didn't want to hear all this negativity. "But after a while you get used to it, don't you?" I asked, praying she would say yes.

"Yes, you do get into a kind of a routine, but you're exhausted all the time. I sat around for months in my pajamas because there was no time to get dressed. By the time I'd fed, burped and dressed her, it was time for the next feed. When Tony got home, I was sitting on the couch in my pajamas with greasy hair. I'd say hello, hand Sally to him, go straight to bed and pass out. We didn't have sex for eight months."

"Eight months!" I didn't mean to make her feel worse, but I couldn't help it. Jesus Christ, enough already with the information. This was awful—there was no way it could be as bad as she was making out. She obviously just didn't cope very well with it. I'd be different. I had loads of energy. I'd bounce back quicker. Mind you, I spent a fair amount of time on the couch in my pajamas as it was. I'd have to get out of that habit and back into a regular routine at the gym.

"Yes, Emma, no sex for eight months. During those months I was a fat, miserable, greasy-haired blob with a sore vagina, leaky boobs and the energy levels of a ninety-year-old."

"My longest stretch without sex was three months, so I do feel sorry for you there," said Lucy, thawing out.

"But, Jess, once you got back into it, it was okay, wasn't it?" I asked, determined to extract a positive response.

"Well, eventually. But it took a long time. After about six months I decided to go into town to get some sexy underwear and some new clothes to make myself feel better. I still couldn't fit into prepregnancy clothes and I needed to get out of the tracksuit I was living in. Between getting Sally ready, having a shower myself and packing all her nappies and baby wipes into the bag and all that stuff, it took two hours. We were just about to set off when she threw up all over herself, so I had to take her out of the car, change her and feed her again. Instead of leaving the house at ten as I had planned, we left at twelve. The traffic was so bad that it took an hour to get into town. Then we spent another hour stuck in a car park queue. By the time I'd parked it was nearly two and I knew she'd be hollering for food again soon. So I just turned 'round and drove straight home. I didn't even get to one shop. I cried all the way home, then just put on the same saggy tracksuit and had another sexless night. When I eventually made it into town I blew a fortune on sexy lingerie and attacked Tony when he came in from work. I had to do something before his penis shriveled up and fell off from lack of activity," said Jess, laughing.

"Why didn't you call me? I could have picked some stuff up for you, or babysat," I said.

"I was ashamed and embarrassed. I didn't want to admit what a disaster I was to anyone—not even myself. When my baby-group mothers came over for coffee they'd all crash on about how much sex they were having and how the orgasms were better now. So I lied as well and said Tony and I were at it like rabbits."

"Well, it's obviously better on the sex front now, as you're pregnant again. . . ." I said, smiling at her.

"That's just it—everything's better now," she said gloomily. "We're getting into a nice routine, we have regular babysitters, go out every weekend and have fun together, and now I'm bloody pregnant again and it's all going to stop and before you know it I'll be back sitting on that bloody doughnut."

"Why don't you opt for a Cesarean? Lots of people do nowadays," said Lucy, always the practical one.

"And don't breast-feed, just go straight to bottles," I added helpfully.

"To be honest, my vagina's so stretched after giving birth to Sally that I reckon this one will just slide out," said Jess.

That was it. I'd heard quite enough. I decided to nip it in the bud and refocus the attention on Lucy—after all, it was the reason we'd met up, and it was a lot less gruesome. "I'd like to propose a toast," I announced. "To Jess's new baby and to Lucy's new promotion—which she totally deserves because she lives in that office."

NINETEEN

A month later I was at the airport waiting for my brother's plane to land, feeling decidedly grumpy. I'd gotten my period the day before. It had been three days late and I had gone through the oh-my-God-I'm-pregnant euphoria, only to be disappointed yet again. Christmas was normally my favorite time of year. I loved the buzz around town as people rushed about in the cold buying presents for loved ones, meeting for drinks and wishing each other well. It was the only time of year when strangers actually risked eye contact and spoke to you—to wish you a merry Christmas.

I always collected Sean from the airport on Christmas Eve. It was our little ritual. We'd been doing it for years. I had always loved seeing all the Christmas decorations at the airport twinkling at me as I drove in. The arrivals lounge was like a carnival as people shouted and cried when their family and friends came through the sliding doors and ran to hug them.

By the time Sean came over to me, I was always tearful—having witnessed numerous emotional family reunions. He found it very entertaining and usually had a tissue on hand for me.

This year was different. I stood at the back of the arrivals hall, watched the travelers coming out and envied them. I watched bitterly as grandparents saw their grandchildren for the first time. I wanted to go over to them and shout, "Do you know how lucky you are? Do you have any idea how difficult it is to produce grand-children?"

A man dressed as Santa came over to me. "Ho-ho-ho, young lady, and a merry Christmas to you. Come on, give Santa a smile."

I wanted to pull Santa's beard off and punch him in the nose. Instead I opted for glaring at him, but he was not to be deterred: "Come on, I bet you have a beautiful smile. If you smile all your wishes may come true. Come on, Santa isn't going to leave until he makes you smile. In fact he's going to sing—come on, join in. *'Rudolph the red-nosed reindeer . . .'*"

The airport was packed and the people standing beside me were staring. I grabbed his arm and whispered under my breath. "Look, Santa, you're barking up the wrong tree here. Now, will you please just fuck off and torment someone else?"

Poor old Santa nearly fell over with shock. I'm sure he'd never been spoken to like that before or since. I felt guilty for being so rude, but he was doing my head in and I really didn't feel like singing "Rudolph the Shagging Reindeer." Thankfully, when I looked up I saw Sean coming toward me. I waved at him. He looked pretty cheesed off himself, which was unusual as he was normally so upbeat and even-tempered.

"Hi, welcome home," I said, hugging him.

"Yeah, great," he said, arms hanging limply by his sides.

"What's up?"

"Just got dumped. Happy fucking Christmas to me."

"Oh, Sean, that's terrible, you poor thing. Come on, let's get out of here and go for a drink. You can tell me all about it."

I was a bit disappointed. I'd been hoping to off-load on Sean, but now it looked as if I'd have to console him. He seemed really down. When we got to the pub, it was jammed with people being cheery and Christmassy, so I brought Sean back home for a few drinks. James was out at some rugby coaches' get-together so we had the place to ourselves. I poured us both a large vodka and cranberry juice and sat down beside him. "Okay, tell me everything. What happened? I want a blow-by-blow."

"She called me at work four days ago, said she was in love with her agent and she was moving to L.A. with him. When I got home all her stuff was gone."

"Did you see it coming? Were you getting on badly? How could she suddenly be in love with her agent?"

"How the hell do I know? The guy is married with two kids. I never suspected anything. Besides, I thought everything was fine. She was getting frustrated with the acting because she wasn't getting any parts, but I never imagined . . . I suppose they did spend a lot of time together and she did seem to have a lot of auditions in Manchester and Birmingham that involved going up the night before to prepare. God, I'm such a dickhead. How did I not see the signs?" said Sean, realizing for the first time that he had been played for a fool. He groaned and covered his face with his hands. I poured him another large vodka.

"God, Emma! I used to pay for all her hotels when she went away to auditions. I gave her a credit card because I felt sorry for her having no money and she said she hated taking handouts from me. She put all her expenses on the card. Jesus, she was shagging that bastard on my money."

As Sean pieced it all together, he grew increasingly despondent. He berated himself for having been so naïve and blind: she had taken him for a complete ride, she had used him for the fool he was—

I jumped in: "Hold on. Stop saying you're a fool. You met a gorgeous girl and fell for her. What's so terrible about that? Okay, it ended badly and she's a stupid cow, but come on, it's not as if the relationship was a complete write-off—or was it?"

Personally I wanted to slate the bitch, but I was trying desperately to boost his nonexistent ego.

As I was trying to think of something positive to say, someone started banging on the front door. I presumed it was James, who must have lost his keys, but when I opened the door Babs was swaying on the step in a Santa hat, holding a bottle of vodka and beaming at me. "Ho-ho-ho, merry Christmas. Don't worry, I've brought my own booze. After the last time I called in and was served that green muck I was taking no chances."

"Come on in, you nutter. Sean's here and we have loads of vodka. He got dumped, so be tactful."

Babs stormed into the room like a whirlwind. "Hey, bro, merry Christmas. I hear you got dumped by that loser you brought to Dad's party. You're much better off without her."

"Hey, Babs, sweet and sensitive as ever," he said, hugging her.

"Come on, Sean, anyone that calls you 'Pooh Bear' has got to go. She was an absolute leper. 'Too good-looking for *EastEnders*,' give me a break. Are you blind or what? The only pity is that you didn't dump her first."

"Thanks for that, Babs. I'm sure Sean feels much better now," I said, handing her a drink and glaring at her.

"And the way she went on about having to get acting lessons for an ad for Barclays Bank! She was a total spa. So what happened, anyway? When did you get dumped?"

"Barbara, can you please stop slagging her off? Don't I get a few weeks' grace? It's only been off four days," snapped Sean.

Babs rolled her eyes. "God, it's like depressed and depresseder in here. Come on, it's Christmas, the season to be jolly."

Sean and I shrugged and sighed, neither of us feeling remotely cheerful.

"Right, there's only one thing for it," said Babs, fishing around for something in her bag. "Here we go. Pop a few of these babies and you'll feel no pain," she said, handing us two pills.

"What are they?" I asked suspiciously.

"Ecstasy," said Sean.

"Barbara! What are you doing with drugs in your bag?" I was shocked at the thought that my sister was not only a drug user but a supplier.

"Don't get all big-sister on me, Emma. I only use them for recreational purposes, or in this case to treat depression," said my young sister, giggling.

I had never tried Ecstasy. I had done a few lines of cocaine years ago at a party, but hadn't been impressed with the results, so I had decided to stick to alcohol. A lot of my friends had gotten into the whole E-clubbing scene when it first exploded, but my main problem was that I can't dance—well, I can do the side-to-side shuffle, but I definitely don't have anything that could be identified as rhythm—so I avoided nightclubs that didn't play good old-fashioned pop. Give me a bit of Kylie or Sister Sledge any day over Armand van Helden's drum 'n' bass mix of "Sugar Is Sweet" or Technocat's "Dance Like Your Dad" mix, featuring Tom Wilson.

Sean said, what the hell, he could do with a buzz—he had obviously dabbled before in class-A drugs because he seemed to know the score. Clearly Babs was an old pro and I didn't want to be a party pooper and, besides, I had always secretly wanted to try E to see what it was like and if it did make you "feel the music," so I took one too.

Sean and Babs then proceeded to rearrange the furniture in the room to give us plenty of space for the dancing. I was a bit worried when they pushed everything up against the wall. What type of leaping was going to take place? Then they went through my CD collection, letting out groans of horror as Shania Twain followed

Barbra Streisand's Greatest Hits, U2's *The Unforgettable Fire,* ABBA, David Gray, Coldplay . . .

"Come on," said Babs, looking at me in shock. "You must have one decent CD, surely. We can't dance to this crap."

"Hold on, found one," Sean said, as he held up Sash's "Encore Une Fois."

It was one of the only dance songs I liked so I'd bought the twelve-inch.

"God, it's so nineties," said Babs dismissively.

"Well, it's going to have to do, because I don't fancy dancing to Garth Brooks," said Sean, laughing.

"I don't feel any different," I said. It was true, I was feeling no effects whatsoever from the E I had taken. I had expected to be bouncing around like Zebedee by now. Babs and Sean looked at each other and laughed.

"Just give it a few more minutes," said Babs, handing me a stick of chewing gum.

"What's this for?"

"You'll need it when the pill kicks in, trust me. Just chew," said my drug-pushing sister.

Five minutes later I felt butterflies in my stomach and a tingling sensation down my arms and then I felt fantastic—really happy and full of energy. Sean put on my one and only decent CD and I leaped like a maniac. I could dance, I could feel the music right through my body—the same body that I now realized I loved. I was dancing like Jennifer Beals (well, her body double) in *Flash-dance.* I had rhythm.

For the next four hours we danced to "Encore Une Fois" over and over again. We hugged each other and told each other we loved each other and we leaped and jived and I chewed on the Wrigley's gum, thus preventing the alarming involuntary jaw movements I made whenever I stopped chewing. I loved everyone, I wanted to go and tell all our neighbors how much they meant to me, but Babs and Sean stopped me. They were having great fun watching their E-virgin sister freaking out to the music.

The unsuspecting James came stumbling in after a heavy night boozing with the boys, expecting an earful from me for being so drunk and so late on Christmas Eve when we had to be up early next morning to spend Christmas Day with Mum and Dad. Instead he walked in to see his wife throwing herself around the room like something possessed, with the stereo on full volume, while his brother- and sister-in-law rolled around on the couch, crying/laughing.

"James," I squealed, jumping on top of him, "I'm so glad you're home, I love you so much. You're wonderful. Come on, dance with me, feel the music." I grabbed his arms and swung him 'round and 'round. He extracted himself from my grip and ran to the bathroom, where he proceeded to throw up violently.

"Classy couple," said Babs, roaring with laughter. "I hope I grow up to be just like you."

TWENTY

*W*hen we woke up we were both fully clothed, lying on top of the duvet. I was still twitching from the Ecstasy and James was lying with a bucketful of vomit at his side.

"And we want to be parents." I giggled as James threw up into the bucket again.

"Don't," he croaked. "I can't laugh and puke at the same time."

We dragged ourselves out of bed and over to Mum and Dad's house, which looked a bit like Santa's grotto. To my mother's great dismay, my father was a huge fan of "the Christmas decoration." Every year he set about decorating the house with great gusto. Rudolphs, Santas and elves hung from the ceilings, surrounded by lots and lots of tinsel. We always had the biggest, bushiest Christmas tree and it always groaned under the weight of the baubles; the pièce de résistance was the buxom platinum angel perched on top. Every year my mother would put her foot down at having flashing fairy lights, much to my father's disappointment.

"Over my dead body am I having tacky flashing lights. It's bad enough with all these ridiculous decorations hanging from every corner and a tree the size of Mount Everest with an angel at the top that looks like a stripper."

That's not to say she wasn't into Christmas, because she was.

She loved Christmas, especially as it meant having Sean home for a few days, and she always cooked us a feast fit for kings.

We arrived late, because James had to pull over every mile or so to retch out the window. He looked positively green. Babs and Sean—our resident drug pros—were fine, but although I didn't feel too bad, I was beginning to panic because my heart was racing at a hundred miles an hour and my pupils were so dilated that my eyes looked as if they were black. I kept checking them in the mirror and taking my pulse to see if the bloody E had worn off. I didn't want it in my system anymore. What if it never left me and I had flashbacks while I was driving, crashed the car and killed someone? Or, worse, what if it leaked into my eggs and made our baby a drug addict or deformed or something? I was breaking into a sweat thinking about it. I needed reassurance so I dragged Babs into the bathroom.

"What?" she asked.

"When does this drug wear off? I'm still twitching."

Babs grinned at me. "Relax, it'll be out of your system totally by tonight. You're just reacting strongly because it's your first time. It's good stuff, though, isn't it?"

"I feel really guilty and paranoid now. What if I've done permanent damage to myself?"

"God, Emma, you're such a drama queen. You took half an E tab, not a heroin overdose. Chill out."

Mercifully, by the time we settled down for present giving, the twitch had subsided and I was feeling more normal. Mum fussed over "poor James and his terrible food poisoning." Every time she left the room Dad put a drink in front of James and winked at him, saying, "Go on, are you man or mouse? Get that into you— the hair of the dog and all that, you'll feel better if you have a drink," and laughed as James turned a deeper shade of green.

* * *

I opened my present from Mum and Dad. It was a book—*The Art of Zen and Meditation: How to De-stress Our Bodies and Minds.* I looked up and Mum nodded. "I think you'll find it most useful. The woman in the shop told me her daughter was transformed by it. Not a bit uptight or snappy anymore, she said."

"I see—and you think I'm like that woman's daughter, do you? Uptight and snappy?" I said, in an uptight and snappy tone.

"That's not what I said." Mum sighed. "Just read it, Emma, it's supposed to help you. Now, Sean, this is for you," she said, and handed him an envelope.

He opened it and grimaced. It was a weekend for two in a luxury hotel in the Cotswolds. He took a deep breath. "This is really thoughtful of you, but I've split up with Amy, so I'll give it to Emma and maybe she can give me her book on the art of Zen. I could probably use it."

"Oh, Sean, what happened?" said my mother, doing a very good impression of someone who wasn't delighted that her son had just escaped from the claws of a girl to whom she had taken an instant dislike. Mum made all the right noises as Sean explained that it had ended rather abruptly—until she heard the part about Amy running off with the married agent. "Nothing but a cheap slut," she said. "Good riddance to her. You're far too good for that kind of a girl. Don't waste your time and energy pining over her, she's a no-good Jezebel."

"What the hell—" Babs interrupted, staring at her present.

"It's called a winter coat, Barbara. It's to cover you up when you go out half naked. In the future you're not to leave this house without wearing it. Do you hear me? I'll not have the neighbors saying my youngest child is a wanton hussy," said Mum, deflecting on to

Babs her anger at Amy for dumping Sean and having an affair behind his back.

I was feeling a bit left out. The coat was lovely and looked very expensive, and Sean's weekend away was generous too. Why did I only get a book?

"And this is for you too, Emma. Just something for work," said Mum, handing me a beautiful set of handmade makeup brushes that I had been coveting for ages.

I had a lump in my throat as I hugged her. "Thanks, Mum, sorry for being an idiot earlier. I promise to read the book from cover to cover."

We spent the rest of the afternoon stuffing our faces with chocolate and drinking wine—even James managed a few glasses and began to feel better. When I went to get us another bottle Dad followed me into the kitchen and began shuffling and clearing his throat. "Emma, I wonder if I might have a quick word . . ."

Whenever Dad cleared his throat you knew he was about to enter into areas where he should never go—areas where he felt exceedingly uncomfortable and you could be sure that he was only broaching the awkward subject with you because Mum had prodded and poked him into it. The last time he had cleared his throat before speaking to me was when I moved in with James—unmarried. My mother didn't approve at all and had badgered Dad into saying something to me. So he had mumbled about rushing into cohabitation without commitment and English boys being a bit fast and the importance of contraception—at which point he was purple in the face and sweating.

This time he looked directly over my shoulder, out the window. "I just wanted to see how things are going, you know . . . on the . . . eh . . . ah . . . well . . . baby front. Your mother feels you're a little uptight and maybe a bit tense, you know, that things might be a bit tense at home and maybe you should try to, you know . . . uhm, relax a bit and be a bit more cheerful with James. These things can take time and best not to get too wound up. Okay? Great, right . . . excellent. . . . Okay, so . . . let's say no more about it."

Typical! My mother had blown everything out of proportion and had obviously decided that James and I were heading for a breakup due to my mishandling of my infertility. God, she was annoying sometimes. What did she expect me to be? The Doris Day of wifely perfection? Aaargh. Still, it wasn't Dad's fault, so I patted him on the shoulder. "It's okay, Dad, James and I are fine, everything's fine. You can tell Mum that we won't be getting divorced any time soon and I'd greatly appreciate it if she kept her nose out of my marriage."

"And pigs will fly, Emma, and pigs will fly. You know your mother. Still, she only interferes out of concern. Anyway, enough about this. Drink?"

When we went back inside, Babs had put on *EastEnders* and was tormenting poor Sean. "Is she good-looking? Yes, I think she is. Is she too good-looking for *EastEnders?* No, I don't believe she is. Okay, what about her? Is she not very attractive? Come on, Pooh Bear, work with me here—"

Sean threw a cushion at her. "Just because you have a nose that makes Barry Manilow's look positively tiny doesn't mean you should be jealous of other women."

"Jealous of that retard Amy? I don't think so," snapped Babs, who always reacted violently when her big nose was mentioned.

"It's such a pity about your nose. You'd be quite good-looking if you had a small one like Emma's," said Sean, turning the screws.

"Well, at least I'm not a loser who gets cheated on and dumped by his one and only girlfriend," shouted Babs.

"Don't get angry, Babs, your nostrils flare when you get het up and you draw attention to your schnoz—and let's face it, that's the last thing you want. By the way, I've always wondered, doesn't it get in the way when you snog?" I asked.

"No, it doesn't, and I'd rather have a big nose than be barren," she roared, and then her hand flew to her mouth. "Shit, Emma, I'm sorry, I didn't mean that. You know how angry I get when you slag off my nose. I'm sorry, honestly, I didn't mean it. I'm sure you're not barren, and if you ever were, I'd give you some of my eggs."

"That's very generous of you, Babs, but we don't want our kids having your considerable nose. If we ever reach that stage I can assure you that the only person allowed to donate her eggs will be Cameron Diaz," said James, defusing the situation.

"Dinner's ready," said Mum, popping her head 'round the door.

TWENTY-ONE

I woke up on New Year's Day, and all I could think about was that it had been a year. A full calendar year and not a baby in sight. Lots of sex, copious amounts of peeing on sticks and temperature taking and no sodding baby. I was sick and tired of the natural methods and of being patient. It was time for action.

I went to see my gynecologist, Dr. Philips. He told me once again that I was not to worry about it, that I was young and healthy and it would all happen soon if I just tried not to focus so much on getting pregnant. . . . Sure a year was nothing, it took six months for your body to adjust from being on the pill, so it was really only six months that we'd been trying and that was no time at all. . . . I just needed to relax and it would all come together. . . .

Relax! Do they not teach them in med school how annoying it is for a patient to be told to relax when they are wound up like a tightly sprung coil?

"The thing is, Dr. Philips, I can't relax. It's just impossible. Please stop telling me that relaxing will make it all happen because it's not something I'm capable of doing. Believe me, I've tried."

"Ah, now, Emma. A lovely young girl like yourself will be pregnant in no time. You just need a little patience. Babies don't happen overnight. Go out and enjoy yourself and don't be wearing yourself out worrying."

Overnight! What was this? Some form of torture? Could the man not see I was going out of my mind? I gripped my bag and willed myself to be calm and not cry. My voice shaking, I said, "Doctor, I realize that I seem a bit impatient to you, but I have now been trying for over a year. I'm thirty-four—which may seem young to you, but does not seem young to me. I want to go on fertility drugs or do IVF or whatever it takes to get pregnant. Please understand that I'm not leaving this office until you refer me to a fertility specialist. I'll go mad if I don't do something."

Dr. Philips looked at me and sighed. He could see he had a lunatic on his hands. "Well, now, Emma, you don't want to be jumping into fertility treatments. Have you tried yoga? Apparently it works wonders. Only the other day I had a patient who had been trying to conceive for three years and then she took up the old yoga and a month later she was pregnant. Your mind-set has a lot to do with it. A positive frame of mind works wonders."

I ground my teeth. "I have tried yoga and found it to be a modern form of torture. It's just not for me, Doctor. I'm a doer. I can't sit around waiting for things to happen. I need to move forward on this. I don't want to spend another year trying with no results. Please, Doctor, I want the fertility drugs."

Dr. Philips shook his head. "I can see there's no persuading you to wait another few months, so I'll make an appointment with Dr. Reynolds at the Harwood Clinic. He's considered the best fertility consultant in the country."

A week later when I arrived at the Harwood Clinic I was impressed. My feet sank into the plush cream carpet in Reception and they had proper magazines to read—*Vogue, Elle* and *InStyle*—not the usual outdated medical journals that talked about ingrown toe-nails and hernia operations. I sank back into the soft red sofa and opened *Vogue*. I was drooling over an outrageously expensive Louis Vuitton bag when a heavily pregnant woman and her doting hus-band walked in. What? I had presumed that only women who couldn't get pregnant came here. The last thing I expected was to have to sit with expectant couples. I tried not to look at them as he placed his hand on her stomach and they giggled in amazement as the baby kicked or farted or sang or whatever it was doing in there. I hated them. I hated them for their happiness and excite-ment. The man caught my eye and smiled at me. I scowled and hid behind my magazine. He might have had lots to be cheery about, but I didn't. They should have separate waiting rooms for women who are pregnant and women who are not, I thought, because we live in two very different worlds. And us barren gals don't want to have to deal with glowing pregnant couples.

After a thirty-minute wait, pretending to read *Vogue* and trying not to have a nervous breakdown as two more happy pregnant couples arrived in the waiting room, I was asked to follow a glam-orous nurse to Dr. Reynolds's rooms. I trotted down the corridor after her, feeling confident that this man was going to cure me and save me from spiraling into insanity.

I walked in and a small, young, scruffy-looking man in a crum-pled suit smiled at me. He looked like a refugee fresh off the boat from Outer Mongolia or somebody selling the *Big Issue* rather than his services as a fertility specialist. He stood up to greet me, still only reaching my shoulders, and gave me a wet-fish handshake. Where was my middle-aged bellower? I wanted one of those loud, noisy, overconfident doctors who bellowed at you and crushed your hand when they shook it. I immediately felt at ease with those men. The louder the doctor bellowed at me, the safer I felt. It was ridiculous, pathetic, even, but it worked. I wondered if they taught them that in college: "Shout: the patients find it reassuring."

Dr. Reynolds was pale and hunched. He had blond, wiry, unkempt hair, thick National Health–type glasses and was chewing the end of a Bic pen. Where was my tall, tanned, athletic-looking doctor? I wanted my specialist to look as though he'd just swooped in from the slopes of Saint Moritz or from a week in the Caribbean on his yacht. Loaded. I wanted him to look loaded. Stylish suit, crisp white shirt, trendy, but not too trendy, tie and a big fat gold pen—they always have big fat gold pens to match their big flash antique desks.

Dr. Reynolds peered at me over his ordinary-looking desk and smiled awkwardly. I wondered for a moment if I had the wrong guy. Maybe the nurse had made a mistake. I looked around the room. It was full of thank-you cards and pictures of women with babies. All very well, my dear Watson, but they might have been planted there. They might have been pictures of his fifteen brothers and sisters with their offspring for all I knew, and he might have written the cards himself.

"Dr. Reynolds?" I asked.

"Yes, that's right."

Christ, it *was* him. Maybe this was some kind of a windup. Maybe James had set it up to distract me from my obsessive path, in a lame effort to "lighten you up." I looked around for hidden cameras.

"So what seems to be the problem?"

"What? Oh, sorry, uhm, well, I can't seem to get pregnant so Dr. Philips suggested I come and see you, so here I am . . ." I mumbled grumpily at the man-child.

"I'm sorry to hear you're having problems conceiving. It must be very stressful for you. I see from Dr. Philips's letter that you've been trying for a year now."

Call me old-fashioned, but at one hundred and fifty euro a pop, I expected more than a curly-haired youth, fresh from sitting his finals.

"Yes."

"No family history of fertility issues? Mother, grandmother?"

"No, none. My grandmother had six children, my mother had three."

"Not to worry. Lots of women in their thirties have trouble conceiving. We'll need to check that everything's in good working order. We often find that it's a simple little thing that's preventing patients getting pregnant and we can sort it out in no time. You'll have to have some tests done. Some of them may be a little painful, but they tend to be more uncomfortable than painful. . . ."

As he talked on about the various tests—all with dreadfully long and complicated names—I began to relax and trust him. He certainly seemed to know what he was talking about. Maybe he was one of those child prodigies who went to college at thirteen and got a first in every subject. He talked on: "Fallopian tubes . . . run a dye through . . . hysterosalpingogram . . . diagnostic radiology . . ."

I must say I was beginning to have a lot more admiration for the cast of *ER*. These words were impossible to pronounce and they had to learn off pages of them. Some of the cast had English as a second language—like Dr. Kovac. It was amazing when you thought about it.

". . . so once we get those results we can look at our options."

Shit. I had no idea what he'd said—I'd completely missed the bit about the tests and was too embarrassed to ask him to repeat himself, so I nodded sagely and pulled my diary out of my bag.

Dr. Reynolds arranged for me to have the hysterosalpingogram the following day (I asked him to spell it for me so I could look it up on the Internet when I got home). He told me to take painkillers and antibiotics beforehand and afterward. It sounded a bit scary.

"Is it sore? Why do I have to take antibiotics?"

"The dye they run through your fallopian tubes, in extreme circumstances, can cause small infections. The antibiotics are to prevent any chance of that happening."

"And the painkillers?"

"They will numb any pain or stinging you may experience. But it's a very straightforward procedure and is over in five minutes. Don't worry, you'll be fine."

Bloody hell! Dye through my fallopian tubes did not sound good. What color dye? What if it didn't come out? Did it just stay there whirling around—bright orange or green dye? Did it come out when you peed? Would you have orange pee? I was deep in thought about rainbow urine as I walked back to the car, when I heard, "Emma? Emma Burke, is that you?"

Fuck fuck fuck fuck. It was my mother's best friend Nuala, whom she hated. They were always needling each other. When Nuala's son came back from a summer in San Francisco and announced he was gay, my mother—who was on a high for weeks—gave her a book called *Coping with a Gay Child.* It was sweet revenge for the time Nuala had tormented her when Babs, aged thirteen, had been expelled from school for shaking the statue of the Virgin Mary during assembly and making everyone think they had seen an apparition. Nuala had been over like a shot to offer my mother her condolences and reassure her that she would pray for Babs's lost soul.

Babs had always been bold, but shaking the statue of Our Lady in front of the whole school was a step too far. My headmistress Sister Patricia had told my mother that Babs was going down the path of delinquency and she was a bad influence on the other girls.

She had to expel her and she strongly recommended that Babs be sent away to a school for wayward girls. My mother had seriously considered entering the witness protection program because of the shame of having a daughter expelled. She had come home in a terrible state and told Babs that she would never forgive her for bringing the family into disrepute.

When Dad came home, Mum told him what had happened and he had done the one thing he really shouldn't—he laughed. In fact, he roared. He thought it was the funniest thing he'd ever heard. Needless to say, my mother was not amused and they argued for hours about sending Babs away to boarding school. Eventually they compromised by sending her to a weekly boarding school, so she was only gone from Monday to Friday. This only made Babs worse because she was locked away in a confined space with all the other female misfits in Ireland during the week and let loose every weekend to chase boys.

"Oh, hi, Nuala. How are you?" I said.

"Well, I'm fine. How are you? Are congratulations in order?" she said, beaming at me from behind her bouquet.

"What? Oh God, no, I—"

"Ah, now," said Nuala, squeezing my arm, "don't worry, I won't say a word. I won't call your mother Granny yet!" she said, beaming at the prospect. "I'm off to see my niece. She's just had a little boy. I'll be in visiting you soon, no doubt."

"No, honestly, Nuala, it's not—"

"We'll not say another word about it. Sure you know I'm the soul of discretion. Your secret is safe with me."

There was no point explaining. I just shrugged and walked over to the car.

* * *

When I got home the phone was ringing.

"Hello."

"So, I have to hear from Nuala Corrigan that my own daughter is pregnant. Do you have any idea how humiliating that is? I nearly choked when she told me. 'Congratulations, Granny,' she says to me. Is it too much to ask that you call me yourself after having me worried sick about you all year? Am I only told the bad news? Is that it? Never the good news?"

"*Stop!* God, Mum, I'm not pregnant. I was seeing a fertility specialist and I met bloody Nuala in the car park. She put two and two together and made ten as usual. If I was pregnant you'd be the first to know."

"Oh, right. Mind you, it'll be all over Dublin by now. You know what she's like. Still, she'll feel a right fool when she finds out you aren't expecting. That'll teach her. I'd better go—I'll have to ring her and put a stop to her gossip. Hold on—what do you mean you were seeing a fertility expert?"

"To find out why I can't get pregnant."

"Emma, let nature take its course and leave well alone. Don't be going having tests and poking around with your insides. No good will come of it. Stay away from hospitals unless it's an emergency. People get addicted to tests and examinations. I'm warning you now, stay well away from hospitals and doctors. You're to stop all this panicking and calm down. You're a young girl with a fine, strapping young husband. You'll be pregnant in no time, but you have to stop getting het up and running to the doctor every five minutes."

"Are you finished or just pausing for breath?"

"I'm just—"

"Mum," I said sharply, "I'm not running to the doctor every five minutes. I don't enjoy tests and doubt very much that I'll ever be addicted to them. I'm just trying to find out why I can't get pregnant. The doctor said it's probably something really simple. So I think it's better to find out now and sort it out, rather than sit around for another year hoping and praying for a miracle. I'm sick of doing nothing. It's driving me insane."

"Oh, you're all the same, you young ones. Everything has to be immediate. You want to snap your fingers and have a baby. Life's not like that, Emma. These things take time and getting yourself into knots is bad for you and bad for your marriage. What does James think of all this running to the doctor?"

"He thinks it's a good idea. He wants me to see the specialist and check if everything's in working order. It's no big deal. Jesus, it's not as if I'm going in for major surgery. I'm just going to have a few simple tests."

"Tests are never simple. Mark my words. Leave your insides alone."

"I'm having the tests done and that's the end of it."

"Headstrong. That's your problem, you were always headstrong."

"Gee, I wonder where I got that trait from."

"Don't be fresh with me, young lady. Now, when are these tests?"

"Tomorrow."

"I'll say a prayer they go well."

"Thanks, Mum."

"Not that I approve."

"No."

"All right, 'bye now."

" 'Bye."

TWENTY-TWO

I looked up "hysterosalpingogram" on the Internet. There were 3,068 entries. I clicked on the BBC health site. I trusted the BBC. It was an institution. The BBC wouldn't exaggerate or dramatize, it would simply give me the facts.

Hysterosalpingogram is a series of X-ray pictures of the female reproductive tract. Dye that shows up on X-ray is passed into the uterus and tubes and spills into the abdominal cavity. Why is it done? An HSG will show the shape of the inside of the uterus and the fallopian tubes, confirming that they are normal and the tubes are open . . .

Thank God they shortened it to HSG. Even native Welsh speakers wouldn't be able to get their tongues around "hysterosalpingogram.'

Although the hysterosalpingogram is not a treatment, gently forcing dye through the tube may dislodge any material which blocks it and pregnancy has been known to occur. Abnormal findings, such as polyps, fibroids and adhesions, can be detected during the test.

It didn't sound too bad. Gently forcing dye through my tubes sounded all right. Although "dislodging material" on the way through sounded a bit painful and it didn't say what color the dye was. I scrolled down to "Procedures and Tips":

You may be advised to take a simple painkiller or some anti-inflammatory painkillers such as ibuprofen beforehand as you can get crampy pains, during or after the test. These should settle quickly. You will undress and put on an examination gown and be asked to sit up on the couch before your legs are put in the lithotomy position.

"Lithotomy position"? What was that? It sounded like one of those complicated yoga positions. I should have tried harder in yoga class—now when the doctor tried to twist my legs into the lithotomy position, I wouldn't be flexible enough. I'd have to get James to help me do some of those training stretches he did with the team. Suppleness was obviously the key to this whole process.

A speculum will be placed in the vagina so that the cervix is visible. While X-ray pictures are being taken, a fine catheter will be passed into the cervix and dye injected into the uterus. It should pass on through the tubes. For 2 to 3 days afterward you may notice a sticky vaginal discharge—this is the dye leaking out and is harmless. Any dye which remains within you will be harmlessly absorbed.

Absorbed! Where did it go? Into your bloodstream? And as for the dye leaking out—it was all very well for the BBC to be all stiff upper lip and refer to it as "harmless," but it sounded gross to me. I decided that the Internet was not good for me. I was one of those people who are better off not knowing. Ignorance is bliss.

When James came home I told him about the test. He was due to go out to football, but I figured when he saw how nervous I was, he'd stay in and comfort me.

"So they blast this dye out your tubes and apparently it's really sore," I announced dramatically.

"That sounds a bit grim," he said, doing up his laces. "Maybe you should leave it for a bit."

"Leave what for a bit? We've been trying for a year. What am I supposed to do? Sit around and wait for another year to slip by? I don't want to be ninety when my kids are in school."

"Okay, okay. If you feel you want to go ahead with it, then fine. You just don't sound very happy about it."

"Well, how enthusiastic would you be at the prospect of having a dye blasted up your penis and out your balls?"

"I dunno, sounds a bit kinky."

"Come on, be serious."

"Look, Emma, if you don't want to do it, then don't do it."

"I have to do it. Whether I want to or not. I have to find out why I can't conceive."

"Okay, well, if you're sure . . ."

"Anyway, that's not all. I met Nuala in the car park and she now thinks I'm pregnant and then she called Mum and then Mum rang me and it was a complete mess."

"Who's Nuala?"

"You know Nuala. You've met her loads of times. She's Mum's best friend."

"Oh, right, the one she's always complaining about."

"Yes. Anyway, can you believe I met her, of all people?"

"No. Look, I've got to go. I'll see you later."

"What? You're not leaving? James, I've had a crappy day and I have to go for a horrible test tomorrow. I presumed you'd stay in and keep me company."

"I'm sorry you had a bad day, darling, but I can't let the boys down tonight. It's a league game."

"If it isn't bloody rugby, it's football. Thanks a lot for your support. I'll just stay in on my own, then."

James grabbed his bag and rushed out the door. Cheers, I thought. Thanks a lot, James. I wanted him to give me a hug and tell me what a brave soldier I was. How my strength and determination amazed him. How he could never endure a test where they blasted dye up his genitals. That he would tell our baby how wonderful I had been in the face of adversity . . .

Instead he had bolted out the door as fast as his legs could carry him.

The next day I arrived at the hospital having taken my antibiotics and three ibuprofen for good measure. The nurse on Reception was very bustly and bossy. She marched me toward a tiny dressing room and told me—very loudly—to get undressed and take off everything, "including your underpants . . . and wait there until I call you. Good girl."

There's something about hospitals that makes you feel ten years old. It doesn't matter how small the test or examination, once you step inside a hospital you feel young, frail and vulnerable. It's all bright lights and people in white uniforms rushing about. Doctors striding purposefully down endless corridors. Huge lifts opening up to reveal cheerful orderlies wheeling terrified-looking patients off to surgery. And it's all mixed in with the smell of bleach and boiled cabbage.

As I sat shivering in my gown—which was wide open at the back—I began to feel really nervous. Just as I was contemplating getting dressed and doing a runner, the nurse came back and told me to go straight down, turn left at the nurses' station, follow the signs to Radiology and then a few more lefts and rights . . . what? Was I supposed to go on this hike barefoot and showing my bare ass to the world? I looked at her and blinked. "I'm sorry, could you repeat that, please?"

She looked at me and shook her head. She could tell I was a potential weeper. "Follow me," she barked.

And with that she took off down the corridor like a bullet with me trailing in her wake, one hand gripping the back of my gown closed and my bare feet padding along the cold linoleum. As we turned the corner I saw a woman about my age shuffling along the corridor toward us. She was also trying to keep some semblance of dignity by holding her gown closed at the back, although she had had the foresight to keep her socks on. We caught each other's eye and nodded grimly. She didn't look too good to me. You could see she was in a lot of pain. I prayed silently that she hadn't just come from Radiology.

"Here we are. This is Emer, she'll look after you," said old Bossy Boots, leaving me with a sweet-faced young nurse.

"Oh, your poor feet must be frozen," said Emer, looking down at my blue toes. "I'll see if I can find you some slippers. Come on in here with me."

She led me into a small room with a bed and some complicated-looking equipment. "Don't be nervous, pet, you'll be grand. It'll all be over in five minutes," she said, patting my arm.

The fact that she was being so nice made me feel even weepier. But I managed to control myself and climbed onto the bed as instructed. The door opened and a confident boomer came in.

"Hello there, Emma, I'm Dr. Tunney, your radiologist. I'll be performing the HSG today. It's a very straightforward procedure. . . ."

I loved Dr. Tunney. He was my kind of medic. I felt at ease with him and began to calm down. Following his instructions, I bent my legs like a frog and waited for him to insert the speculum. Once it was in place, a catheter went in.

"Now I'm going to inject the dye, Emma. This may sting a little. . . ." said my hero.

From hero to villain in three seconds—I have never experienced pain like it. The dye felt like scalding barbed wire being blasted through my insides. I was so shocked by the pain that I stopped breathing.

"It's all right, Emma, it's nearly over," said Dr. Tunney, seeing my face turn blue. "I need you to breathe deeply for me, in and out, in and out."

I managed a few gasps, but the pain was excruciating. Tears were streaming down my face. They took several X-rays and then the pain began to subside as the dye stopped and the catheter and speculum came out. I lay on the bed panting and sobbing quietly from the shock. How could anyone describe that torture as "stinging"? Then it hit me. The two people who had told me it was "straightforward" and "painless" were men. Nurse Emer had never said it wasn't going to hurt, she had just said it would be over quickly.

Dr. Tunney said he would send the results to Dr. Reynolds that afternoon. I didn't give a damn about the results—I just wanted to get the hell out of there. Emer helped me off the bed. My legs were shaking so badly that she had to half carry me back to the cubicle. She was very sweet and went off to get me a cup of sugary tea. I sat down and tried to calm myself. After a minute or two I felt a bit better. I got dressed, drank my tea and left the hospital. As I drove home I wondered if I was a bit delicate. Did other women find that procedure painless? Did I have a very low pain threshold? Was I a big girl's blouse?

Although I had sworn off the Internet a mere twenty-four hours previously, I logged on to see if I could find any accounts or articles by women who had experienced a hysterothingy. After an hour trawling through the infertility websites on the Internet, reading story after story of "miracle babies," I finally hit on the Georgia Reproductive Specialists site. GRS, based in Atlanta, claimed to be committed to providing full-service infertility and reproductive endocrine health care with a focus on patient-centered, compassionate care. They said:

If you are relaxed and in the hands of a gentle physician, the cramping is usually mild. However, if the dye does not flow through the fallopian tubes, additional pressure may be necessary to see if the tubes are really blocked. This can cause more intense discomfort.

I felt a bit better. Maybe I wasn't such a basket case. Dr. Tunney had obviously been a bit heavy-handed with the pressure he'd applied. In the future I'd go to the American websites for my information. They were more understanding, caring and compassionate than the stuffy old BBC.

I switched off the computer, climbed into bed with a hot-water bottle and called Lucy. "Hi."

"Hey, how's it going?"

"Okay, you?"

"Fine. You don't sound too good. Are you okay?"

"I've just come back from a horrible test," I said, my chin wobbling as self-pity kicked in.

"Oh, Emma, was it painful?"

"Yeah, it was. And I'm sick of the whole thing, Lucy, I really am."

"Was James with you?"

"No, there's no point in him coming, there's absolutely nothing he can do."

"Well, what about me? I'd be happy to come with you."

"Thanks, but to be honest, it's easier to nip in and out on my own. I hate all the poking and prodding of my insides. It can't be good for me."

"It sounds awful. Can I get you anything or do anything?"

"Yes, distract me by telling me about your life. Any word from Donal? What's the latest?"

"Well, he called the other day and asked me to go racing on Sunday."

"Horse racing?"

"Greyhounds, I think."

"And?"

"And I said yes. It's not as if my diary is full and he was pretty good-humored about the *Vagina Monologues* date, considering he was totally humiliated in front of a room full of screaming women."

"Ha-ha-ha. I love that story. Every time I think of him shouting 'cunt,' it just cracks me up." I giggled.

"I know. I wish I'd had a camera—his face was a sight."

"So what are you going to wear?"

"No idea, haven't given it a second thought."

"Liar!"

"My Prada boots, black trousers and my beige winter jacket," Lucy admitted.

"I love those boots, they're amazing. He won't be able to keep his hands off you."

"Let's hope so. I haven't had any action in months. Anyway, enough about me and my nonexistent sex life, will I call out later to see you?"

"No, it's fine, really. James will be home soon so I can ear-bash him about my day. You've cheered me up already. Good luck on Sunday, keep me posted."

"Will do. Mind yourself."

TWENTY-THREE

*T*hree days later I was back with Dr. Reynolds at the Harwood Clinic for the analysis of my results. The pain of the test had subsided and I was feeling better physically, but was nervous in case they had discovered something drastically wrong with me. After giving me his wet-fish handshake, Dr. Reynolds asked me how the test had gone.

"Well, to be honest, I found it pretty painful," I admitted.

I had planned to tell him that it had been one of the worst experiences of my life and in the future he should warn his patients because his idea of a "slight stinging" was ludicrous and he should try shoving some barbed wire up his penis the wrong way and see how that translated into "mild discomfort." But when I was sitting in his office, facing him, I lost my nerve and opted for a toned-down version of events.

Dr. Reynolds nodded sympathetically. "Well, let's take a look at these X-rays, shall we?" he said, and placed two on a screen. He stood to one side, as if giving a lecture to a bunch of medical students, and began pointing to various shapes on the screen. "Now, as you can see here, the uterus appears to be normal, which is good news. The right fallopian tube seems to be open—we can see the dye passing through the uterus and the right-hand tube and spilling into the abdominal cavity. The left-hand tube, however, is not so clear. It's impossible to tell from this X-ray whether the dye is spilling out or not. I'm afraid it's unclear as to whether this tube is open or not."

"What does that mean?"

"It would be advisable to redo the test so we can double-check the left-hand side."

"Sorry? Did you just say redo the test?" I asked, horrified at the prospect of having to go through that again. "Hell will freeze over before I ever put myself through that torture again. There must be a less painful way of finding out about that tube. Besides, why can't you see from the X-ray? Did Dr. Tunney not do it correctly? Why should I have to have another test? I don't understand how this is all so inconclusive."

I was beginning to panic.

"I realize it's frustrating for you, but sometimes the X-rays don't tell us all we need to know."

"I'm not having that test done again. Does it really matter anyway? You only need one good tube to have a baby. Don't you?"

"Well, in theory, yes, you do only need one functioning fallopian tube, but it's important to know if they're both working correctly. There is a less painful way of investigating the status of the fallopian tubes and abdomen. We can perform a laparoscopy. It's a procedure that is usually done as day-case surgery under general anesthetic—"

"No."

Dr. Reynolds looked at me.

"Sorry, Doctor, but I don't want any more poking and prodding down there, it can't be good for you. We've established that I have one functioning tube and that's enough for me," I said firmly.

I didn't want to undergo a general anesthetic to establish what we already knew—I had one good tube and probably two good ones. If Dr. Tunney had done his job properly we'd know for sure about the second. They should send him on a photography course to fine-tune his skills. His blurry X-rays were no good to anyone. I wanted to move on to the next stage. I wanted fertility drugs.

"What can I do to make sure I produce eggs? What can I take?"

"Well, if you don't want to have a laparoscopy I could put you on a course of clomiphene with ovarian follicle tracking."

"Okay . . . what does that entail?" I said suspiciously. I didn't want any more pain.

Dr. Reynolds explained that clomiphene citrate increased FSH and LH output from the pituitary. Basically, he told me that it prompts your body to produce eggs. And you could take it in tablet form a few times a month. It sounded good to me—no pain at all.

"The majority of pregnancies occur in the first few treatment cycles and there's no reason why it shouldn't happen quickly for you. I must explain, however, that there is a slightly increased chance of multiple pregnancy with clomiphene."

Fantastic. I'd definitely have twins now, maybe triplets. This was perfect. I'd not only get pregnant quickly, but have a family in one go. I beamed at Dr. Reynolds. "No problem at all."

He smiled at me. "Yes, that's what most of my patients say. But I must warn you that multiple pregnancies can be dangerous for the babies and the mother so it's not the ideal situation. However, as I said, there is only a slight chance of it occurring."

Fine, whatever, let's just get on with it, I thought. I wanted him to give me the drugs there and then, but he wasn't finished with the bad news yet.

"You also need to be aware that there continues to be debate on the question of a relationship between the use of clomiphene and later development of ovarian cancer. . . ."

Cancer! Did he say cancer? I tried to concentrate as Dr. Reynolds explained that some analysis had been done ten years ago on a group of women in Seattle and some of them had developed malignant tumors in their ovaries and they thought it might be connected to clomiphene.

"However," he continued, "treatment with clomiphene for less than a year was not associated with increased risk and the consensus is that the risk has probably been overstated, but it is important that you know about it."

So the ones who got the cancer had been on the drug for over a year. Well, that was fine, because I'd be pregnant within three months. Still, I didn't want to go through all of this and die a few years after giving birth and have my beautiful triplets being brought up by some young blonde whom James had married on the rebound. I decided to double-check on the risk front.

"So the risk is minimal?" I asked.

"Absolutely."

"Totally?"

"Completely."

"Okay."

"Now, the follicle tracking," said Dr. Reynolds, not giving me much time to recover from the cancer scare, "will show us if the ovaries are functioning well with the clomiphene. It allows us to track the size of the follicles in the ovary over several days to predict timing of ovulation."

"And how does that work?"

"It's a series of internal ultrasound scans."

I didn't like the sound of that. External was fine. Internal most certainly was not. I winced.

"I can promise you that the scans are not painful at all."

Well, I'm not going to Dr. Tunney, I thought. If he can't take a decent photo he's likely to shove the internal scanner up my ass instead of my vagina.

"Who will be doing the scans?"

"I can arrange for you to have them done at a private clinic down the road here. They have the most up-to-date scanners and I've had positive feedback from all the patients I've sent there."

Well, it would be good to know exactly when I was producing the eggs and it would help us perfect our timing, so I decided it was a good idea. "Okay, fine. When do I start taking the drugs?"

"You'll take them between days three and seven of your next cycle," said Dr. Reynolds, writing me a prescription. "Then call the clinic and make an appointment for tracking on days nine, eleven, thirteen and fifteen of your cycle. They may want you to come back for another one on day sixteen or seventeen, depending on your ovulation date."

It all sounded a bit intense. I hadn't enjoyed my one previous internal examination at all. Mind you, it had had a lot more to do with the radiologist being so rude than the fact that it was painful. It hadn't really been painful—more uncomfortable, really. Besides, at least this method left no room for ambiguity and it would help us focus on the right days to have sex.

"Thanks," I said, taking the prescription.

"Good luck," said Dr. Reynolds. "I'll see you in a few weeks to review the first month."

When James came home later, I followed him around the house and gave him a blow-by-blow account of my day. ". . . And I have to take these mad drugs that make me produce loads of eggs and there is a strong possibility that I could develop ovarian cancer from the drugs and die after giving birth to triplets."

210 / Sinead Moriarty

James stared at me, frowning. "Cancer? As in, cancer?"

"Yes."

"Isn't this a bit extreme, Emma?"

"No. It's the only way."

"What about good, old-fashioned sex?"

"We've tried that. Remember?"

"So you're going to give me three strong sons, then die and leave me to bring them up alone?"

"Daughters—and you can only remarry after five years of grieving, but not to a blonde and definitely not to that cow who's always flirting with you after the matches."

"What cow?"

"You know—Paddy's sister, Louise."

"Why not her?"

"Because I'm not having my three daughters brought up by some fool who can barely string a sentence together. You can marry a nice brunette—maybe a teacher or something. But she can't have any kids of her own, I want her to be fully focused on my girls."

"But look how well it worked out for the Brady Bunch. He—*like me*—had three boys and she had three girls."

"Yes, but your new wife's boys will want to be getting into my girls' knickers and I'm not having that."

"Why do I have to wait five years?"

"Any sooner would be disrespectful to me and my family. And by the way, I want that Billy Joel song 'She's Always a Woman to Me' sung at my funeral."

"That's a dreadful song. It's so cheesy."

"It's not your gig, it's mine, and I want that song."

"Yeah, but you won't be there—so I'll have George Michael's 'Freedom' played instead."

"Not funny."

"Neither is taking drugs that are going to give you cancer," said James.

"They won't. I was exaggerating. Some woman in the back of beyond got ovarian cancer ten years ago or something and everyone made a big deal about it because she had also taken these drugs. It's a one-in-a-zillion chance. Don't worry, I have no intention of leaving you to marry some busty young one."

TWENTY-FOUR

*L*ucy wasn't unduly worried about her date with Donal. She had been greyhound racing at Shelbourne Park in Dublin on a corporate night out and had been surprised by how much fun it was. She had expected it to be really boring, but instead she had ended up dining in a private room overlooking the racetrack and had spent the evening sipping wine and placing bets without having to leave her chair. She had even ended up winning a few quid.

Donal had said he'd pick her up early on Sunday as they were going to a race meet in Tipperary. Lucy presumed it was going to be some type of corporate rugby-lunch thing. She hoped the race course dining rooms in Tipperary would be as nice as the ones in Dublin. She thought the same company owned them all. As she had discussed with me, she was wearing her high-heeled black boots, tight black trousers, black cashmere sweater and her favorite beige suede jacket with fur trim.

When Donal arrived, he took one look at the boots and said, "You can't wear those shoes, they'll get wrecked. Besides, you'll never be able to wear those heels all day."

Lucy was a believer in suffering to look good. The boots were very high and exceedingly uncomfortable to wear, but they looked great with the trousers and she was planning on staying seated for most of the day. Besides, she had a box of Band-Aids in her bag for emergencies.

"I'll be fine. I could walk for Ireland in these. They're actually very comfy."

Donal looked down at the pointy heels and shook his head. "Well, if you're sure . . ."

"Yes, I am. Come on, let's go," said Lucy, locking her front door and pulling her jacket closed against the howling wind.

Donal drove like a maniac and talked incessantly about how convinced he was that his dog, Blackie, was going to win. He owned half of her; the other half belonged to the trainer, Jimmy McGee. According to Donal, Blackie had been running well over the last few weeks and they were confident she was going to win the big prize today. He reckoned he could make up to ten thousand euro if things went well. Lucy was delighted: if he was counting on winning that kind of money it'd be champagne all 'round, and being with a dog owner was bound to make the day more exciting. She just hoped Donal didn't expect her to trudge down to the ring before the race like the owners did at horse racing: it was lashing rain and she didn't want her hair to go fuzzy.

When they had reached the outskirts of Fethard, Donal swung into a small rundown house and hopped out of the car.

"Where are you going?" asked Lucy.

"To pick up Jimmy and Blackie," said Donal, as he ran up to the front door.

Two minutes later a man of about fifty, in an oversize tweed jacket and cap, climbed into the back of the car, with a large greyhound in tow.

"Jimmy, this is Lucy."

"Howrya," said Jimmy, pulling his lips into a toothless grin. "This here's Blackie," he said, patting the dog fondly on the head.

As Lucy turned her head to say hello, Blackie leaped forward and slobbered over her face. Lucy was not an animal lover and, with the dog licking off her makeup, she was not about to change her mind. She pretended to pat the dog while pushing her into the backseat.

"Isn't she something?" said Donal, beaming at Blackie. "Well, Jimmy, how's she been the last week?"

"Great, Donal. She's been great now. I took her out this morning at six to loosen her up and she was flying, so she was. I tell you, we'll be winning big-time today. I feel it, so I do."

"Woo-hoo," whooped Donal, thumping the steering wheel. "Come on, the Blackie!"

Blackie—excited by the whooping—threw herself and her wet, mucky paws into the front seat on top of Lucy and her cashmere sweater. Lucy stared down at the balls of delicate wool wedged between Blackie's filthy paws. She silently cursed Donal and his stupid mutt.

They drove on, then took a sharp turn left into the middle of a wet field that was jam-packed with cars, dogs and people in Wellington boots and wind cheaters. Lucy looked at Donal. "Please tell me this isn't it? This isn't the venue. Where's the racetrack? Where's the bar?"

"There's no track in coursing. This isn't greyhound racing, it's coursing," said Donal, looking confused.

"But you said we were going to the dogs," said Lucy, panicking at the thought of spending the day knee-deep in mud.

"Yeah, the dogs. Greyhound coursing *is* the dogs. Come on, you'll have fun. It's a great day out."

Donal got out of the car and caught up with Jimmy and Blackie, who were already mingling with the other owners and trading odds with the bookies. Lucy sat in the car and tried to breathe deeply. She was in the back end of Tipperary, in the middle of a mucky field, wearing nine-hundred-euro Prada boots. There had to be a clubhouse or bar of some sort. She climbed out of the car and tottered after Donal, her heels sinking farther into the wet grass with each step. She felt like a complete idiot. All the other women there were wearing Wellies, jeans, chunky sweaters and rainproof jackets. The group Donal was talking to turned to stare at her as she stumbled toward them. "Hi," she said, smiling brightly. "Can someone please tell me where the nearest toilet is?"

An attractive woman of about her own age—dressed in appropriate clothes for coursing—who had been talking to Donal when Lucy hobbled over, turned to her and said, "Of course. You go straight up the hill and—you see that big tree there? Well, if you go behind it you'll find a beautiful marble bathroom with fluffy pink towels and a woman to wipe your arse."

Everyone, including Donal, roared laughing as Lucy stood, lopsided—one heel sunk farther than the other—going a deep shade of scarlet. She smiled, tried to come up with a witty retort, but was too humiliated to think straight. She turned 'round and limped away, their laughter ringing in her ears.

She stumbled back to the car, cursing her boots, her jacket, the weather and Donal for bringing her to this godforsaken place. She sat back in the car and tried not to cry when she saw her reflection in the mirror. She was trying to smooth down her hair and wipe away the mascara, which was lying in streaks down her cheeks, giving her a distinct look of Ozzy Osbourne, when Donal appeared at the window. "Are you okay?"

"Do I look okay? I'm in the middle of a fucking field in the pissing rain. I ask a simple question and suddenly I'm the joke of the county. Thanks a lot for sticking up for me back there. Who is that cow, anyway?"

"Ah, don't mind her. That's just Mary's way."

"Charming. How do you know her?"

"We went out a while back."

Great, thought Lucy. The good-looking blonde was his ex. And, worse, she was one of those outdoorsy girls who don't wear makeup but always look lovely. Their cheeks are always flushed from brisk country walks and they always have their hair tied back with little wispy bits falling gently onto their fresh faces. "I see. Any other exes I should be aware of?"

"No," said Donal, smiling at her. "Now, do you need to pee?"

"Yes, badly."

"Okay, follow me," he said, taking her by the hand and leading her away from the mass of people.

He brought her to a portable toilet, which was hidden behind a hedge. It was smelly and filthy—but at least I don't have to squat behind a tree, thought Lucy, as she hovered over the toilet rim. When she came out, she looked down at her boots, which were now covered in urine as well as muck. "God, I must look like an idiot in these," she said.

"A right eejit."

"Thanks for rubbing it in."

"The way I see it, you have two choices here. You can either stay in the car for the day, or put on a pair of my old runners and a rugby jersey and get stuck in."

"If I had a book to read, I'd opt for the car, but I don't, so show me the runners."

They went back to the car and Donal rummaged around in the boot. Finally he pulled out an ancient pair of trainers and a crumpled rugby jersey, which reached Lucy's knees. She put them on and turned 'round. "Well, how do I look?"

"Like a supermodel. Now, come on, I need to focus on the

race," said Donal, grabbing her hand and dragging her back down. He introduced her to a few people—including the dreaded Mary, who ignored her—and went off to find Jimmy and Blackie. Lucy quietly asked the friendly-looking man, Liam, beside her what went on during a race.

"Well, d'you see, there are two dogs competing against each other in every race. The slipper there—he's the fella that holds the dogs back until the hare has a good head start of about eighty yards—releases the dogs to chase the hare. When the dogs catch up with the hare, he has to twist and turn to get away from them. Points are then given by the judge—you can see him over there on the horse—to each dog, depending on how they coped with turning the hare."

"Do they not have to catch the hare? Do they kill it? Isn't that really cruel?"

"Oh, for God's sake, lads, we have one of those city girls with a bleeding heart here," said Mary loudly. "She'll probably start crying about the 'poor little bunny rabbits' in a minute. Where did Donal find you at all?"

Lucy glared at her, but was determined not to get caught up in a slagging match. She didn't want to turn into a fishwife yet. She'd leave that for later, when she'd really let Mary have it. "As I was saying, do they catch the hare?"

"The object is not to kill the hare, but to test the dogs against each other. Are you with me?" said Liam. "The dogs only chase by sight, so once the hare escapes they pull up and it's over. The judge awards points to decide which dog won. And that winner will go on to run against the winner of another heat and so on."

Lucy wasn't quite sure what was going on. How could you judge a dog on how it made a hare turn? It seemed very odd. Suddenly everyone rushed forward to the edge of the coursing field—

spectators were not allowed inside it—as Blackie's name was called. Bookies offered last-minute odds and cash changed hands quicker than lightning. Blackie was to race against a fierce-looking dog called Bootsy; she was given a red collar and stood to the left with Donal and Jimmy. Bootsy was given a white collar and stood to the right with his owner. Then the slipper appeared, put the two dogs on a special leash and brought them into the coursing field. The hare was released from a cage at the side of the field and after a few seconds the slipper let the dogs go.

Lucy shouted, "Come on, Blackie!" and everyone in the place turned to glare at her.

"Pathetic," muttered Mary, under her breath.

Nobody spoke or moved a muscle as the two dogs tore off after the hare, darting this way and that. Forty seconds later it was over. Everyone peered at the judge to see what color handkerchief he had raised. It was red. Now everyone (except Lucy, who was afraid to open her mouth) cheered and slapped Donal and Jimmy on the back. Mary rushed forward to give Donal a lingering kiss and fuss over Blackie, who had run back, looking very pleased with herself.

Thank God it's over, thought Lucy. At least we can go now. The drizzle had made her hair similar to Tito Jackson's on a bad day and one of Donal's runners had a hole in the sole, so her right sock was soaking. Donal came over to her, beaming like a kid. "Wasn't she great? Did you have a bet on?"

"No, I completely forgot. I got caught up in trying to understand the rules. Never mind, let's go and celebrate."

"Good idea," said Donal, heading to the car. Lucy trotted after him, delighted at the prospect of a cozy country pub with a log fire. Donal opened the boot and tossed her a can of beer. "Cheers. Here's to the next race."

"What next race?"

"The next race against the winner of this one."

"You mean it's not over?" said Lucy, feeling utterly dejected.

"Not at all. If she does well we'll have two more to go. Fingers crossed. Cheers," he said, knocking back his beer.

Lucy was about to say she'd had enough and was going to take the car, book into a nice hotel, have a long soak in a bubble bath and would meet up with him later, when Mary bounded over. "I'll have one of those, thanks," she said, pointing to Lucy's beer. "Well, did you hear this one shouting during the race? She was nearly asked to leave by the steward. I was mortified for her."

"Ah, sure it's Lucy's first time. She'll get used to it," said Donal, winking at the rain-sodden Lucy.

"I dunno about that, Donal. Some girls aren't made for coursing and I think this one would be more comfortable in a five-star hotel."

"This one," said Lucy, trying not to lose her temper, "is standing right here in front of you. And I would appreciate it if you didn't talk about me as if I wasn't here."

"Ooh, now, no need to be so touchy. Very sensitive, are we?"

"No, Mary. Not sensitive, just civilized. Maybe if you spent less time in fields with dogs you could work on your social skills."

"Donal," said Mary, hands on hips, glaring at him, "are you going to let her speak to me like that?"

"If you dish it out, Mary, you have to be able to take it," said Donal, grinning at Lucy. Mary stormed off. "Come on, you city slicker. Two more races to go and then we'll go somewhere nice to celebrate and dry off."

Lucy smiled at him. Suddenly the rain and muck didn't seem so bad. Blackie won the next race but lost in the final to an outsider called Bosco. There were murmurings that Bosco's trainer might have slipped him some steroids. Apparently he had doubled in size in a year, but no one could prove it, so Bosco and his trainer Benny Kean won the cup and made a killing from the bookie. Donal ended up winning a thousand euro, which he split with Jimmy. Everyone was heading to the local pub for celebration drinks, but as they were driving out Donal turned left instead of right like everyone else.

"Where are we going?" asked Lucy.

"As a reward for being a good sport in the rain all day, I'm taking you to the Sanderson Hotel in Tipperary for a hot bath, dinner, drinks and, hopefully, if I get you drunk enough, a night of passion."

And that was exactly what happened. . . .

TWENTY-FIVE

I began to take the clomiphene and, having eagerly swallowed the first tablet, I decided to read the accompanying leaflet. It described the possible side effects of the drug, which included ovarian hyperstimulation and enlargement, possible rupture, visual disturbances, hot flashes, abdominal discomfort, nausea and vomiting, depression, insomnia, weight gain, rashes, dizziness and hair loss. I stared at it in shock. Jesus Christ! I was going to be bald, sweaty, fat and depressive. I rang Dr. Reynolds in a panic. He assured me that these were extreme side effects that rarely—if ever—affected his patients and especially not on the low dose of fifty milligrams that he had started me on.

Feeling calmer, I decided to throw out the information leaflet in case James found it. I knew he'd make me come off the drugs immediately if he read those symptoms. I'd wait until he found a clump of my hair on the pillow before I went into any explanations. For the next four days I took my drugs, and later, on day nine, I went into the clinic for my first follicle-tracking examination.

Once again I found myself naked from the waist down, flat on my back with my legs akimbo. The male radiologist, Tom, was young, fit and extremely good-looking, which made it all even more uncomfortable. When I'm embarrassed I tend to overcompensate by talking incessantly in an overcheery manner. So when Tom began explaining the procedure to me, I kept interrupting him with crummy lines. It was pathetic.

"As you are no doubt aware, follicle-tracking scans will show us if the ovaries are functioning correctly. With these scans we can—"

"Oh, I see, yes. Come on, the eggs, come on, the Easter bunny, ha-ha . . ."

He looked at me, smiled without smiling and continued. "—track the size of the follicles in the ovary over several days to predict timing of ovulation and advise you of the optimal time for conception."

"Will I have to bring my husband with me next time so we can get to it immediately in the broom cupboard, ha-ha-ha?"

It was awful. I knew I was making a fool of myself, but I couldn't control it. I was just so nervous.

Tom was a real pro and once again continued his flow as though I had never interrupted him. "We'll also be measuring the thickness of the womb lining. This gives an indication of egg quality and likelihood of a successful pregnancy."

He then took a big tube of lubricant jelly and squidged a lump of it over the top of one of those large vibrator-type things and inserted it into my vagina. The bad Tommy Cooper impressions ended there and then. I was shocked into silence. A computer screen was turned toward me and as Tom twisted the camera thing around, he began clicking furiously with the mouse, dragging measuring lines across the screen and printing out little black photos. All I could see was a big black mass with the occasional black blob. He was intent on measuring any black blobs that appeared on the screen. After about five minutes of frenzied measuring, clicking and printing, the camera was taken out and I was handed a tissue by the nurse to wipe away the lubricant while Tom politely turned his back . . . gross.

Once I was dressed, Tom sat me down and began showing me the printouts. They were small, dark and blurry. I had no idea what I was looking at. "You can see here," he said, pointing to a cluster of blobs, "that the follicles appear to be similar in size. When one grows significantly bigger than the others, we can be confident that you're ovulating and an egg will be released. It's too soon to tell with your follicles yet. I'll make an appointment for you to come back in two days' time."

"What if in two days' time I still have no big one?"

"It could mean that you're ovulating later in your cycle or that you're not ovulating at all. We won't know until we've tracked you a few more times this cycle."

"What if I don't ovulate?"

"Well, then, Dr. Reynolds will probably increase the dosage of clomiphene."

Great—more drugs. I'd be a fat, sweaty baldy in no time. So much for the sex: James wouldn't want to go near me.

Two days later I was back in the clinic and a different radiologist was doing the same test. I had to answer the same questions about how long I'd been trying to get pregnant and how long I'd been taking clomiphene.

"Where's Tom?" I asked, annoyed.

"We rotate," said Judy, the new radiologist. "There are three of us so we do different days each week. Now, tell me, what dosage of clomiphene are you taking?"

When she had all my details she inserted the ultrasound camera and we stared at the screen. No big blobs. She made an appointment for me to come back in two days' time on day thirteen of my cycle. Two days later I went through the same process with Liz, the third radiologist. We went over the same questions and again stared at a screen with no obvious big blobs appearing. I was told to come back in two days' time—on day fifteen—to see if I was ovulating later in my cycle. On day fifteen it was Judy again and there were still no big blobs.

"I'm afraid, Emma, it doesn't look like you're going to ovulate this month. I'll send a report to Dr. Reynolds and he'll discuss your options with you."

I left the clinic feeling despondent. What the hell was wrong with me? Why couldn't my stupid ovaries produce eggs? How come everyone in the world was able to get pregnant except me? Was I barren and they just couldn't figure out why? Was it ever going to happen? Should I just hang up my boots and pack it all in?

When I got home a package was waiting for me. It was a box with Dutch stamps on it. I didn't remember ordering anything. Maybe it was a present from James. I opened the box and un- wrapped the gift. It was a large pink bunny rabbit with beads. . . . Oh my God, it was a vibrator! I looked at the message inside the box: "To brighten up your sex life. Sorry for calling you barren at Christmas. Babs."

I had never been one of those modern women who had vibrators in their bedside tables. I suppose I had always had some kind of boyfriend/leper/loser on the scene, and thus a fairly regular sex life so I had never felt the urge. My pre-trying-for-a-baby sex life with James had been extremely active, frisky and fun—we couldn't keep our hands off each other. We didn't need battery-operated devices: we were doing just fine using the equipment God had given us.

Mind you, I'd been tempted to try a vibrator after Lucy told me that hers gave her better results than any man she had slept with. This one was called the Rampant Rabbit Pearl vibrator. I switched it on and giggled as the little beads spun 'round and the rabbit ears vibrated. The promotional leaflet claimed:

> *There is a good reason that this is the most popular sex toy in the world, just ask any woman who has one. A long, thick jelly-finish shaft, vibrating, rotating pearls, multispeed vibration and the soft bunny ears to tease the clitoris—it's fantastic.*

I hid it in my wardrobe. After all my internal tests, I couldn't face inserting anything else inside me for the time being, but maybe at a later date . . .

Having analyzed the tests, Dr. Reynolds decided to increase my dose of clomiphene to one hundred milligrams. I went for four more internal ultrasounds and still no big blobs appeared. A month later my dosage was increased to one-hundred-fifty milligrams—still nothing, so it went up to two-hundred milligrams. I could now feel the side effects. The sweating was the worst. One minute I'd be completely normal and the next I'd be drenched in sweat and my face would be bright red. Truth be told, my mood swings were getting worse too.

I was doing my regular makeup job with Amanda Nolan on *Afternoon with Amanda* the morning I was due to go in for my first ultrasound on day nine of the new two-hundred-milligrams dose. I arrived late, having had to buy a shirt on the way in because a particularly violent hot flash had left me dripping. As I was putting on Amanda's mascara, I began to think about the test and how desperately I wanted one of the blobs to be bigger than the other when I heard Amanda squeal.

"Ouch."

Shit! I had stabbed her in the eye with the mascara wand. "I'm sorry, Amanda. Are you okay?" I asked, handing her a tissue. "God, I'm really sorry—let me see your eye."

"I'm fine, Emma, but what's wrong with you? You're like a cat on a hot tin roof. You can't seem to concentrate for more than ten seconds these days. Sit down and tell me what's going on."

I told her about my treatment and how invasive it was and how I hated the tests and how after four months on the drugs my blobs were not getting bigger and how I was all sweaty and hot and bothered all the time and how I felt weepy at the slightest thing. "In fact, I pretty much feel either blind rage with the world or just really tearful, like now," I said, beginning to cry. "There's no happy medium. I ate the face off James last night because he'd bought round teabags instead of pyramid-shaped ones. I'm turning into a monster and now I'll probably lose my job because I've just blinded the star of the show."

"No you won't," said Amanda, passing me a tissue and patting my arm. "Come on now, Emma, give yourself a break. This is extremely hard on you. It's harder for the woman than the man because she's the one who has to have all the dreadful tests and take the nasty drugs. You're not to beat yourself up. It's perfectly normal to be feeling emotional—you're taking hormone-inducing drugs, for goodness' sake. But you'll have to do something to help yourself along. Are you having acupuncture?"

"No."

"Well, you need to start immediately. Acupuncture is known to help fertility. Now, I go to a great girl called Sheila who treats me for my hay fever. Here's her number. Call her and tell her you're a friend of mine. She's a miracle worker and it'll help you unwind from all those other tests."

"Thanks, Amanda," I said weepily. "Thanks for being so nice."

"Come on now, blow your nose and make me look beautiful. Only this time try not to injure me in the process."

I booked an appointment with Sheila on day eleven. I arrived feeling very sorry for myself. I had just been for another ultrasound, and as usual no big blobs had appeared on the screen. Sheila answered the door in a floor-length turquoise kaftan. She had long red hair tied back in a big plait and she smelled of incense. "Hello, Emma, come on in," she said, beaming at me.

I followed her into a room at the front of her house. It was painted a pale shade of lilac and smelled of lavender. Sheila sat me down and gently talked me through the last year and a half of my life. It was like therapy. I felt I could tell her anything. I talked and talked, and she nodded sympathetically and took notes, lots of notes, pages and pages of notes—I had a lot to say. We discussed my digestion, lifestyle, stress levels, eating habits, drinking habits, sleep patterns . . . my whole medical history as well as my family's.

I wanted to move in with Sheila and spend the rest of my life in this calm, lavender-scented room. She was totally sympathetic and said all the symptoms I was feeling were normal and a lot of her patients were having the same treatment I was and finding it equally stressful. She explained that acupuncture had been practiced in China for many thousands of years, but had only become known in the West fairly recently. She said that the success rate of acupuncture in aiding fertility was extremely high, especially when done in conjunction with hormone treatment. She added that every individual was treated uniquely as the exact combination of causes of imbalance within the body is different for everyone.

"A number of factors have to be taken into consideration, and that's why I had to ask you about any treatment you've had, your

230 / *Sinead Moriarty*

family's medical history and your current emotional state. Now, I'm going to ask you to lie back while I do a pulse reading to determine the flow of energy in your body and I'll also check your tongue."

"My tongue?" Shit, I hadn't washed my teeth before coming—what if my breath smelled?

"Yes, we can learn a lot from the tongue. Its texture and coating will indicate your general state of health."

"Okay, but what about the needles? I'm not very good with needles. Does it hurt?"

"You will feel only the tiniest pinprick, I promise."

Normally—particularly in light of the recent lies I'd been spun about tests not being painful—I wouldn't have believed her. But something about Sheila made me trust her. Besides, she was a woman and women don't lie to one another about pain.

I lay back on the bed in the middle of the room and tried to breathe deeply as instructed. Sheila looked at my tongue and didn't recoil, so my breath mustn't have been too bad, and then she felt my pulse. She told me that my qi—which was my vital energy and is made up of yin and yang—did not feel balanced. My energy was not flowing freely and evenly. My flow of qi was blocked due to the emotional and physical stress I was under.

She didn't need to look at my tongue to figure that one out. One look at my blotchy face was a dead giveaway. I tried to slow down my breathing and relax.

Then Sheila took out her needles and began inserting them into my arms, hands, feet, ankles, tummy and head. The only time I winced was when she came at me with a needle that she wanted to insert into my face—between my eyebrows. I thought she was going to stab me in the eye. My arm jerked up to stop her. The needle ended up impaled in the palm of my hand which—judging by the look of horror on Sheila's face—was not one of the energy points she was targeting. She extracted it and reminded me of the importance of remaining calm. Then, wedging the offending hand down with her leg, she inserted the needle in my forehead.

She turned down the lights and told me to relax. Within five minutes, despite the fact that I was half-naked, with needles sticking out of all corners of my body, I fell asleep. Twenty minutes later Sheila had to wake me up. I felt wonderful, as if I was floating. I felt relaxed and at peace. It was fantastic. I loved Sheila. I loved acupuncture. I felt positive for the first time in ages. It was going to work. Now that my qi was unblocked, my blobs would get bigger.

TWENTY-SIX

*I*t was a miracle. Two days after the acupuncture, when I went for my next internal ultrasound, I saw a big black blob on the screen. Tom measured it and smiled. "It looks good, Emma. It's significantly bigger than the others. Come back in two days and we should know for sure."

I was elated. I was going to live in China forever. Acupuncture was the way forward. Sheila had performed a miracle.

Two days later and the blob was huge. I was ovulating. Alleluia. I raced home and rang James. "I'm ovulating. Come on, quick, come home, we need to have sex now."

"I'm in the middle of a meeting. I'll call you back when I'm finished."

"*No.* I need you to come home now, James."

What was he doing? It was vital that we had sex now. Right now, while I was ovulating.

"I'll call you later."

"No, James, come—"

He'd hung up. I flung the phone across the room. It had taken four and a half months to get to this stage and now he was going to ruin it by coming home late and the egg would be gone, or shrunk or whatever. We needed to have sex now. I was hyperventilating as I paced the room. The hot flashes were coming fast and furious. I was damned if I was going to wait another minute. I grabbed my car keys and drove like a lunatic to the rugby club. Grannies dived into bushes for cover as I rammed the car up on the pavement to overtake slow drivers. I was bright red and sweaty by the time I got there. I stomped up the stairs to James's office.

I could hear voices, but nothing was going to stand in my way. I was a woman with a mission. I flung open the door. James and two older men in suits turned to stare at me.

"Hi, sorry to disturb you, but I need to speak to James urgently," I said, glaring at James, who was glaring back.

"Sorry, gentlemen, will you excuse me, please?" said James, coming over to me and frog-marching me out of the room. "What the hell are you doing, Emma? I'm in a very important meeting. I told you I'd call you back later."

"I don't give a toss about your stupid meeting. I've spent the last four-and-a-half months taking hormones and undergoing the humiliation of having my legs constantly in stirrups. I've just been told that I'm ovulating, so we need to have sex now. Not later on, not in an hour—*now.*"

"Keep your voice down," said James, dragging me farther away from his office. "I'm in the middle of a meeting with my boss. We're discussing the revamp of the clubhouse. I can't leave the meeting, so will you please just go home. I'll talk to you later."

"I don't care about your stupid boss. We have to have sex now. Come on, stop talking and come into the loo with me. It'll only take a minute," I said, dragging him toward the ladies'.

"*Emma,*" said James, now as red in the face as I was. "Go home and calm down. An hour or two will make no difference."

"That's the whole bloody point. It does make a difference. Come on, just come in here for a quickie."

I grabbed his shirt and began to tug. James pulled away and we began a tug of war, until I heard a rip and fell backward onto the ground with half of James's shirt in my hand. Buttons flew everywhere. James looked down at his now exposed chest.

"Well, that's just fantastic. Thanks, Emma. You've managed to make a complete fool of me. I have to go back into that meeting with a ripped shirt," said James, trying to tuck the shreds of his shirt back into his trousers.

"I'm sorry, but—"

"I don't want to hear it. Just go home," snapped my fed-up husband, as he stomped off holding his shirt closed with both hands.

I went and sat in the car and cried. I knew I was turning into a nutter, but we did need to have sex as soon as possible. What was the point of going through the treatment if we weren't going to follow it up with the sex? Part of me was annoyed with James for not understanding how important it was to get our timing exactly right. But I knew I'd have to make it up with him if there was any hope of having sex that day so I bought him a new shirt and when he came home I was wearing just the shirt and a pair of high heels. He walked straight by me—ripped shirt flapping—and went upstairs to have a shower. He was obviously still raging. I waited for him to come out and contemplated whether to bring out the Rampant Rabbit to surprise him, but decided against it. James wasn't a sex toy–type of guy—at least, I didn't think he was. As I tried to picture him in leather chaps brandishing a whip, the real James came into the room wrapped in a towel.

"Sorry about earlier. I got you a new shirt. D'you like it?"

James had his "serious chat" face on.

"Emma, this has got to stop. I understand that the drugs are making you moody, but storming into my office and ripping my shirt off in front of my boss is just not on. You have got to calm down."

"I know I went too far today, but I can't help it, James. I'm pumped full of hormones. Do you have any idea what that's like for me? I think half the time I'm going insane. I'm either sweating like a racehorse or crying or wanting to murder someone for looking at me sideways. I don't know if I'm coming or going. It's like I have no control over my emotions. I'm sorry about today, but what's the point of putting myself through this hell if we don't have the sex?"

"We will, just not in the middle of a meeting. A couple of hours isn't going to make any difference. You've got to get that into your head. And getting yourself into a state about it isn't going to help either. Larry said his wife went through IVF and the most important thing of all is to be relaxed and positive."

"Larry?"

"The architect who was in my office today with my boss."

"You discussed our private business with a complete stranger?" I said—turning into my mother.

"It was hardly private after you stormed into my meeting and ripped my shirt off. I had to explain why I was half-naked when I went back in. Thankfully, Larry had been through something similar so he understood because Eddie just looked shocked."

"Fuck Eddie and Larry and his stupid relaxed wife," I snapped, hormones taking over again.

"Eddie's my boss, Emma."

"I don't care, I—" I stopped. I realized that if we had another argument, we wouldn't have sex, and sex was more important than me trying to ram the point home that the hormones were making me crazy. Let's face it, he could see that.

"So do you like the shirt?" I purred, as I began to unbutton it.

"What?" said James, taken aback by the sudden U-turn in the conversation.

The phone rang.

"Leave it," I said, as James picked up the receiver.

"Hi . . . no. No plans . . . yeah, sounds good . . . see you there."

By the time he hung up I was having a savage hot flash and the shirt was stuck to my back. I was furious at the interruption. "Who was it?" I snapped.

"Donal. We're going to meet him and Lucy for drinks now, so you'd better hop into the shower."

"But we can't, James, we—"

"Emma," said James firmly, "we're going to go and have a few drinks, relax and enjoy ourselves, and when we come back we'll have sex. Now, go and get dressed."

I looked at my watch. It was now five hours since the test and by the time we got home it would be eight or nine hours. Still, it was better to have relaxed sex than fighting sex. I didn't want an angry baby. It would be nice to see Lucy. I hadn't seen much of her lately as she'd been traveling a lot with work and spending her spare time with Donal. They seemed to be getting on well. It would be the first time the four of us had been out together, so it would be fun, I thought, trying to jolt myself into a good mood.

Half an hour later we were sitting in the pub beside a cozy fire and I was feeling better. Lucy looked happy and comfortable with Donal. It was weird at first, seeing them together as a couple. They were in the honeymoon phase where nothing the other person did annoyed you. All the little idiosyncrasies that would later drive them 'round the twist were still "cute." It was like when I first met James and I thought the way he chewed each bite of food thirty times before swallowing it was sweet and now it drove me insane. I always finished my meal at least half an hour before James. He labored over every bite as if it was his last. Lately—no doubt due to the hormones—I had been tempted to put my hand into his mouth and shove the food down unchewed. At least I had managed to control that particular urge.

Donal was telling the story of Lucy meeting his niece Annie the week before, and how well they had got on and how Annie thought Lucy was beautiful and cool and glamorous. . . . I looked at Lucy as he was telling the story—she was positively glowing. It was nice to see her so happy. She looked at me and I beamed at her. She beamed back. I was thrilled for her: she so deserved to meet someone who thought the world of her. I nodded toward the loo and we both got up and went in for a chat.

"Oh my God, Lucy, he's besotted with you. It's great," I said, hugging her.

"Do you really think so?"

"Of course I do. The way he looks at you and talks about you—he's smitten."

"I really like him, Emma. I can't believe it because at first I thought he was such an oaf. But underneath it all he's lovely—all manly and protective. We still fight, but I'm definitely falling for him. Big-time."

"I'm so glad. You deserve to be happy. It's as if you've been going out for years. You're so yourself with him, it's great."

"It's the first time I can remember feeling totally relaxed with someone. I'm not constantly worried about holding my stomach in or wondering if my makeup is perfect or if I'm wearing the right clothes. I actually don't care because he doesn't care about that stuff. We've only been seeing each other properly since we went coursing and that's four months ago, but I feel as if I've known him for years . . . and the sex is fantastic."

"Four months? My God, Lucy, I can't believe we haven't seen each other in so long. It's crazy."

"I know, and chatting on the phone isn't the same as meeting up. It's just been really hectic with work and Donal."

"Look, you've been busy and so have I. I seem to spend all my spare time in hospital these days. We'll have to make a deal to meet up once a month for dinner. I want to know everything about you and Donal. He's obviously really serious about you—the fact that he introduced you to Annie is a huge sign."

"I was really pleased about that, and thank God she liked me."

"And why wouldn't she? You're fantastic. It's great, Lucy, it really is. You deserve every bit of it," I said, getting all tearful.

"Stop, you'll start me off," said Lucy, her eyes welling as she gave me a hug. "Now, enough about me, how are things with you? Are you okay?"

I didn't want to moan. It wasn't fair for her to have to console me when she was so happy. "Fine, thanks. The hormones seem to be working at last, so fingers crossed."

"Good. I know it'll all work out for you, Emma. It will, honestly. You'll be a mum in no time."

I nodded, not trusting myself to speak, and we went back in.

Two drinks later and I felt really drunk. I was totally light-headed and slurring my words like George Best on a bad day. After three glasses of red wine it was a bit odd that I was so smashed. The others thought it was funny and laughed about what a cheap date I was, but I knew it was the drugs because I never normally got drunk so quickly. James decided he'd better bring me home, so we were back in our house at ten o'clock. Him, very slightly merry. Me, very drunk.

I stumbled upstairs, got undressed, put on the new shirt I'd bought him and the high heels and fished the Rampant Rabbit out of the wardrobe. I went downstairs, jumped on top of James, who was lying on the couch, and stuck the vibrating Rabbit ears up his nose. The look of shock on his face set me off and I fell off the couch laughing, the Rabbit still shaking in my hand.

"What the hell is that?"

"It's the . . . ha-ha . . . it's the . . . ha-ha . . . best-selling sex toy in the world. Look, it has different speeds," I said, howling as I increased the vibration.

"Where did you get it?"

"Babs ordered it on the Internet to spice up our sex life."

"Why does she think it needs spicing up?" said James, looking a bit put out.

"Dunno. 'Cos I'm not pregnant, I guess," I said, giggling at the jellyfish thing vibrating.

"I see. All right, then, up you come," said James, lifting me over his shoulder like a fireman, legs buckling under the weight. "Bring the Rabbit—I've always quite fancied a threesome."

TWENTY-SEVEN

I spent the next two weeks constantly poking my boobs, to see if they were tender, and feeling nauseous—although I didn't know if that was because of the drugs, stress or the longed-for pregnancy. As those weeks went by I felt different. I felt a change in my body. I was tired, my breasts were tender and I was convinced I had that funny metal taste in my mouth that pregnant women talk about—although it might have been my fillings. I had never been more sure of anything in my life: I was pregnant. So when my period was late, I charged out to buy two pregnancy tests.

This time I waited until I was three days overdue and then I did the first test. I waited a few minutes and looked at it—negative. I wasn't put out. I knew I was pregnant. I did the second test—negative. It doesn't matter, I told myself, this often happens. It's probably too early for the tests. I called Dr. Reynolds, told him I was overdue and wanted to check if I was pregnant. He told me to come in for blood and pregnancy tests.

I did. I wasn't pregnant.

I locked myself in the toilet of the Harwood Clinic and cried myself sick. I had been so sure, so positive . . . and now nothing. Back to square one. I was devastated. I left the clinic, not caring about my blotchy face and red nose, and was about to get into the car when my mobile rang. Thinking it was James, I answered it. I wanted him to tell me it was going to be all right.

It was Tony.

"Hey, Emma, just calling to say Jess gave birth to a bouncing boy last night. Eight pounds three. We're over the moon. I was se cretly hoping for a boy, but you know the way you don't want to say anything. Anyway, we're going to call him Roy—after Roy Keane."

I held the phone away from me, as I threw up beside the car.

"Emma? Are you there?"

"Sorry, Tony, I dropped the phone. Great news," I said, trying not to gag on the chunks of vomit still in my mouth.

"Yeah, we're thrilled. Jess said you can come and visit any time. She's dying to show him off."

"Okay, yeah, I'll be in later."

"Great. I'd better go, I've a list of people to call. See you soon."

I sat in the car and tried to suppress the wail I could feel just below my chest. I knew that if I let it out I wouldn't be able to con-trol it. I breathed deeply—in and out, in and out. As I calmed down, my anguish was replaced with anger and resentment. Why the hell did Jess have it all so easy? How come she was able to pop out kids like a rabbit? Why did it all go so smoothly for her and Imogen and everyone else in the whole bloody world? Why? Why? Why? Why? I'd have to go to the stupid hospital now and smile and coo and pretend it was the best news I'd ever heard. I wanted to kill someone. I wanted to drive the car into a wall. Aaaargh. How much more of this did I have to endure?

Stop it! I shouted at myself. Think of people worse off. Think of women who have had five miscarriages or their baby has died when it was six months old or they were in a car crash and are paralyzed. Think of poor Christopher Reeve in his wheelchair. Stop feeling sorry for yourself. This is not the end of the world. Think of the starving people of Africa. . . . I didn't feel better, I felt worse. Now I was beating myself up for being self-pitying and dramatic—so on top of feeling miserable, I now felt guilty about it.

When I got home, Lucy rang. "Hi, Tony just called."

"Yeah, it's great news," I said, failing miserably to sound cheerful.

"Are you okay?"

"Yeah, I'm fine."

"Really?"

"Yeah. I had a moment of feeling sorry for myself, but I'm fine now," I lied. "I'm going to pop in later to see her."

"I was going to go after work, about seven. Do you want to meet me for a drink first? Bit of Dutch courage?"

"Thanks, but after the last reaction I had to drink, I think I'd better stay off it. I'll meet you in the reception area at seven."

By the time seven o'clock came I had got my tardy period and was feeling even worse. I was going to call off the visit, but I felt that it would look like sour grapes. Jess knew I was trying to get pregnant. We had never discussed it, but she knew me well and my erratic behavior wasn't exactly subtle. Besides, she had said it to Lucy, who had said it to me. So I knew she knew, and she knew I knew she knew, but nothing had been said. I preferred it that way. What was there to discuss? She was fertile, I wasn't, end of story. I didn't want her to feel bad about having a baby and she didn't want me to feel bad about not being pregnant.

Lucy arrived at the hospital with a big pot of Clarins body-shaping cream, while I had brought a bunch of flowers.

"Body-shaping cream?" I asked.

"It's practical. She'll want to get back into shape quickly after this baby, considering the last time it took them eight months to have sex. It's supposed to be fabulous for reducing fat and puffiness in the waist and hips."

"Good thinking. Tony will be pleased anyway," I said, smiling.

"Are you ready?" she asked, squeezing my hand.

"Yeah, let's go."

As we walked through the maternity ward I began to understand why desperate women snatched babies. All around me tiny pink newborns were swaddled in blankets. Some were being held by their mothers, some were being fed, others just lay quietly in their cots, ready and waiting to be swiped as their exhausted mothers slept beside them. It would be so easy to stroll over, pretend I was a friend or relation and walk out the door with a baby of my own. I could tell James that it had been left on our doorstep in a basket with a note saying, "Please love me." I would persuade him to move back to England—away from the Irish police—and we would live happily ever after in a pretty cottage by the sea in Cornwall.

"Emma," said Lucy, tapping my shoulder, "it's this way."

I followed her into a room with two beds. In the far corner Jess was looking tired but happy. She was breast-feeding her little bundle of joy, staring down at him with her face full of unconditional love. I felt my stomach twist. I took a deep breath and plastered on a smile. "Hey, there. Congratulations. Oh, look, isn't he gorgeous? How are you feeling?"

"Fine. Thanks for coming in. The flowers are beautiful."

"I think Lucy's cream will probably come in more handy," I said, as Lucy handed it to her.

"Thanks, Lucy, I'll need this badly."

"Well, it's for Tony too," said Lucy, winking at Jess as Tony walked in carrying fresh romper suits for his son.

"What's for me?"

"Nothing," we all said, laughing.

"Birds!" said Tony, shrugging. "James not with you?" he asked me.

"No, he's training tonight."

"Pity. I'd murder a pint."

"Who said 'pint'?" said Mr. Curran, Jess's father, as he arrived with her mother. "Jesus, Jessica, do you have to do that in front of me?" he said, putting his hand over his eyes when he saw his daughter breast-feeding.

"What's she supposed to do, Dessie?" asked Mrs. Curran. "Starve the child so you feel more comfortable? Honestly . . ."

"Right, Tony, about that pint," said Mr. Curran.

"Thanks a lot, Dad, you've only just arrived. Would you like to see your grandson before you bolt out the door?" said Jess.

"I can see him from here. Sure he's a grand little fellow. We'll be back in an hour when you've finished all that and I'll have a squeeze of him then."

With that, Mr. Curran legged it out of the ward before anyone could stop him, Tony hot on his heels.

"Men!" said Mrs. Curran, raising her eyes to heaven. "Well, Jessica, he's a little dote, so he is. How are you feeling, pet?"

"Not too bad, Mum," said Jess, smiling at her mother. "It was easier this time."

Mrs. Curran nodded knowingly.

I had always loved Mrs. Curran. When we were growing up she was the mother who was always at home in the kitchen baking bread or cakes. I used to like going back to Jess's house after school because we'd always have hot scones fresh from the Aga or home-made brown bread. It was heaven. Because Babs was so much younger than me, Mum was always busy looking after her and didn't have time to bake. But Jess was the youngest in her family and Mrs. Curran was married to that Aga. It was a big red one and you had to shovel the coal into the little door on the left-hand side. You could see the fire burning away when you opened it. Mrs. Curran said that the Aga was the only way to cook real food. She thought microwaves were the curse of our generation.

"Emma, it's been ages since I saw you. You look wonderful. How's life treating you?"

"Well, thanks, Mrs. Curran."

"I hear you married a lovely Englishman. Isn't that great?"

"Yeah. I don't know how James puts up with me sometimes."

"I'm sure he's delighted with you. Any kids of your own?"

"No, not yet . . . you know . . . just sort of . . ."

"*Mum!*" snapped Jess. "Don't annoy Emma with stupid questions."

It was a conversation stopper if ever there was one. We all looked at the floor.

"I think I'll go and get us some coffee," said Mrs. Curran, breaking the silence. "Emma, will you give me a hand?"

We left the room and, when we were out of earshot, Mrs. Curran said, "I'm sorry, Emma, I didn't mean to be insensitive. I can tell I hit a nerve. It's not easy, is it? It's not always as straightforward as we hope. It took me a long time to have Jessica's brother. I had three miscarriages before I had him and I remember how hard it was to be around babies."

I nodded. I was afraid to speak. I could feel a lump forming in my throat. It would have been better if she had been horrible and insensitive. Being nice to me was dangerous territory.

"I didn't mean to upset you, pet. I know how hard it can be. But don't worry, it will happen for you. It will."

I had begun to cry. I knew that I had to get out of there before I really broke down. I managed to blurt out, "Have to go," and ran down the corridor, bumping into ecstatic fathers and mothers as I went. I couldn't breathe. I felt as if I was drowning. I made it to the car and tore out of the car park down the road. I was crying so much I couldn't see a thing. I just needed to get home before I completely fell apart. I needed the safety of my house. I jammed my foot down on the accelerator. Faster, I had to go faster.

It was only when the police car drove up beside me, siren blaring, and almost ran me off the road that I realized it was me it was after. A very angry policeman stormed over to my car and thumped on the window. I rolled it down.

"In a hurry, are we, madam? Step out of the car, please. Have you been drinking?"

I climbed out of the car and shook my head. "No. I was visiting a friend in hospital." The shock of being arrested had dried up my tears.

"Breathe in here, please," he said, pointing to a little tube attached to a bag.

The result was negative, but the policeman was still furious.

"I've been chasing you down for the last two miles. Did you think you were going to get away from me by driving faster? Do you know you were going at eighty miles an hour in a forty-mile speed limit? Think you can make up your own rules, do you? I'm going to charge you with reckless driving."

"But I didn't mean to . . . I just—"

"There's no excuse for driving like a maniac and endangering people's lives."

I couldn't control it. It had been coming all day. A wail of anguish escaped from my throat. I sat down on the side of the road and sobbed uncontrollably. The policeman was taken aback. He clearly hadn't dealt with a hysterical woman before.

"You don't understand . . . this has been the worst day of my life . . . seventeen months and nothing . . . no baby . . . and I went to see my friend and her new baby . . . and it was just so hard . . . so many mothers and babies . . . all so happy . . . the love in their eyes . . . so I had to leave . . . and I was crying and driving . . . I couldn't see 'cos of the crying . . . I have nothing . . . no baby . . . just horrible tests and drugs that make me go mad . . . and my husband hates me . . . well, he doesn't hate me, but I'm driving him mad . . . I'm driving myself mad . . . it's just so hard . . . why is it so hard to have a baby?"

The policeman's face softened. He sat down beside me and patted my shoulder. "There, there now. My wife went through the same thing. Three years of tests only to be told at the end of it that she couldn't have kids. So we adopted a little girl from Romania four years ago. A gorgeous little thing, she is. My wife went through hell. I know how hard it can be."

"Really? You adopted?"

"We were told we'd never have children naturally, so it was the only option for us. I'm sure you'll have some of your own. You're a lot younger than my wife was."

"I don't feel young, I feel about a zillion years old," I said, sighing.

"You're only a slip of a thing with your whole life ahead of you. It'll work itself out, these things always do. Come on now, we can't sit here all night, I've criminals to catch," he said, standing up.

I stood up too. "Are you going to arrest me? Am I going to have to go to prison and become a lesbian so I don't get killed?"

He laughed. "No, you aren't going to prison. I'm letting you off with a warning. Come on, I'll escort you home."

"Will you put on your siren? I've always wanted to have a police escort."

When James heard the siren he came rushing out of the house

thinking I'd been in an accident. Policeman Kieran Mooney escorted me to the front door and told James he had a wonderful wife and he was to look after me because I had had a very stressful day. Then he warned me never to drive when I was upset. Cry first, drive later.

TWENTY-EIGHT

*A*few weeks later I was sitting in the kitchen reading a
book that taught you ways to remain calm. James had
bought it for me after the police-escort incident. I was reading a
page a day and some days I have to say it annoyed me more than
calmed me down. The day before, I had read a piece on slowing
down. The book recommended speaking at a more relaxed pace
and slowing down your breathing to become instantly calmer. I
had tried it on James when he came home, but he said I sounded
like a stroke victim and it was far more scary than calm.

On this particular day the book was telling me how to relax my
facial tension. I was following the instructions: "Slightly raise the
eyebrows—this relaxes the brow muscles. Place your tongue against
the roof of your mouth—this relaxes the jaw muscles, and then
smile to relax the cheek muscles."

As I sat there grinning like a Cheshire cat with my tongue stuck
up in the air, the doorbell rang. It was Babs sitting on an enormous
pink suitcase, looking decidedly grumpy.

"What's going on?"

"Mum and Dad have thrown me out of the house with only the
shirt on my back."

"Big shirt," I said, nodding at the suitcase.

"A few personal effects, that's all. You can't begin a new life without clothes or a hair straightener. I didn't bother bringing makeup 'cos I figured you'd be able to give me loads."

"Are you planning on staying for a while?"

"Only until I can get enough money together to buy my own place. By the way, can you lend me a tenner to pay for the taxi?"

I sighed and gave her the money. She came back beaming. "So, what'll we have for dinner? I fancy Indian."

"What did you do?" I asked, intrigued to know how far she had gone. It must be pretty bad if they had kicked her out.

"Nothing."

"Bullshit."

"Okay, well, it's all your stupid fault, anyway."

"What?"

Babs told me that Mum had decided to try to help me with my fertility issues so she had been looking at the *Encyclopaedia Britannica* for information on fertility drugs. "But sure those books she has date back to the dinosaurs, so she couldn't find anything helpful. Then she starts asking me about the Internet and how it works and how you get information and all that. I tried to explain it to her, but it was impossible. . . ."

Every time Babs showed Mum how to do something she was shouted at for going too quickly and not respecting her elders. Mum kept reminding her that when she was teaching Babs to read, she had spent hours sitting patiently with her as she struggled with each letter, and now her ungrateful pup of a daughter didn't have the decency to give her mother a few computer lessons. She accused Babs of deliberately using technical terminology to throw her off-guard.

"So I gave up and told her to get professional lessons. I even found her a course to do and she signed up. Then she decided to turn your room into a study and started to clear out your stuff and put it into my wardrobes. . . ."

Whereupon Mum had come across a small box buried under a spare duvet that she just happened to open and, to her horror, inside she found a stash of dope. Needless to say she hit the roof. By the time Babs got home from college that day, Dad had been summoned and she was met with a rare, but formidable, united front. A huge row ensued, which ended up with Babs packing her large pink suitcase and "running away" to my house.

As she finished telling me the story, the phone rang. We both looked at it and said, "Mum."

I picked it up and quickly held it away from my ear, so that my eardrum didn't perforate with the high-pitched squeal.

"DO YOU KNOW WHAT THAT BRAT HAS DONE? BROUGHT DRUGS INTO OUR HOME! HARD DRUGS!"

"Mum, calm down, it's not that bad—"

"WHAT? Not that bad. Don't give me your new-wave nonsense. I know drugs when I see them. I've seen *Crimewatch*—I've even seen that *Trainspotters* film. Don't try to pull the wool over my eyes. They all start with the pot and the next thing you know they're on heroin, lying in the gutter with a needle hanging out of their arm. Your sister has gone too far this time. Even your father is shocked. Hard drugs . . . in my home. The shame of it. A drug addict for a daughter. If Nuala gets wind of this I'll never be able to show my face in public again. Drugs are a slippery slope. No wonder she's thin, jigging away on those ecstatic pills, morning, noon and night. There are young girls dropping dead all over the country from taking those. I know all about those pills, Emma, I wasn't born yesterday. I know about these things."

"Mum, I realize you're upset about the pot, but it's a very mild drug. It'll be legalized soon. It's not a hard drug, it's only for fun. She's not a drug addict."

"For fun! Fun, is it, to throw away your life on drugs? Fun, is it, to fry your brain and end up dead or like that Ozzy Osbourne? Drugs kill, Emma, it's a well-known fact. Here's your father now. The poor man has aged twenty years since he found out that his youngest child is a drug addict."

Dad came on the phone, sounding very cheesed off. "Can you keep her there for a few days till your mother calms down?"

"Sure, but only a few days, I've enough on my plate without Babs lounging around my house sponging off me, thanks very much."

"Of all the effing times—this has to blow up the weekend of the Ryder Cup and I've a big bet on Europe to win it. I'll wring your sister's neck. I won't have a moment's peace for the next three days. It'll be a miracle if I get to see one bloody hole played. Your mother wants me to go to some shagging parents-against-drugs meeting tomorrow."

I stifled a giggle. Dad was clearly in no mood for humor. I did feel sorry for him: he was obsessed with golf. It was his one true love. Every two years, when the Ryder Cup was on, he took over the television for three days. No one was allowed even to look at the remote control. All soap operas, reality-TV shows and sitcoms were out of bounds. It was golf, golf and more golf. The only time I had ever seen my father cry was thirteen years ago when Bernhard Langer missed a six-foot putt on the very last hole in Europe's bid to retain the trophy. He went from being hailed as the "genius golfer from Germany" to "that feckin' useless Kraut."

I told him I'd keep Babs for a few days until Mum calmed down, then send her home to face a few months of daily urine and blood tests. He didn't even laugh at that. He was a broken man. His Ryder Cup weekend was in tatters.

When James came home he tripped over the pink suitcase.

"What the hell? Emma, what is this doing here?" he snapped,

assuming I had placed it there to test his aptitude at the hurdles on the way into the kitchen. Then he saw Babs and it became clear. "Ah, I see we have a visitor. I sincerely hope this is a farewell visit by you, Babs, as you are on your way to the airport to emigrate for . . . a year, judging by the size of that suitcase."

"Wrong. I got kicked out of home because my mother found some blow in my bedroom, so I'm moving in here for a few days while I decide where to go to begin my new life."

"Why don't you just go straight to South America and stay with some of your fellow barons in Colombia?" said James, finding himself very amusing as he grabbed a beer from the fridge.

"Ha-ha," said Babs, rolling her eyes. "I think I'll hide out here for a while first, thanks."

"Well, it's an ingenious plan. Interpol would never look for you in your sister's house."

"Hilarious! Don't give up the day job, James, Billy Connolly isn't exactly quaking in his boots."

"Oh God, please shut up. I'm not listening to this sniping for the next few days," I said, jumping in before they got worse. "Now, what do you fancy for dinner?"

"I'd like some of that revolting green tea and some tasty steamed vegetables," said Babs, pushing her luck.

The raging hormones kicked in. "You ungrateful little wench," I said, grabbing her suitcase and hurling it out the front door, in an amazing display of superhuman strength. It must have been another side effect of the drugs I hadn't previously noticed. Maybe that was what Bruce Banner took before he turned into the Incredible Hulk—plain old hormone enhancers. "Go on, piss off, I'm sick of you. I've enough shit to deal with without you annoying me."

Babs looked genuinely shocked and for once was speechless. She looked at James.

"Come on, Emma, she's sorry. Aren't you, Babs?"

"Yeah, I am. Sorry, Emma, I was just joking. If you want me to eat the vegetables I will, but can I at least have a beer to wash them down? I really don't think I can stomach drinking the green muck. Maybe it's because my nose is so big, but the smell of it makes me want to puke."

"I'll cook if you like," said James.

Christ! If Babs was apologizing and James was offering to cook, I must be really scary. Still, it made a nice change. "Okay, I'd like Szechuan beef."

"Did I say 'cook'? I meant 'pay for,' " said James, as he grabbed his car keys.

"You sit down and put your feet up, Emma, we'll be back in ten minutes," said my newly humbled sister.

This was great—I should roar at her more often.

Five days later I drove Babs home to face the music. Dad was furious with her for causing him to miss the entire Ryder Cup. Mum, meanwhile, had been watching every film on drugs she could find in the video shop—including *Goodfellas* and *The Basketball Diaries*—and had spent hours calling the "My child's a drug addict, what can I do?" helpline. She had just stopped short of buying a sniffer dog. Babs was frisked at the front door, then hustled into the house for some serious questioning, *NYPD Blue* style. For the first time in my life, I actually felt sorry for her.

TWENTY-NINE

A month and a useless big black blob later, I was still not pregnant. Our wedding anniversary was coming up, and I was trying to decide where to go for a nice romantic mini-break. Suddenly it came to me—I had to stop waiting for miracles to happen and go and find one. There was only one place I knew where miracles happened. I went to the travel agent and booked three days away as a surprise for James. Needless to say, I had planned the three-day break around my supposedly fertile time of the month. When James came home I handed him an envelope wrapped in a red bow. "Happy anniversary."

"But it's not until next week—or did I . . ." he said, looking panic-stricken at the thought of having forgotten an anniversary with a wife who currently went off the deep end if he brought home the wrong teabags.

"No, you haven't forgotten—it *is* next week. I just wanted to surprise you early with this little holiday so you can plan your training 'round it."

"Oh, right," said a relieved-looking James. "Where are we off to, then?"

He opened the envelope and pulled out the itinerary. "Two re-turn flights to Paris. Fantastic, I love Paris. . . . Oh, hang on, and

258 / Sinead Moriarty

then onward by train to Lourdes. Lourdes?" asked James, looking at me.

"Yes."

"Joke?"

"No."

"We're going to Lourdes for our wedding anniversary?"

"Yes."

"This is a windup."

"No."

"Emma."

"What?"

"What the hell is this?"

"We're going to Lourdes for a few days. It's no big deal. I thought you'd be pleased. It's something a bit different and the weather should be nice. I've booked a hotel with a swimming pool. I think it's time we had some divine intervention. I know you're not Catholic and I'm a lapsed one, but God is all-loving and forgiving and miracles happen in Lourdes. Apparently if you have really bad skin diseases and multiple sclerosis and stuff, they dunk you in holy water and you're cured. So I think it's worth a shot for us to go to the baths and pray at the grotto to Our Lady. She can relate to having children. Sure, wasn't Jesus a miracle—a virgin birth and all that? So, anyway, I just think it might help and miracles do happen in Lourdes, I read about them, and Auntie Doreen says that pilgrimages are really inspiring—"

"I'm not going on some wild-goose chase to Lourdes to spend three days with a bunch of religious fanatics. We'll stay in Paris and have a nice, relaxing time drinking wine and chilling out."

"I can't drink on these stupid drugs and, as you well know, relaxing is not my forte these days. I have spent the last six months with my legs in stirrups drugged out of my mind to no avail. So I'm going in search of a miracle. This is the trip I want and this is where I'm going," I said, snatching the itinerary out of his hand.

"I see, and if this doesn't work, what's next? Fatima for Christmas? Medjugorje with your auntie Doreen for New Year's Eve?"

"There's no need to make a mockery of it. Just because you Prods don't believe that Mary was a vital part of the equation doesn't mean that She wasn't. In case you haven't noticed, it's Mary who performs the miracles. It's Mary who appears to people and gives them hope. Protestants are just too chauvinistic to appreciate the power of a woman in religion. In my world, Mary rocks," I said, in a speech that Sister Patricia would have been proud of.

"Oh, I'm well aware that She rocks. Didn't Doreen see Her rocking in some field a few years ago just before she turned into a pilgrimage junkie? I have the utmost respect for Mary, but I'm not spending three days in Lourdes waiting for Her to start swaying or dancing or whatever She does when She appears. Nor am I diving into dirty bathwater in some far-fetched belief that it will help us conceive. We'd be much better off in a nice hotel in Paris having lots of sex."

"James," I said, in my scary voice, "I'm going to Lourdes with or without you. My mind is made up. As an anniversary present to me I'd like you to come, but I'm going regardless. Miracles do happen and, anyway, maybe if I go to Lourdes and see really sick people and stuff, I'll stop feeling so miserable and be distracted and not even think about getting pregnant and then get pregnant. You know, reverse psychology. I want you to come with me. It'll be fun."

"Fun? In Lourdes with sick and dying pilgrims?"

"Okay, not fun exactly, but fulfilling and spiritual, and maybe we can help out with the sick while we're there."

260 / Sinead Moriarty

"Now you're really selling it to me. Go to Lourdes and wipe people's arses. Why don't we leave now? Why waste any more time? Let's go tomorrow."

"Fine. Don't come. I'll go on my own. Just like I go to all my appointments on my own. Just like I take the drugs on my own. Just like I get the bad results on my own—"

"Okay! I'll go," said James, sensibly shutting me up before I blamed him for the hole in the ozone layer and the destruction of the Amazon rainforest. "But this is a once-off, Emma. Never again. Next year I'm booking the trip and we're going to watch United playing in Old Trafford."

"Of course. Next year we'll do whatever you want. Old Trafford sounds nice. Is it in the Cotswolds?"

James sighed and picked up the newspaper.

A week later we were on the TGV shooting across the French countryside, surrounded by young people with guitars singing folksy songs and talking excitedly about the wonder that was Lourdes. I thought it was nice and joined in with the few songs I recognized—"Bridge Over Troubled Water," "Annie's Song," "He Is Lord" . . . I nudged James to sing along, but he refused and spent the entire journey glaring out the window. He was obviously determined not to enjoy himself. Mind you, he had never been a sing-song person. When we had family gatherings and Dad got a bit drunk, he'd launch into his Tom Jones impression and sing "Delilah," hips swinging, and winking at his imaginary Las Vegas audience. We'd all sing along, but James always looked a bit uncomfortable, and when he was forced to sing something himself, he always sang that really annoying rugby song, "Swing Low, Swing Chariots," or whatever it's called: he knew we all hated it and that we would interrupt him after the first line. I always sang "The Sun'll Come Out Tomorrow" from *Annie*. Mum would sing a very emotional rendition of "Somewhere Over the Rainbow" in a high, squeaky voice, which always made us howl with laughter, although I'd say the ghost of Judy Garland was writhing in torment at the crucifixion of her song. Sean sang "The Piano Man" and, unlike the rest of us, he could sing. Babs thought singing was for dorks and always went to bed when it began. It was one thing she and James had in common.

When the train pulled in, I waved good-bye to the international do-gooders as they went off to comfort the sick. They told me that there was always help needed in Lourdes and said I was welcome to join them any time to lend a hand. James stood grumpily to the side, fiddling with his case. I could see he was worried that I was going to volunteer him for duty.

Our hotel was surprisingly nice. Not plush, but nice and clean and airy with a decent-size pool. It was on the outskirts of the town, and while there were statues and pictures of Mary in abundance, you didn't feel as though you were in the grotto. We dumped our bags and headed for a swim. It was lovely and warm outside and the pool was heated. James began to cheer up.

Later that evening, on our way to the grotto, I filled James in on Bernadette and the apparition. *The Song of Bernadette* had been my headmistress Sister Patricia's favorite film and we had been subjected to it at least five times a year in religion class. Personally I thought that at twenty-four Jennifer Jones was a little old to be playing the young Bernadette, but Hollywood had thought otherwise. I explained to James that on February 11, 1858, fourteen-year-old Bernadette had been minding her own business, focusing on her breathing—because she suffered from chronic asthma—when Mary appeared to her. It was the first of eighteen apparitions and soon people from all over were coming to the grotto of Massa-bielle. Bernadette became a nun and devoted her life to God. Well, she had to, really—it wouldn't have looked too good if she'd gone off to Paris to shake her booty at the Moulin Rouge.

There was a long line of people waiting to go past the grotto and pray for their special intentions. Everywhere you turned there were sick people, but everyone looked peaceful and serene. It was nice. Even I began to feel calm. We shuffled along and when we got to the grotto I prayed for my miracle. It was very soothing. By the time we had finished, the torchlight procession had begun. We sat on a wall and watched it go by. Everyone carried candles and sang in different languages. It was really beautiful.

When we got into bed later that night, I suddenly felt odd about having sex. It didn't feel right—even though it was day thir-teen of my cycle. I had just been to one of the holiest places in the world and somehow sex seemed wrong, or bold, or something. I felt as if I was committing a crime. James said it was just my old Catholic guilt surfacing, but it was important to remember that I was married, trying to procreate and had left the Rampant Rabbit at home. I wasn't even just in it for the fun—I was actually trying to get pregnant. "Even the pope couldn't fault you, Emma. It's clean sex with your husband without contraceptives or sex toys."

He was right. Besides, it was day thirteen and I needed to focus. I got up and took down the picture of Mary and Saint Bernadette, and turned the statues lining the room to face the wall. Now at least I didn't feel we were being watched.

The next morning I dragged James out of bed early to go to the baths. I knew the queues got very long and I wanted to catch some sun in the afternoon, so we went down early. The queue for the men's baths was separate from the women's so we arranged to meet up for coffee afterward.

When I got to the top of my queue I was ushered into a crowded room, told to undress and tie a damp, ice-cold sheet 'round myself. Then I went into a freezing room with a bath in the middle and women on either side. I was unceremoniously dunked in the bath-water. It was subzero and my body was in total shock. I was told to go and get dressed, but offered no towel. The really weird thing was, I was dry. Bone dry. It was as if the water had vanished—a miracle in a way. Everyone in the changing room was looking at one another in wonder. I got dressed and ran to meet James. If Mary could make special nonwet water, surely She could give me a few good eggs. He was waiting for me, drinking coffee and reading the paper.

"Hi," I said breathlessly, slumping down into the seat opposite him. "Wasn't that just the most spiritual experience ever?"

"Yeah, absolutely," he said, just a little too enthusiastically.

"I mean the water. Isn't it incredible?"

"Mmm, yes, I thought so too."

"Were there men there to dunk you?"

"Oh, yes, there was dunking. Coffee, darling?"

"Yes, cappuccino, please."

James ordered me a coffee, then began to tell me about something he had just read in the paper.

"Isn't it amazing the way the water is so warm?" I interrupted.

"Amazing. Almost hot, if you think about it."

"You liar! James Hamilton, you're a big fat liar. You didn't go to the baths."

James knew he was sussed. "No, I didn't, and I have no intention of going. I didn't want to have an argument with you this morning about it, so I played along. But, Emma, I will never be having a bath here so don't start. I came to Lourdes to keep you company, not to convert."

I knew I was wasting my time so I let it go.

That afternoon, as we lounged by the pool, we saw a little boy in the shallow end, paddling around with armbands on. He looked about six and he was bald. He watched in awe as James swam the length of the pool under water. He beamed at him when he came up for air.

The poor little boy, I thought, my eyes welling with tears. He must have cancer. All his hair has fallen out. He's obviously come to Lourdes for a miracle cure. I felt like a fraud. Coming to Lourdes with my silly problems when this little boy was about to die.

"Hello," he said shyly to James.

"Hello to you," said James, wiping water out of his eyes.

"My name's Peter, I'm learning to swim. Soon I'll be able to swim like you," said the little boy, in a strong Scottish accent.

"Good for you," said James. "Do you want me to help you?"

Peter's face lit up. "Yes, please."

A young girl in her early twenties came over to the edge of the pool and told Peter not to bother the nice man. James assured her that it would be his pleasure to help Peter learn to swim. She smiled at him and introduced herself. "I'm Peter's mum, Linda."

James introduced himself and I strolled over to meet them too. Linda looked pretty good in her bikini and I wanted to get a closer view. She was young and attractive, but looked worn out.

"Hi, I'm Emma. Your little boy is lovely."

"Thanks, he can be a handful at times, but I wouldn't be without him."

"Look, we're going to be here for the afternoon, so why don't you lie back and enjoy the sun while we keep an eye on him for you? Take a break, I'm sure you could do with one," I offered.

"Are you sure?"

"Positive."

"I won't say no. Thanks," she said, her face full of gratitude at my meager offer of help. I felt truly humbled as I watched her walk away and sink into her sun lounger. What a brave lady she was.

We spent the rest of the afternoon by the pool as James patiently taught Peter to swim while Linda read and dozed in the sun. My heart melted as I watched them together. James was brilliant with him and Peter worshiped him. It was perfect. James was really getting into the spirit of Lourdes. He was helping a dying child. Mary would definitely help us out now. By early evening Peter could do a few strokes on his own and he was chuffed to bits.

They were leaving at five the next morning so we said good-bye to Peter when Linda took him off to bed. He clung to James and began to cry. James lifted him up. "Hey, little man, no tears now. I want you to go home and practice your swimming. And when you win a gold medal at the Olympics for Great Britain, I want you to remember that I gave you your first lesson. And the gold medal goes to . . ." said James, swinging Peter upside down.

"Peter!" squealed the little boy.

"You've been great," said Linda, smiling at me. "Thanks for looking after him."

"It was a pleasure," I said. "He's such a lovely kid. How long has he been ill?"

"Ill?"

"Sick."

"Peter?"

"His hair and—"

"Oh, that. There was a lice outbreak at his school so I decided to shave his head so the little bastards couldn't fester in his hair.

Did you think he had cancer?" said Linda, throwing back her head and whooping.

"Well, I just thought because you were in Lourdes that—"

"Och, no. We just came with my nan for a bit of a break. She comes every year and my mum couldn't take her this year so we came instead. Come on, Petey, let's get you to bed."

THIRTY

A week after we got back, I was ironing in the kitchen when I saw something moving at the window. I looked closer, thinking it was a bird or a cat. It was a statue of Our Lady, dancing from side to side.

"Emmaaa, can you hear me? I want you to spread the word about religion."

I looked down to see Babs kneeling under the windowsill, giggling hysterically. "Very funny. Come on in," I shouted.

"Well?" she said, plonking herself at the kitchen table.

"Well what?"

"Did you see Her? Did She speak to you or at least sway for you?"

"Neither."

"Are you pregnant?"

"I won't know until next week."

"Do you think you are?"

"Dunno. One day I do. The next I don't."

"I can't believe James went with you. He must think you're mad. Going to Lourdes for your wedding anniversary! Even Mum thinks you've lost the plot. Still, at least if James leaves you, you can move to Lourdes and become a nun."

"It's great to see you too, Babs."

"I'm just telling you what everyone thinks. I even got a call from Sean! The first time he's ever called me for anything. He thinks you're losing it too."

"So you all think I'm going insane?"

"Pretty much, yeah."

"Well, you can go back and tell them all that I'm perfectly sane, and that next time they send an emissary they should choose more carefully."

"Look, I don't know about the baby stuff and how hard it is, but you have been pretty moody lately and you're always going mental for no reason. It can't be good for you or your marriage."

"So you're a marriage counselor now?"

"Fine, I'll butt out. I'm just filling you in on what's being said about you. To be honest, I'm delighted, it takes the pressure off me. Mum's so distracted about you that she hasn't had a go at me for weeks. She didn't even give out when I came home with my belly button pierced."

"Really?" I found it hard to believe that Mum hadn't hit the roof when she saw that.

"Yep. I'm telling you, her main concern now is you. It's great, so keep it up, sis. By the way, any chance you could do my makeup this Saturday? I'm going to a ball and I want to look sensational. My next boyfriend is going to be there."

"Ex?"

"No, next. I spotted him last week. Very sexy and knows it, so I have to look really good and you have to do lots of shading to make my nose look smaller. Okay?"

"Okay. If I decide to stick my head in the oven before then, I'll let you know so you can make alternative arrangements."

"Well, at least you haven't totally lost your sense of humor. I'll tell Mum, she'll be pleased. See ya."

" 'Bye."

* * *

The next day when I went to open my post, there was a letter from Sean. I recognized his handwriting. He hadn't written to me since I went on a French exchange to Toulouse, aged fifteen, and hated it. Mum had made him write to me every day to cheer me up. The family I was sent to were friends of friends of my auntie Tara's. They were awful. The girl—Cécile—was a stick insect with no personality. The mother kept telling me I was fat and fed me nothing but steamed vegetables and lettuce. I've never been so hungry in my life. The undernourished Cécile spent half the day weighing herself and shoving her fingers down her throat after every meal, and the other half lying on her bed and discussing diets on the phone with her equally obsessed friends. I hung out with the housekeeper, Dominique: she used to sneak me in chocolate bars to keep me going, until Madame Leroux caught her and fired her. So I ended up starving and feeling guilty because I had lost the lovely Dominique her job. Eventually after I'd cried to my mother on the phone every night for two weeks—even she grew weary of telling me it was character-building—she changed my ticket and I flew home early.

Sean's letter said:

Dear Sis,

Hope you don't mind me sending you this. I'm not trying to stick my oar in, but Mum tells me—on a daily basis—that you are having a tough time with this pregnancy lark and I saw this in a magazine in the dentist's yesterday, so I ripped it out—much to the bemusement of the receptionist. If you are interested I'd be happy to pay for the consultation and treatment. Let's face it, I can't even hold down a relationship, so the chances of me being a father are slim to none. Your kids will be the closest thing I get to parenthood, so I'm doing this for selfish reasons too. Anyway, see what you think and let me know. The offer is there. This woman seems to be doing great things and all the stars go to her so you'd be in good company! Keep away from the aspirin.

Sean

Inside was an article about a woman called Zita West. She was a midwife who had been one of the first people to take acupuncture into NHS hospitals. Her clients included Kate Winslet, Cate Blanchett and Davina McCall—sounded good to me. I was still going to Sheila for my acupuncture once a week and still finding it the only thing that helped me relax. I read on. The article said:

West is shocked by how few women are really in tune with their bodies, especially their menstrual cycles . . . losing weight can increase your chances of conception as can detoxifying the liver. . . . West also asks women to refrain from using tampons, which can alter the mucus in the vaginal tract, and keep out of the gym and swimming pool when they are on their period— when, according to Chinese medicine, the body should rest.

I like the sound of resting, but, come on, Zita, no tampons? It's not very practical. All the same, her clients were breeding like rabbits so she must be good. I wondered how much she cost—a lot, judging by the people going to her. I was tempted, but it was unrealistic. Flying to London to see her would be a needless extravagance. Besides, I was getting fed up with conflicting advice. Everyone had an opinion and lots of them differed. It was really sweet of Sean, but I wasn't going to take him up on the offer—even though I would have enjoyed hanging out in the waiting room with Cate and the gang.

* * *

Another week of waiting, hoping and praying later—I got my period. The miracle of Lourdes was that I didn't throw myself under a bus out of frustration, disappointment and utter despondency. James had gone to London to try to persuade the London-Irish scrum half to come and play for Leinster, so I decided to call in to my mother for some sympathy and TLC.

She opened the door and as soon as I saw her, I began to wail. "Muuuuuum, I'm . . . uh-uh-uh . . . not pregnant again."

"Oh no! You poor old thing. Come on in," she said, giving me a hug. "Sit down there now and I'll get you a glass of wine."

"Thanks," I sniffled, as she poured me a goldfish bowl–size glass. "I can't bear it, Mum. It's not fair. Everyone else is getting pregnant except me. What's wrong with me? What's wrong with my stupid body?" I said, slipping easily into self-pity mode.

"Now, Emma, stop that nonsense at once. There's nothing wrong with you or your body. You're a healthy young girl and you'll have a healthy baby one of these days, but you'll have to try to calm down. Look at the state of you. It's not good for you to be so stressed out. You'll have to try to distract yourself. Take up tennis or join a folk group or something. Babies take time, you can't be impatient."

"It's been over a year and a half. I'm not being impatient. I'm sick of waiting. Why isn't it happening? It's not bloody fair. I think I'm going mad."

"Now, listen here, you'll have to get a grip. All this obsessing, drug-taking and moodiness is not good for you or your marriage. I'm sure James is finding it a strain too. I hope you're not taking your frustrations out on him. The last thing a man needs when he gets home from work is a nagging wife," she said, conveniently ignoring her behavior toward Dad for the past thirty-five years. Every time the poor man walked through the door, he was given odd jobs to do around the house, or ordered to get a haircut, polish his shoes, throw out the tie he was wearing, lose weight, help his children with their homework, feed the goldfish and—if it wasn't snowing—mow the lawn. But clearly my mother was suffering from early onset Alzheimer's as she lectured me on being a good wife.

"What you need to do is be nice and cheery when James comes in. No husband wants to be greeted by a long face. When he gets home show an interest in his life and don't be always giving him bad news. Mark my words, Emma, James is a very handsome young man and successful too. He's a good catch and I'm sure there are plenty of young ones who would be only too happy to turn his head."

"What am I? A useless old bag who no one wants? What am I supposed to do, Mum? Follow James around all day in bright pink dresses, telling him how marvelous he is? What about me? What about my life? My support? Who's going to tell me how great I am? How brave and uncomplaining I am? What if I never have kids? What if I'm barren and I just keep trying and trying and never get pregnant? I want a family, Mum. I want kids. That's what life's about. But it doesn't look like it's going to happen. That thought terrifies me. I need your support."

"You have my support, you silly girl. I'm worried sick about you. I know how much you want children. Aren't I down on my knees every night praying for you? I've even got your father to start praying too. I'm just saying that you need to calm down or you'll make yourself ill and you'll put a strain on your marriage. And everyone says that stress is a disaster when you're trying to get pregnant."

"But what if I never have a baby?"

"Of course you will."

"But what if I don't, Mum? I have to face the fact that I may never get pregnant. I have to look at my options. I'm thinking of adoption."

"Adoption? For goodness' sake, Emma, stop running before you can walk. You're thirty-four, not forty-four. Stop panicking. Now, do you want me to cook you a shepherd's pie?"

It was my favorite comfort food and she had always made it for me when I was younger—when I had the flu, or the time I broke my arm, or if I had a fight with Jess or Lucy or whatever minidrama was going on at school.

"Yes, please," I said, tears welling as happy childhood memories flooded back. Oh, to be young and carefree again.

"Okay. You pour yourself another glass of wine and I'll make the dinner. Don't worry, pet, it'll all work out. You'll see," she said, getting a bit tearful herself as she pulled a Marks & Spencer shepherd's pie out of the freezer.

THIRTY-ONE

*I*t was time to go back to see Dr. Reynolds. I had been on the fertility drugs for seven months. I had looked at numerous fuzzy screens, showing small, medium and large blobs—all useless. It was time for action. James came with me for support. I asked him to bring along some paper and a pen to take notes, so we could discuss our options afterward without forgetting anything that Dr. Reynolds had said.

Dr. Reynolds told us how sorry he was that the treatment hadn't worked. He said he was surprised as he was sure it would be effective, seeing as how we were both young and healthy. "But I think it's clear that it isn't working so we need to look at our options."

I nudged James to start taking notes.

"I mentioned the possibility of a laparoscopy before and I think at this stage it's the best thing to do. The procedure is straightforward and relatively painless as you are under general anesthetic. It takes about twenty minutes so you'll be home within a few hours."

"Okay," I said warily. Painless tests were a myth. "What exactly does it involve?"

"We'll bring you in and once you're asleep we insert a fine needle into the abdomen, then pump in gas to push away the intestine. The laparoscope—which is a fiberoptic telescope—is then inserted through a small incision under the belly button and we inspect the inside of the abdomen and pelvis, including the outside of the womb, the tubes and the ovaries."

"Incision?" I didn't want to end up with a big scar and no baby to show for it. I was all for Cesarean sections (too posh to push, and all that—it sounded very civilized to me), but I didn't want a scar for no reason.

"Don't worry, it's a tiny scar that only ever requires one small stitch. If we find any abnormalities during the procedure we deal with them there and then, thus avoiding a further operation. In your case I doubt we'll find anything dramatically wrong, as we know from your X-rays that all seems in order."

"Will it be painful when I wake up?"

"You'll need to rest for a day after the operation. I recommend taking some light painkillers and there may be some vaginal discomfort and a little bleeding, but it will be minimal."

Minimal my ass, I thought. So far nothing had been painless, despite all promises to the contrary. I sighed as I faced the thought of yet more time spent in the clinic. Still, at least this way they'd know for sure if something was wrong, and I'd be knocked out, so chances were I'd feel little pain. "Okay, what if you don't find anything that explains why I can't seem to get pregnant? What then?"

"Well, then I think we'll have to look at IVF. But let's take it a step at a time. I'll set up an appointment for the laparoscopy and we can look at our options after we've analyzed the results.

"Any more questions or concerns?" he said, looking from me to James, who was doodling on the piece of paper he was supposed to be taking notes on.

"Uhm. No, thank you, Doctor, that all seems pretty straightforward," said James, delighted the meeting was over so he didn't have to listen to any more chat about vaginas.

My appointment was made for ten days' time. James and I went for a coffee and I asked to see his notes so I could remember exactly what I was in for. He reluctantly passed over the sheet of paper.

Laparospuppy—Gas pump, No pain. No scar. Call Glen Red-grave—offer him five grand more. Need his skills. Scrum half—key position. Check budget with Eddie.

"James! Did you listen to a word he said?"

"Yes. The information is there, it's just a summary of it."

"For goodness' sake, you were supposed to be taking detailed notes."

"Well, he said it was all very straightforward so I just jotted down key points—like the name of the procedure so you can look it up later on the Internet."

"What exactly do you think a 'laparospuppy' is?" I said.

"It's when they open you up and you surprise them all by giving birth to a small dog."

A couple of days later, Lucy called me and asked me to meet her for a drink. She sounded a bit strange on the phone, but when I probed her for more information, she went all KGB on me and said she'd talk to me when she saw me. She was waiting for me when I arrived, looking a bit hot and bothered. Before I had even taken off my jacket and sat down, she blurted out, "Donal has asked me to move in with him."

"What?" I squealed. "When? How? Tell me everything."

Lucy told me that she and Donal had gone out two nights before for dinner and ended up getting pretty smashed. They stumbled back to Donal's house, and when she woke up in the morning she realized that her shirt was covered in red wine. She had an important meeting to go to and no time to wash it, so she panicked.

Donal turns around and says, "Relax, I think there are some shirts in that drawer over there." Lucy presumed he meant his shirts, but when she looked inside there were three blouses, face creams, a hair-dryer and other girly stuff. So she asked him whose they were.

"Oh, they must be Mary's," said Donal, as cool as you like.

"Mary I met at the dog coursing?" Lucy said.

"Yep," he said.

"Mary your ex-girlfriend?" she said.

"The very same," he said.

"I see," said Lucy, managing to keep calm. "What are they doing here?"

"I dunno, I suppose she left them behind."

"And you expect me to wear one of that stupid cow's shirts to work, do you?"

"Well, you said you needed a clean shirt, and sure isn't that a clean one? I was only trying to help."

"Help!" roared Lucy, losing her cool. "By offering me your exgirlfriend's clothes? How am I to know she doesn't come up and stay and that's her regular drawer? I notice I don't have a drawer. Your bloody ex-girlfriend does, but I don't. I have to traipse around carrying spare knickers and a toothbrush in my bag. I'm sick of it, Donal. I'm sick of living out of a suitcase," Lucy announced dramatically.

"But we nearly always go back to your place," said Donal, looking puzzled. "You hardly ever stay here."

He had a point—they almost always ended up in Lucy's place, because she preferred it that way and he didn't care where they were. Having sex in Lucy's bed rather than his was fine with Donal.

"Well, I'm here now, and you're foisting your ex's clothes on me."

"I'm not foisting anything on you. If you want a drawer, take one. Help yourself to any drawer you like, but stop shouting—it's too early for shouting."

"Why are you keeping her stuff? If it's over, throw it out. As a matter of fact, I'm going to do it for you," said Lucy, grabbing Mary's things from the drawer and throwing them into a plastic bag.

"While you're cleaning up there, would you mind giving the place a bit of a Hoover and maybe throw on a wash if you have time?" said Donal, grinning, as he snuggled back under his duvet.

"Funny? How would you like it if you found my ex's clothes hanging in my wardrobe?"

"If he happened to be the same size as me and I needed a shirt, I'd be delighted."

"That cow is twice the size of me and I'm the furthest thing from delighted. I don't like surprises. I don't like having your past shoved in my face. I'm too old for this crap. I want my own bed and my own shower and my own bloody wardrobe. Here," said Lucy, tipping the bag upside down on Donal's bed, "clean up your own mess."

Later that afternoon Donal called Lucy for a chat. "Howrya?"

"Busy," she said coolly.

"Just wanted to check what that scene was earlier—I'm not very good at reading women's minds. Were you pissed off about Mary's shirts being in the drawer? About me thinking Mary's shirts would fit you and you thinking you're much thinner than her? Or about you not having a drawer in my wardrobe? If it's because the shirts were there, I've thrown them out. If it's because I thought they'd fit you, well, I'm not very good at women's clothes and judging sizes and if it's a drawer you want, you can have one, in fact you can have two. I just want to be clear which issue I'm dealing with. Or did I miss the point entirely, and were you doing that thing where women pick fights about something when they're actually pissed off about something completely different?"

Lucy smiled despite herself.

"Lucy? Are you there?"

"Yes. Look, I was just tired and hungover and I was annoyed to find Mary's stuff still in the drawer. It felt like I was a stranger in your house or something. All this spending the night in each other's places is becoming a drag. Not having our stuff in the same place is just a hassle, really," said Lucy, dropping large hints without actually asking him to move in.

She had been thinking about it all day. They spent almost every night together—mostly in her place—it would be so much easier to move in together. It would mean Donal wouldn't have to rush home to get changed for training and she wouldn't have to go to work in a stained shirt, and it'd be nice to wake up together every day. She really liked Donal. Truth be told, she was falling in love with him, but she wouldn't ask him to move in with her. It seemed too keen, too pushy.

"Ah, sure it's not so bad. I'll buy you a toothbrush today and if you tell me what size you are I'll get you a shirt to hang up in the wardrobe too. How about that?"

"Fine. I have to go," said Lucy, raging with him for missing the point.

An hour later, a huge package arrived at Lucy's office. It was one of the large wooden drawers from Donal's wardrobe tied in a red ribbon with an envelope taped to the inside. She opened the envelope and a key fell out. The note said, "Subtlety was never your strong point. I'd love you to live with me."

She called him. "Hi."

"You got it, then?"

"Yes."

"Well, are we moving in or what?"

"Only if you move into my place. It's much nicer."

"I can't, Lucy. Annie has her room all done up in my place. It's the only home she knows and I don't want to uproot her again."

"Of course," said Lucy. Damn, she hadn't thought of that. She couldn't force the issue: Donal's little niece needed stability. She'd have to move into Donal's house. "I understand, but I'm getting decorators in. Your place needs serious work."

"That's fine with me. I'll see you later. We'll ring Annie at school tonight to tell her. She'll be thrilled."

She's not the only one, thought Lucy, as she beamed out the window, flipping the key in her hand. Finally, a proper boyfriend, one who understood her and wanted to live with her!

When she called over to her new home later that evening, they phoned Annie at her boarding school. Donal told her the good news and Lucy could hear her screaming on the phone. But they weren't happy screams: she was screaming blue murder.

"*No way,*" she roared. "She's not moving into my house. That's our house, Donal, it's for you and me and no one else. I don't want her moving in and changing everything. You'll never have time for me anymore. It's not fair. It's not what you promised. You said it'd just be you and me after Mum and Dad died. I'll kill myself if she moves in, I swear I will. I don't want her in my house. I hate her. I hate you. You'll get married and have babies and then I'll be ignored."

"Jesus, Annie, calm down. I'm not getting married and I'm not having any babies. Lucy is just going to move in is all. She stays almost every night anyway. It'll make no difference to you. You got on great with her when you met. I thought you'd be delighted."

"Well, you were *wrong*. I'm not. I don't want her in my house. I don't want anyone else in my house. You'll abandon me just like Mum and Dad, I know you will," screamed the hysterical Annie.

Lucy shrank back into the couch. Christ, Little Orphan Annie had a big pair of lungs for one so young. She too had thought she'd be pleased. They had got on well when they met. She'd thought the kid liked her, but now she was causing havoc.

"Come on now, Annie, calm down, nothing will change, I promise. I'll always put you first, you know that. Have I ever let you down? Well, have I?"

Put her first? Lucy didn't like the sound of that. She felt sorry for the child being orphaned and all, but she didn't want to play second fiddle to some hormonal brat who apparently hated her.

"No," admitted Annie grumpily.

"And I don't intend to start now. Lucy's going to move in for a month or two and we'll see how it goes. I'm sure we'll all get on famously. When you come home in a few weeks we'll go out and talk about it. If it doesn't work out Lucy will move out," said Donal, winking at Lucy in an effort to reassure her. "This is your home first and foremost, you know that, kiddo. Come on now, calm down, it'll all work out."

"Fine, she can move out when I come home, then. Tell her not to unpack. She's not staying, and if she dares go into my room, I'll kill her."

"Okay, I'll give you a call on Saturday," said Donal, desperately trying to get off the phone before any more damage could be done.

"That went well, I thought," said Lucy.

"She's a bit highly strung. She's terrified I'll have no time for her now I've you here. She's never had to share me with anyone before. You're my first official lodger," said Donal, smiling. "Don't worry, she'll come 'round."

He didn't sound convinced and Lucy knew how awful teenage girls could be. Suddenly their cozy cohabitation looked distinctly rocky.

Lucy finished telling me the story and took a slug of wine. She looked pretty shaken. On the one hand she was chuffed that she and Donal were getting so serious, but she hadn't planned for the sweet Annie to turn into such a monster.

"Just ignore her," I said. "She's a mixed-up kid who's scared that Donal will stop paying her attention if you move in. She doesn't mean it, she'd be jealous of anyone he loved. I'm sure it'll be fine. You'll just have to be supernice step-girlfriend/surrogate-aunt-thingy. How often does she get out of school?"

"One weekend in six."

"Well, that's not so bad. On those weekends you can come and stay with us."

"Thanks. I'm afraid I might be more Cruella de Vil than Mary Poppins. I'm not very good with kids. At least if it was you, you've had experience dealing with a younger sister."

"You can borrow Babs any time. She'd try the patience of a saint. I'll send her over to you tomorrow for some practice. Annie will seem like Pollyanna after Babs."

THIRTY-TWO

$\mathcal{I}$ woke up in the recovery room after the laparoscopy with Dr. Reynolds smiling down at me. I felt wonderful. If this was what class-A drugs were like, I was definitely a candidate for drug addiction. I felt as if I was floating and had the urge to laugh loudly. Dr. Reynolds said that the procedure had gone very well and that nothing unusual had been discovered. I appeared to be perfectly "normal" inside. He went off to tell James I was awake, while a nurse took my blood pressure, pulse and temperature.

Two hours later I was back home in bed with James fussing around me. He made me cups of tea and filled hot water bottles and brought me magazines and books and kept plumping my pillows. The sight of me being wheeled off in my backless gown had obviously shaken him. What might have been only a small procedure was still an operation and James was upset by it. "How do you feel now?" he asked me, for the millionth time.

"I'm fine, James, honestly. Sit down and relax. You, on the other hand, look like you could do with a drink."

He smiled. "Sorry, darling. Seeing you being carted off to theater gave me a bit of a fright. I hate you having to go through all this. It's so bloody unfair."

"Yeah, I know." I sighed. "And to be honest, I'm disappointed they didn't find anything. I wish they had—then at least they could have fixed it and we'd know why I haven't been able to get pregnant. Now we're just back to square one again. I hate the fact that it's all so vague and inconclusive. Anyway, it looks like IVF now."

"We don't have to do this, you know," said James, stroking my hair. "We could just take some time out, go on hols and try to forget about it. Give you a rest."

"No, I want to keep going," I said. "I'm on a roll now. I'm a bit scared of IVF, but loads of women go through it and have babies, so it's worth a shot."

"But what if it doesn't work?" said James. "What then? Do we just keep trying?"

"I don't know. I'm happy to give it one shot, but I'm not sure if I want to do it loads of times."

"Are you sure you want to go ahead with it?" he asked again, his face full of concern.

"Yes. It's worth trying, but if it doesn't work I think we should consider adoption. I've been thinking about it a lot lately and I think it would be a good option."

James didn't say anything.

"What do you think?" I pushed.

"I think we should take one step at a time. Adoption can be tricky."

"What do you mean?"

"Well, it's not your own flesh and blood. It's someone else's child and you don't know what those people are like. The child could be damaged in some way."

"Oh, for goodness' sake, look at Mia Farrow and all her lovely children. They always seem really happy in the pictures you see of them."

James looked at me in shock. "I hardly think Mia and her

brood are the ideal family. Didn't Woody end up having sex with his adopted daughter? It's not exactly a normal family unit."

"Okay, well, maybe that was a bad example, but look at, uhm . . ." Damn, I couldn't think of anyone—my brain was still fuzzy from the anesthetic. "I can't think of them now, but there are loads of successful people who were adopted and loved and went on to achieve great things. I'll think of them in a minute," I said, racking my brains to come up with some names.

"Look, get some rest. You've just had an operation and you need to take it easy. Call me if you need anything," said James, kissing my forehead as he switched off the light. The conversation was over. I'd think of some adoptees tomorrow, I thought, as I fell into a deep sleep.

Two weeks later we were back in Dr. Reynolds's office. He went over the findings—or lack thereof—of the laparoscopy, and told me all my bits were essentially in the right place. I had "unexplained infertility." There was no reason for me not to get pregnant, except for the small fact that, despite my best efforts and some fairly strong drugs, I couldn't seem to. I was a prime candidate for IVF, said Dr. Reynolds. My chances of success were high.

"What exactly is the rate of success?" asked my now alert and professional note-taking husband.

"The internationally accepted success rate of IVF is seventeen percent per treatment cycle," said Dr. Reynolds. "However, with youth and health on your side, your chances are much higher. I would say you have a twenty-five percent chance of conceiving first time. This can be considerably higher if you're having acupuncture in conjunction with the treatment. I hope you'll keep up the acupuncture, Emma."

I nodded. Of course I'd keep it up. It was the only part of the process I didn't dread.

"I do, however, have to warn you that it is expensive and there are risks involved."

"How expensive?" I asked.

"You're looking at about six thousand euro per treatment."

"What risks?" asked James.

"Fertility treatment can result in an increased risk of multiple pregnancies. Ectopic pregnancies are twice as common in IVF pregnancies and ovarian hyperstimulation syndrome can occur, but only in very rare cases. However, these are all very unlikely outcomes," said Dr. Reynolds, smiling at us.

James looked at me and asked me if I was sure I wanted to go ahead with it. I nodded. It was too late to back down now. I wanted to give this a go. I was going to give it my best shot. I wanted a baby.

"What exactly happens?" I asked. "Is it really painful?"

Unfortunately I had been on the Internet chat-room sites and had read some pretty dire reports about the pain and emotional trauma of IVF. I had also read of the miracle babies, but as usual had fixated on the pain and stress.

"We'll give you drugs to stimulate your ovaries into producing more eggs, not dissimilar to the drugs you've been on. These will need to be injected—which is where your husband comes in. Once the drugs kick in and the eggs mature, we'll retrieve them and fertilize the good ones in a test tube with your husband's sperm and then implant them in the womb."

"But how do you get the eggs out?" I asked, as James, on learning he had to inject me, had gone very quiet.

"Once the eggs are mature we'll begin the retrieval. We'll put you to sleep and an ultrasound probe, with a fine hollow needle attached to it, will be inserted into your vagina. Under ultrasound guidance, the needle is then advanced from the vaginal wall, punctures the back of the vagina, entering each follicle, and sucking out the fluid, which contains the egg. . . ."

My insides began to squirm at the thought of what lay ahead. Jesus Christ—puncturing? Did he actually just say "puncturing" and then follow it with "sucking"? And not even bat an eyelid? Were all doctors just sadists in white coats?

"This fluid will be given to the embryologist, Dr. Bradley, who will examine it under a microscope and count the eggs. When all the follicles are emptied, you'll be taken to the recovery room to rest. The whole procedure takes about forty minutes and you'll be out for the count so you won't feel a thing."

I was speechless. The mere description of it all had left me reeling. I glanced at James, who was looking decidedly peaky. Dr. Reynolds appeared oblivious to our discomfort and went on to describe the procedure for the embryo transfer. I had to have a full bladder; a speculum would be inserted to clean the cervix. A catheter was to be placed through the cervix into the lower segment of the uterus. A fine plastic catheter into which the embryologist had transferred the embryos would then be placed through the outer transfer catheter and advanced near the top of the uterus. Once the placement was correct, the embryos would be expelled from the catheter and inserted into the uterus.

"And then we let nature take its course," said Dr. Reynolds, having the gall to smile at us again as we sat white-faced with shock.

I tried to swallow, but my throat was dry. "Am I under general anesthetic for the embryo transfer?" I croaked.

"No, there's no need. It's very straightforward. We can offer a mild sedative if you like. Some of our patients take Valium. It's up to you."

"Put me down for the maximum dose," I said.

Dr. Reynolds then gave us a fact sheet about IVF, prescriptions for all the drugs I needed and made an appointment with the nurse to show James how to inject me with the hormones. He recommended we wait until my next cycle to give my body a rest after the laparoscopy.

Six weeks later we were in the bathroom at home, and after an hour of painstaking measuring of the vials, analyzing the needles and re-rereading of the instructions, James had finally filled the syringe and was now aiming the needle at my thigh. His hands were shaking and sweat was forming rapidly on his brow.

"Ouch. What the hell are you doing?" I snapped, as he hit me on the thigh with his free hand.

"Flicking the area to numb it before I inject," he said, pointing at the instruction leaflet on the floor to defend his actions.

"Well, it hurt. Do you have to be so rough? The bloody injection's bad enough without you bruising my leg first with all the flicking. Just stick it in and get it over with, and don't hit a nerve."

"Maybe I should get some ice to numb the area. That might help," he said, putting the needle down and heading out the door.

"James!" I roared. "Will you stop faffing around and stick the bloody needle in?"

"Okay. I was just trying to make it less painful. I think that icing the leg would be a good idea. It says here on page three—"

"STICK THE BLOODY THING IN BEFORE I KILL YOU!" I shouted, snatching up the instruction leaflet and flinging it across the bathroom.

"Fine," he said, expertly ignoring my histrionics. "Ready, then? And a one and a two and a—"

I grabbed his hand and shoved the needle into my thigh. It was James's turn to shout: "For God's sake, Emma, you'll hurt yourself."

I had expected it to be really painful. I had wound myself into a frenzy about the daily injections I was going to have to endure, but it was all right. Not painless, but not too bad. I looked down at my thigh where the red mark was. Well, let's face it, there was plenty of flesh available to soften the blow. James, breathing deeply to stay calm, inserted the drug into my leg, gently pulled out the needle and stuck a Band-Aid over the mark. "Sorry," I said, "you were making too much of a production of it. I don't want it to take longer than absolutely necessary."

"Fine. Tomorrow I'll just stab you," he said, picking up the torn leaflet.

"That would be lovely, thanks."

For the next two weeks James injected me, and as the level of hormones in my body increased I became ever more volatile and my mood swings had to be seen to be believed. On the fifth day when James arrived five minutes late to give me my injection because he'd got stuck in traffic, I accused him of having an affair and told him I wanted a divorce. Then I locked him in the bathroom and refused to let him out until he swore on his mother's life that he wouldn't divorce me because I couldn't bear him children. On the eighth day we went grocery shopping but had to leave the supermarket when I saw an old woman shopping alone and began to sob hysterically about the sadness of loneliness.

On day eleven I was back in the clinic having my fourth ultrasound and blood test in ten days. The waiting room was full of hopeful, desperate women like me. I felt right at home. I preferred these women to the pregnant ones. At least we were all in the same barren boat. We nodded and smiled at each other. I was surrounded by kindred spirits. The room was full of unspoken empathy. A small blonde woman to my left turned to me and asked me how my follicles were coming along. I said they seemed to be doing okay, they weren't A students, but they certainly couldn't be admonished for lack of effort.

"I've got twenty beautiful ones," gushed the blonde. "I think it's partly to do with the fact that my husband is so good at giving me the injections. Mind you, I have fantastic veins, which helps. The nurses said my follicles are the best they've seen. I meditate and use visualization techniques daily, it's very effective. . . ."

Suddenly I felt wretched again. I had seven measly follicles and Fertility Barbie had twenty. Obviously Ken was doing a better job at injecting Barbie than James was doing with me, or maybe it was my veins. I'd never really thought about my veins before. I looked down at my arms as Barbie rattled on. What made a good vein? Were bulgy ones good? I looked at hers; they seemed pretty normal to me. Before I could throttle her, the nurse called me in for my tests. I had ten follicles and my estradiol was two thousand. This, judging by the smiles and nods from the nurse, was good news. She told me to sit by the phone, as I'd be ready for my hCG injection soon.

HCG (human chorionic gonadotropin) is a crucial part of the IVF cycle and is given about 35 hours before egg retrieval.

So said my IVF guidelines book. While it was all good news, I was dreading the egg retrieval, so I wasn't exactly dancing around the room when Nurse Nancy called the next day to tell me exactly when I needed to have the hCG shot. James injected me at the exact time indicated and we went into the clinic two days later for the procedure. While I was being punctured by giant needles and sucked free of eggs, James was going to be masturbating at his leisure in a nice room the clinic provided, with wall-to-wall porn to help him along the way.

I don't remember much about the retrieval, as I happily wafted off into a deep sleep for the duration of the process. I woke up in the recovery room feeling groggy and sore and glad it was over. I was sent home with a goody bag that included antibiotics to prevent yeast infection, steroids to protect the prospective embryo from attack by white blood cells and—just in case I thought I was getting off lightly—vaginal progesterone suppositories.

The embryologist called me the following morning to discuss how many eggs to transfer. He suggested that we let eight of the embryos grow for a few days before choosing the best ones. He reckoned we'd be able to transfer three in three days' time. I was hoping he'd shove all of them in for good measure, but he assured me that three embryos was the standard number and would give me an excellent chance of getting pregnant.

Three days later I was back in for the embryo transfer, full bladder, gown and hat on, legs in the air. I had been given the Valium I had requested and Dr. Reynolds allowed James to come in with me to hold my hand—and, I suspect, to take any abuse I might dish out. When I saw the speculum coming toward me, I lay back and closed my eyes, willing the Valium to kick in. It was sore and uncomfortable and I wept with relief when it was over: I was finished with extractions and insertions. I was told to go home and rest for two days, then continue as normal.

"Normal." How easily the word slips off the medical profession's tongue. After weeks of injections, puncturing, steroids, suppositories, sucking of eggs out and pumping of eggs-plus-sperm back in, I was supposed to go home and be normal. I went home and was very abnormal. Although abnormal was now my normal.

For the next two weeks I cried a lot, slept little and tried not to obsess over anything that could be construed as a symptom, limiting myself to poking my boobs six times a day. I shouted at my mother for getting my hopes up when she told me about some friend of a friend's daughter who had given birth to beautiful twin girls after her first IVF treatment. I shouted at James when he said he had a good feeling about the treatment. I chased a magpie for two miles in desperation for it to find a friend—one for sorrow, two for joy—but the bastard bird was a one-man show. Then I cried because I felt sorry for it being alone in the world. I even began speaking to the embryos, begging them to cling on and hang in there.

But as the two weeks drew to a close, I thought seriously about the possibilities of failure. Could I go through this again? What about surrogacy? No, I didn't want another woman giving birth to my egg and James's sperm. It'd be like he'd had sex with her or something. Besides, any of the surrogacy women you saw on TV were rough as old boots and the thought of having to hold some dodgy bird's hand while she pushed my baby out was way too weird. Adoption was the only solution I could imagine going through with. Still, I thought, maybe this time we'll get lucky. Maybe this time we'll be celebrating.

THIRTY-THREE

*T*wo weeks after the embryo transfer, I went for a blood test to see if I was pregnant. The result was negative. There were no tears. I felt nothing. I was numb. Numb to pain, numb to being upset, numb to bad results. It had been nearly two years of disappointment. I had no tears left.

Dr. Reynolds told me not to worry. He said my chances were excellent of getting pregnant during the next session of IVF. He told me not to be despondent. He said I was healthy and young and had time on my side. He came out with the same platitudes that I had been listening to for months. I sat in his office listening but not hearing. I looked over his shoulder out the window.

"Approximately three out of four embryos don't survive the period of early implantation long enough to become viable pregnancies, so don't be too discouraged by this first failure. I can assure you it will happen. We just need to be patient. . . ."

Patient! I thought wearily. Be patient. Relax. Stop worrying. Chill out. I couldn't listen to it anymore. I stood up while Dr. Reynolds was in midsentence. "I don't think I can do this anymore. Thank you for your time and for being so nice, but I don't think I'll be seeing you again," I said. My voice sounded as if it were coming from somewhere behind me, like an echo.

"I understand that you're disappointed, but please sleep on it.

Don't make any rash decisions yet. Call me in a few days and let me know how you feel then," he said kindly.

"Yes, fine."

I left the clinic and walked slowly to the car. I noticed things I had never noticed before. Details. The pictures on the walls, the plant pot, the color of the receptionist's nails as she bade me good-bye . . . I sat in the car for a long time, my mind a blank. I had no energy. I felt completely lifeless. Even breathing was an effort. Eventually I summoned the strength to drive home, where I lay on the couch and stared at the ceiling. The phone rang.

"Hi, Emma, it's me," said Lucy, to my answering machine. "Just ringing to say I've got a booking for nine at Chez Gérard. Did you get Jess a present or will we just pay for her dinner? I suppose thirty-five is a bit of a milestone. Anyway, I'll see you in the bar for drinks at eight."

I had forgotten Jess's birthday. I used to be really good at re-membering birthdays and special dates. I had been a thoughtful person before I had become an obsessive psychotic. I looked at the clock. It was six. We were meeting in two hours. Two hours is one hundred and twenty minutes, I thought. One hundred and twenty minutes is seventy-two hundred seconds. In the time it took me to calculate that, twenty seconds had elapsed. I sighed and closed my eyes. Maybe I could sleep now.

I couldn't. I was too tired to sleep. My bones were tired. I felt one hundred years old. Weary of everything. Lifeless. I wondered if I was having a nervous breakdown. Was this what it felt like? Did you just lie down and never get up? I thought about ringing James to tell him about the IVF failure, but I couldn't summon the en-ergy. Besides, all I did was tell him bad news or shout at him these days. I used to entertain him with funny stories about my day. I used to be witty and full of life. I used to make him laugh all the time. Now all I did was cry, shout or rant about the injustice of infertility. In fact, I couldn't remember the last time I had made him laugh with one of my stories or impressions. It was always him trying to cheer me up and I could see that the novelty was wearing off.

I wouldn't blame him if he left me. He had married a fun-loving, energetic, sassy fireball—a girl who loved to go out and have a good time, someone who lived every moment—and he had ended up after three short years with a certifiable, moan-a-minute drip. Something had to give. I couldn't go on like this. I couldn't put myself or my marriage through any more strain, not to mention my poor family. My mother bore the brunt of a lot of my anger and frustration, as did Babs. Although I wasn't so worried about Babs—she just ignored me or roared back. But my mother had suffered enough of my mood swings. It was time to make a decision. Did I really want to continue pumping myself full of drugs that made me utterly miserable? Did I want to spend the next God-knew-how-long hoping and praying every month for a miracle? Did I want to know exactly what day I was at in my cycle for another two years? It had to stop, and I was the only one who could control it.

But then what? If I stopped my treatment I'd be back to square one and I knew that if I did that and went back to "nature," no matter how much I pretended to myself that I wasn't trying to get pregnant I would still obsess about it. But if I decided to adopt, I would be involved in a process that would guarantee me a baby at the end. Unless, of course, the social worker thought I was an unfit parent. There was no use waiting for Imogen and Henry to die in a car crash and leave me the twins (actually I always saved Henry, but left him able to cope only with Thomas). No matter how much I fantasized about it, the likelihood of it happening was slim to none. So we'd adopt a baby from China or Cambodia like Angelina Jolie. It wouldn't be our flesh and blood. It wouldn't be a mini-me or a mini-James, but it would be a baby and we'd be helping the world. The problem was that when I had brought up the possibility of adoption with James, he had got a bit shifty and said we should keep trying ourselves. He hadn't seemed to like the idea. He'd not said as much, but he hadn't been very enthusiastic. What to do? I lay there and tried in vain to weigh up my options, but I was too weary to decide anything.

I looked at the clock—it was half seven. I had spent an hour and a half procrastinating on the couch and now I was going to be late. I hauled myself up and sat listlessly under the shower, sighing as if the cross of Calvary was welded to my back. I had to snap out of it. I tried to give myself a pep talk. "Come on, Emma, it's not that bad. You could have AIDS or no legs. Come on now." Fuck AIDS and fuck leglessness. I was sick of feeling guilty about being miserable. I'd allow myself to wallow for a few more minutes.

The shower perked me up enough to get dressed—albeit at the pace of a snail. I drove myself into town: I wanted to be able to leave early. I'd have a quick bite to eat, then crawl back into bed.

Lucy and Jess were there when I arrived. They were drinking champagne.

"There she is. Hi, Emma," said Lucy. "Hey, are you okay?"

"Uhm . . . yeah, why?"

"Your hair is soaking wet."

"What?" I said, feeling my hair, which had been dripping down my back, soaking my shirt. I had forgotten to dry it.

Lucy and Jess looked at me with concern.

"Sit down and have a drink, you look like you need one," said Lucy gently, leading me to my chair.

"Emma sweetheart," said Jess, holding my hand, "did you get bad news on the IVF?"

I nodded. They both welled up.

"Oh, Emma," said Lucy, hugging me.

"I'm so sorry," said Jess. "Look, I've been thinking, why don't I give you some of my eggs? I'd like to help. Honestly. The only thing I'm good at is making babies, so let me help."

I shook my head. "Thanks, Jess, but I'm not going to do it anymore. I don't know what I'm going to do, but no more IVF. It's horrible."

"Drink?" said Lucy.

I nodded. What the hell? I needed a drink. I needed to blot out the day. I downed the glass of champagne they put in front of me and held it out for a refill.

"What happened?" asked Lucy.

"Let's not talk about it. I'm not going to ruin Jess's birthday with my boring infertility. I'm sick of it myself. Tell me funny stories. Tell me gossip. I don't feel like talking. I want to listen to fluff tonight. Is that okay?"

"Absolutely fine," they said, and they proceeded to entertain me with all the stories they could think of. I drank and drank and drank. I nodded and I laughed and occasionally I spoke—but it was all a blur. I felt as if I were hovering above the table, looking down on the scene. Now and then I'd catch Jess and Lucy glancing at each other. They looked worried. I continued to drink—my hair eventually dried and my shirt did too.

Four hours later we stumbled into the pub next to the restaurant and sat up at the bar to order cocktails. It was my idea. I didn't want to go home until I knew I'd fall into a dreamless sleep. Tonight I wanted to forget who I was. But no matter how drunk I got, I still kept thinking, What am I going to do? How am I going to face tomorrow? I decided to order shots. As I was throwing a tequila slammer down my throat, I lost my balance and fell off the bar stool onto the marble floor, landing on my head. Finally, I thought—

Silence.

THIRTY-FOUR

I woke up three hours later in hospital with James by my side and a large white bandage 'round my head. We were in Accident and Emergency, and the smell of urine and vomit was nauseating. Drunks shouted at each other and a fight broke out in the corridor. We were behind a curtain in a tiny cubicle. I looked at James: he was a deathly shade of pale.

"You're all right, darling," he said, holding my hand. "You had a slight concussion and you cut your head so they had to bring you in for observation. How are you feeling?"

"I'm not pregnant, James. It didn't work," I said. The tears—missing earlier—were free-flowing now.

"I know. Lucy told me. Why didn't you call me?"

"I'm going to be thirty-five in six weeks. I am a thirty-four-and-three-quarter-year-old woman in hospital because I got so drunk that I fell off a bar stool and bashed my head. I'm such a loser. How did I end up here? What happened to me, James? I want to be old Emma. I want to be fun Emma. I want my life back. I want to be me again. I hate myself. I hate what I'm turning into," I said, sobbing.

"But you are you. You've just had a really difficult time lately. We're going to stop the IVF. You need a break, darling. It's been really tough on you."

"I'm sick of it, James. I'm sick of it and sick of me. It's so bor- ing. I'm so boring. I'm sick of feeling like shit. I'm sick of being grumpy and mean. Don't you want us to be back to normal?"

"Of course I do. That's why I think you need to stop all the treatment. I hate seeing you upset. Let's just forget about children for a while."

"But I can't," I wailed. "I've tried to, I really have, but I can't stop obsessing. It just takes over, you can't control it. James, I think the only way to get my life back and still have children is to adopt."

James looked away. "Come on, darling, let's get you home. We'll talk about this tomorrow. Put your arm 'round my neck. There you go."

I was too tired to argue. I leaned against him as he gently lifted me off the bed and helped me out to the car.

The next morning, Mum called over to check up on me. "How are you, pet?" she asked.

"Not great."

"You've had a bad run. I'm sorry about the IVF."

"Thanks, me too."

"Well, Emma, getting drunk and falling over are not the solu- tion."

"I'm aware of that."

"Your uncle Eddie's a drinker, so it's in the family. You need to be careful of that. These things can be hereditary, you know."

"I'm not an alcoholic."

"It creeps up on you and before you know it you're hooked. It's a slippery slope, Emma. It's especially easy to get addicted when you're down in the dumps. That's the worst time of all to be drink- ing. You're far better off out in the fresh air going for a nice walk."

"I'm not an alcoholic."

"Mark my words, young women your age are very susceptible to alcoholism. It's a dangerous age you're at. The best thing to do is keep away from it altogether."

"I'm not an alcoholic. I had a few drinks last night that went straight to my head because I'm an emotional wreck. I'm sitting here with a throbbing head, feeling really bad about everything, and I don't need you to rub it in."

"Snapping at people and aggressive behavior in general are some of the first symptoms of a problem drinker."

"Mum!"

"I'm not saying you are one, I'm just saying be careful. Anyway, how's James after last night?"

"He's fine. He's not the one who split his head open. In case you hadn't noticed that was me, your daughter, the person sitting opposite you right now."

"There's no need to be smart. The poor boy is worried sick about you. He's finding it hard too, Emma. Remember that."

"I know. I'm sorry for shouting at you. I just need some time to figure out what I'm going to do next, and having you telling me I'm on the cusp of being a wino isn't helping."

"I'm just worried about you. I think you need to stop taking all these hormones and get back to a normal life. Let nature take its course."

Over the next few days, I kept a low profile and thought long and hard about the future. What were we going to do? What was I going to do? I wanted to enjoy life again, not spend every hour of every day wondering where I was in my cycle, or silently praying that this time I'd be pregnant, and constantly feeling let down and depressed when I wasn't. It was time for a change. I had to move on to the next stage in my life.

The more I thought about adoption, the more it seemed like the perfect solution. I wouldn't have to take any more drugs, go for any more tests or endure any more horrible procedures. We'd just put our names down on a list, fill out a few forms and in a couple of months have a baby. I wouldn't have to go through pregnancy or labor. It was perfect. Why on earth hadn't I thought of this earlier? Not only would we have a baby, but I wouldn't have to spend nine months going to the loo every five minutes, swelling up like a balloon and then spend thirty-six hours huffing and puffing in a labor ward. My vagina would remain a normal size and I wouldn't have to hang out with other mothers from my antenatal classes and lie about having sex with my husband. And, speaking of sex, James and I would be able to get back to having a normal sex life! Oh my God, this was perfect. And on top of that we could adopt a baby from a war-torn country and save its life. The more I thought about it the better it got. Adoption was the solution to everything. Fantastic.

When James arrived home that night, I met him at the door with a bottle of champagne. "Welcome home, darling. I've got great news. We're going to adopt a poor baby from an orphanage in China or Brazil and give it a wonderful life. It's all going to be okay. Everything's going to be perfect. We're going to be great parents."

James sat down. He spoke slowly and deliberately. "It's certainly an option, but not as straightforward as you may think. There are lots of things to consider with adoption."

"Like what?" I asked, fully confident that I would be able to allay his every concern.

"What if the baby has AIDS or some hereditary disease we know nothing about? These orphanages don't give you a proper medical history. We could be biting off more than we can chew. You don't know anything about their families. The mother could have been a heroin addict and the baby might be too. It could be autistic . . . there are so many things that can go wrong. It's a very big leap of faith."

"Of course it is, but so is having a baby of your own. I'm sure Charles Manson's parents didn't think he'd turn into a savage killer, but he did. If we have a baby of our own it could get AIDS from a blood transfusion or become a drug addict when it's a teenager. You can never know what's going to happen. Adopting a child is a risk—a really scary risk—but if we love the child and give it a happy home, well, then, chances are they'll turn out all right. Your environment is what forms the person you turn into, not genetics."

"Not necessarily. You can inherit some pretty bad genes."

"Well, look at your mad uncle Harry, all his kids all turned out to be totally normal—humiliated by their father, but normal." I had an answer for everything. James's Uncle Harry, his father's elder brother, was a certifiable loon, who walked around his local village flashing at people. Mr. Hamilton had constantly to bail him out of the local police station. But Harry had three sons who were all totally normal and well balanced.

"True," said James, softening.

"Look, James, I know it's scary, but we'll just have to deal with problems as they arise. And we could go back to having a normal sex life. No more handstands. No more coming down to your office and sexually assaulting you in front of your boss. No more green tea. And you can masturbate as often and for as long as you like. Come on, James, it'll be great. I'll be me again."

He looked down at his hands. "It's not a decision to be taken lightly. We need to look into it properly before making up our minds. It's a big commitment. Let's just sleep on it."

"Fine, sleep on it all you like, but my mind is made up. This is the right thing for us. I have never been so sure of anything before in my life," I said, smiling at him as I put the champagne back into the fridge for a later date. Nothing was going to ruin my buzz. I hadn't felt this alive in months. I knew James would come 'round. I just needed to do some research and dazzle him with facts and figures. I'd do a power-point presentation if I had to. I went upstairs to log on to the Internet and gather my evidence.

While I was bouncing from adoption website to adoption website, I heard James on the phone.

"Hi, are you free for a pint? I need to pick your brain . . . yes, there's a first time for everything . . . say half an hour in Hogan's? . . . see you, then."

James came up and told me he was going to meet Donal for a drink. While he was in the shower, I called Lucy. "Hi, it's me," I whispered.

"Why are you whispering? Are you okay?"

"Fine, thanks. Look, James is meeting Donal for a pint to talk to him about adoption."

"Really?"

"Yeah. I want to adopt and James is a bit reticent so I think he's going to ask Donal about Annie and what it's like bringing up a child that isn't yours, blah-blah-blah. So you have to make sure he says all the right things. It's the perfect solution for us, Lucy. If we adopt we can get back to having a normal life again. But I want James to be as enthusiastic as I am."

"Okay, what do you want Donal to say? I'll have him word perfect for you."

"He has to say that it's great, and that although bringing up someone else's child is difficult, so is bringing up your own child. That things can go just as wrong for biological children as they can for adopted children. That after a while you forget the child is adopted and think of it as your own. That it's a great idea because it means I won't have to have any more horrible operations and tests and will be back to myself again. That James would be an amazing father and the adopted child would be blessed to come into our home. That it's a no-brainer and he has to go for it."

"No problem, I've jotted them all down."

"Gotta go, James is coming. Thanks, Lucy."

"Don't worry about a thing."

Two hours later James came in from the pub and pulled the bottle of champagne out of the fridge. Swaying slightly, he said, "Darling, I've just been talking to Donal about adoption. He said it's great, that although bringing up someone else's child is tough, so is bringing up your own child. He said things can go wrong for biological children as well as adopted children. That after a while you forget the child is adopted and think of it as your own. That it's a great idea because it means you won't have to go through any more nasty operations and tests and will be back to your jolly old self again. That I will be a great father and the adopted child would be lucky to come into our home . . . and what was the other thing Donal said Lucy wrote down for him to say?" He fished a crumpled piece of paper out of his coat pocket. "Oh, yes, that it's basically a no-brainer and we should go for it," he said, winking at me.

"Well, was he persuasive at least?" I asked sheepishly.

"Yes, very."

"You see?" I said, beaming at him. "I told you it was the right thing to do. I knew you just needed a little extra persuasion. And wait till I tell you about the fantastic website I found called 'Famous and Remarkable Adoptees,' which lists all the amazing people who've been adopted. Ella Fitzgerald and Richard Burton and Marilyn Monroe—and, oh, yeah, Moses. He was adopted by the Princess of Egypt and look how well he turned out. And other people like, uhm . . ."

James came over and kissed me. He was smiling. "Well, if it was good enough for the Princess of Egypt, it's good enough for me."